'An exhilarating writer!'
THE NEW YORK TIMES

'K. W. Jeter is one of the m͏͏
writers of imaginative fictio͏
only our admiration but o͏
RAMSEY CAMPBELL

'Scary as hell . . . a wonder͏
T. M. WRIGHT

'K. W. Jeter just keeps gett͏ing better'
Science Fiction Review

'Brain-burning intensity'
The Village Voice

'Stunning.'
Philip K. Dick

K.W. Jeter lives and works in California. He is the author of many novels including *The Night Man*, *Dark Seeker*, *Mantis* and *In the Land of the Dead*. Ramsey Campbell has called him 'one of the most versatile and uncompromising writers' of horror fiction.

Also by
K. W. Jeter in Pan Books
Soul Eater

THE NIGHT MAN

K. W. Jeter

Pan Books London, Sydney and Auckland

To John Jordan,
one of the better sort of football player

Publisher's note
This novel is a work of fiction. Names, characters,
places and incidents are either the product of the author's
imagination or are used fictitiously, and any resemblance
to actual persons, living or dead, events, or
locales is entirely coincidental

First published 1990 by New American Library, New York

First published in Great Britain 1991
by Pan Books Ltd, Cavaye Place, London SW10 9PG

9 8 7 6 5 4 3 2

© K. W. Jeter 1989

ISBN 0 330 31560 9

Printed and bound in Great Britain by
Cox and Wyman Ltd, Reading, Berkshire

Before

"This place looks like death."

Felton watched the young guy turn to his companion and smile. They were both young, thin, wearing those big sunglasses—some French name—that the kids who went away to college always came back with.

"Like death sautéed in shit, over a low flame." The two of them smiled at each other. Dressed in black suits, under the hammering sun; the sweat trickled under Felton's shirt, seeping through the dust and grit lodged in the folds of his own heavy flesh. The Santa Ana winds had come up, turning October into a baking rerun of summer. The two young guys weren't sweating; they smelled like some expensive cologne, something green and sharp rendered out of twenty-dollar bills.

Felton didn't know whether he was supposed to smile as well, whether he was supposed to share in the joke. It was his property they were talking about, after all. But if he didn't . . . He worked up a smile for them. If he didn't, it meant the deal was off, he wasn't going to unload the place.

They stood in the middle of a field of iron poles, rusting under the flaking layers of paint. The poles came up to about chest-height. They stretched in rows over the humps and valleys of asphalt; you could spot the ones that had been hit by cars, leaning a few degrees out of vertical. Right in the middle of the field was the snack-bar building, with its glassed-in front section and the projection windows up above, facing the big screen, the white rectangle clipped out of the blue sky. Nothing else, just the big wide field of asphalt heating up soft and tarry under the sun.

The young guy, the one who did all the talking, picked up a speaker from the holder at the top of one of the poles. He smiled at it, weighing it in his hand, as though he were about to come out with some "Alas poor Yorick" line. Another joke. He didn't, but just hung the speaker back up by its L-shaped hook.

"Quite a place." He turned the smile around toward Felton. "When was the last time anybody showed a movie here?"

Felton shrugged. His shirt stuck to his damp shoulder blades. "It was a while back."

"Yeah—" The other one spoke. "Must've been *Gone With the Wind.*"

The first one smiled over his shoulder at his buddy. The same smile between them. Felton wondered if they were faggots, the way they appreciated every fucking little thing the other one did. But they'd be the kind who'd always have dynamite-looking chicks hanging off them, in the evening when you saw them, when they weren't doing business. The women would be like the suits and the French sunglasses, and the purring car they'd driven up in; things worth having because *you* didn't have them. A little ticking flash appeared at the corner of his vision as he looked at the two young guys; it went in time with the fist clenching and unclenching under his breastbone.

They weren't impressed; that's what the smiles meant. He'd have to say something, to drag the sale back among them, lay it at their feet, like a fox terrier that's just killed a gopher.

"It turns a profit. I mean, even without showing movies. We got the swap meet in here on weekends. Brings in a lot of people." Felton lifted his damp hand and drew an arc, a blessing on the invisible booths and folding tables, the campers and pickup trucks and cars with the trunk lids jawed open, the rope lines strung between two-by-fours, the gauzy pastel baby clothes, the dangling T-shirts with heavy metal emblems or PARTY NAKED or SHIT HAPPENS printed on them; the polished rocks presided over by old desert rats with cowboy hats shading their wrinkled leather faces and bolo ties with big slices of turquoise pulled up tight around their stringy necks; the two-dollar cuff-link sets, three for five dollars, your choice of initials; and the real junk, the old Avon bottles and chipped dinnerware and souvenir salt and pepper shakers that never sold but came back every weekend, that gave the old folks the excuse to sit out under the sun with their folding chairs and picnic coolers and snoozing dogs, to gossip with each other and watch the crowd shuffling by, waiting for someone to pick up a set of pink Tupperware bowls and ask the price, nod and set the bowls back down, shuffle on . . . the three-dollar admission fee was cheap enough for that much entertainment.

"Right—swap meets." The young guy nodded, looking about. "That's a real growth industry." He walked a couple yards away, stopped, and gazed out past the chainlink fence and the waist-high brown weeds bunched up on either side.

Felton turned to the other one. "What exactly are you fellows looking for? I mean . . . is a drive-in what you want?"

The other looked up from the clipboard he carried. Shrugged. "We've got a group of investors that we do some scouting for. Pick up some properties here and there."

"For what?"

Looking at the clipboard again. "Different things. Condo development, industrial parks . . . stuff like that."

Stuff like that . . . It all smelled like money. The sweat under Felton's arms oozed over his ribs, like two soft damp hands. "This is a great location. For stuff like that."

He didn't get a reply; the young guy was writing something on the clipboard.

The first one had gone over to the snack-bar building, poking around, smearing the dust from one of the big plate-glass windows to peer inside. He walked around, slapping the dust from his hand, then rattled the locked door toward the back. "What d'you keep in here?"

Felton obediently trotted over, the sun raking through the thin strands on his scalp. He unlocked the door and pushed it open. "I use it for my office. When I'm out here." As if he had some bigger office in town or something, with a mahogany desk and a secretary out front.

The young guy prowled around, picking up a video-cassette from one of the open cardboard boxes. "You keep these out here? I'd have thought they'd melt away." The office was a baking oven, the shut-up air thick and stifling; the young guy in his black suit remained sweatless.

"They're for the swap meet." A trickle of salt ran down into the corner of Felton's eye, stinging him.

"You sell them?" Clipboard had slid into the office,

too, sniffing about the boxes and the trash mounded in the corners.

Felton nodded. "Just . . . you know . . . as a sideline."

"A sideline . . . Sure . . ." The young guy nodded; he understood. Why a sideline would be needed. Felton wished he hadn't said it. It was embarrassing to be understood like that. He watched the young guy pick up a couple more cassettes from the box, looking at the gray Xeroxed labels on the front, the gray pictures. "There much of a market for stuff like this? Out here?" He held the cassettes up so Felton could see the labels.

He felt himself reddening, heat from under the skin meeting the warm sweat on top. The smudgy label on the cassette in front showed a skinny blonde's hair dangling across a pair of hairy thighs, as she stuffed her partner into her mouth; her spit looped in a string over a nest of curling black hair. The other cassettes were more of the same; the Xeroxed labels made the naked people look like photos of accident victims in an old newspaper.

"There's some—you know, people like that sort of thing." What was he supposed to say?—They're not mine, I don't watch that sort of thing. Why should he apologize to these little fuckers? The first guy was showing the videocassettes to his buddy, and that little knowing smile, the big joke, passed again between them. The one with the clipboard had nodded toward the rows of tape machines and televisions against the wall, and the smile went on; they thought he was some lonely old bastard, fat and womanless, coming out here to his private stash in the sun-baked little room, jerking off in the middle of the empty asphalt and forest of little iron poles. He wanted to tell them about the parties, about the kids coming around—the team; he was buddies with the team; that was important—but he held it back. They'd think he was lying, making stuff up. Business talk was better: "Uh . . . you gotta know your market." That sort of thing.

"That's right." Smile. "You should always know your market." Laying the cassettes back down on top of the box.

The urge to pound his fist into the young guy's smile pulsed up inside him, drawing his spine tight. He followed the two of them back outside.

"What's that over there?" The young guy pointed through the sun's glare. His buddy with the clipboard looked where he pointed.

Felton shaded his eyes with his hand. His head ached, the light jabbing in under his eyelids like glass splinters. How much longer were these guys going to dink around out here? "That's the connector loop. To the Interstate. You got good freeway access here."

"Everyplace has got freeway access. Nothing but freeway access. No, I meant over there; those buildings." The young guy stretched his arm farther out.

Past the fence and the road that circled around—there was just a hillside sloping away, all dust and weeds. Where the hills tapered down to the flat, another fence could be seen, and a few distant buildings.

Felton nodded; they would have to ask about that. "That's, um . . . a county facility."

The young guy turned and looked at him.

" 'County facility?' What is it, a hospital or something? What do you mean?"

"Looks like a school." Clipboard stood on his toes, balancing himself with one of the speaker poles. He'd spotted the green, sprinklered fields, the wire-mesh baseball cages. Flagpole in front.

"They put barbed wire around the schools out here?" The first one pointed with his thumb to the tops of the distant fence.

"It's thé, uh, the juvenile hall, actually." Fuckers.

"Really?" The two of them peered across the fences and dry riverbed at the buildings. Felton's heart drooped lower as he saw the one making another note on the clipboard. "You get a lot of escapees coming over here?"

He shook his head. "No. There's the barbed wire, right?" Which was bullshit. The county probation department didn't maintain the fence the way they should; the barbed wire was missing in sections, rusted away, or gone slack, drooping below the level of the regular wire mesh. He'd stood right here one time, and seen one of the juvie kids, in the standard uniform of T-shirt and faded blue jeans, turn from where he'd been playing left field and sprint for the fence, climbing right over it and dropping onto the access road on the other side, then loping down the riverbed as easy as a marathoner with a ways to go and nobody at his heels. The dumbfuck juvenile hall counselors hadn't even gone running after the kid, just watched him scramble over the fence and light out for the open spaces. They hadn't even stopped the baseball game; they'd sent another kid out to take over left field, while one of the counselors went inside to call up the police and tell them to watch out for one more rabbit on the road. Happened all the time.

So much for condos; Felton watched the one guy writing on his clipboard. People didn't care much for little gangsters and car thieves dropping into their back yards. Or maybe the developers could go with it, advertise it as a plus: Scenic View of Well-maintained Sports Fields. Watch Future Olympic Stars Practicing the Long Jump and Fifty-yard Dash.

The two young guys headed back to their car, at the far edge of the asphalt. Felton tagged after them.

"Thanks for the guided tour." The one who did most of the talking stood with his hand on the car's door handle. "We appreciate your taking the time."

He couldn't help himself; it just came blurting out. "So what do you think? Some real potential here, huh?" In his own ears it sounded pathetic, desperate.

The young guy shrugged. He stripped off his jacket and tossed it inside the car, a blast of cold air rushing from the open door. They'd left the engine and the air-conditioning running all the time they'd been walking around the place with him. "We might make a recommendation on it. Decent-enough location, nice level piece. Could do something with it."

He couldn't let it go. He felt dizzy standing under the sun, as though his brain had melted loose, shrinking in its bone can. "What are you talking about? I mean, in the range of?"

The other guy was leaning on top of the car, watching him. The first one stripped off his tie, threw it into the back seat on top of the jacket. "I suppose our people could go, oh, maybe ten thousand." He undid the top buttons of his shirt; when he got in and drove away, the air-conditioning would chill the light sheen of perspiration on his skin. "I don't think much more than that."

"Ten thousand?" Felton couldn't swallow; his tongue had become thick and dry. "You mean, like ten thousand above the asking? Ten thousand profit to me?"

The smile floated up again. "No. We mean ten thousand flat. For the whole thing."

"Fuh-fuck that shit." He couldn't believe what he'd heard. That wouldn't even get him out of the hole.

He'd take a bath on the place, at that price. These little fuckers were jerking him around. A joke price; he knew it. That's what all the smiling and shit meant. The sweat seeped over his red face. "You're outta your minds."

"Maybe so." The young guy slid behind the steering wheel, the other smiling sonuvabitch already in the car, working the buttons on the tape deck. "If you've got a better offer hanging, maybe you oughta take it." Don't call us. "Anyway, thanks for showing us around." We'll call you.

Felton watched the car driving away, rounding the corner for the narrow lane that led out of the drive-in and onto the road beyond. He thought he could hear the two of them laughing, the inside of the car filling with laughter, strong and cold as the rush from the air-conditioning.

That was the afternoon wasted. He trudged toward the snack bar, to lock up the office. Ten thousand . . . What a pile of crap. It was worth more than that. To him.

And it was Friday already; he felt grateful for that. Like the old folks who came out to the swap meet on the weekends, who hinged their whole lives on the one day of the week. If you could get to that day, it meant you were still alive.

He peered in at the tapes, and the VCRs and televisions hooked together, before closing the door and turning the key in the lock. That much was ready. He'd have to swing by the liquor store for the cases of beer.

Just thinking about it made him feel better. Screw those smiling queers and their goddamn ten thousand. The team was coming tonight. That was all that really mattered. He felt like going out to the road in front and pulling down the FOR SALE sign that had been there for so long. He'd never sell this place—he knew, now, that he didn't want to.

Squeezing the keys in his fist, hard enough for the metal to push a sharp red thread up his arm, he walked across the asphalt, through the stubby iron forest, back to where he'd left his own car.

Part One
Party Night

1

A woman had vomited up a man.

That's what it looked like to Larry. The woman's blond hair dangled across the man's thighs, his skin pallid white. The man lay there on his back, in a room with a mattress on the floor and nothing else; he raised his head to watch, with heavy-lidded disinterest, the last stages of his birth, the cylinder of red flesh sliding from the woman's lips. The curls of black hair were shiny with sweat and the thick strings of her spit looping over a ticking vein. The woman was naked also, her breasts two white shapes that dangled as she crouched on hands and knees, the last little bit of him emerging with another string stretching to the corner of her mouth as she pushed herself back. She wiped it away and stared out at Larry with dead eyes, waiting for him in that small room.

One of the other guys on the team laughed, a big hoarse guffaw. "Jee-zuss *Christ*—lookit that one go, will ya? Haw!" He tilted his head back and took a long gurgling pull at a can of beer.

Larry rubbed the can in his hand across his own brow, the cool damp drawing away a bit of the heat under the skin. He felt sick, the beer he'd drunk welling up in his throat, sour under his tongue. The room, Felton's "office," clamped around him, hot and stinking of the other guys' sweat, like the locker room at

school. But without the stinging smell of the disinfectant the janitors swabbed across the concrete floors,
or the warm, biscuity smell of the towels stacked up
in the laundry cage. Here, in this place, you had all
the jock sweat overlaid with spilled beer and the sticky-
sweet odor of whatever their girlfriends had sprayed
on themselves. Plus that other smell, like sweat but
mustier, ranker, seeping under the jeans and T-shirts
as the night and the party wore on. There was already
enough of it in the room's close air, triggered by Felton's tape collection, to clot in Larry's throat.

He turned away from the television and the VCR
sitting on top of it, and shoved his way through the
other varsity jackets like his own. If he were going to
be sick, it was better to do it far enough way from the
party that his teammates didn't know—he couldn't
stand their razzing, all that laughing and shit.

Near the door, with the night air soft and cool
against his throat and face, he could swallow the knot
of sour phlegm back down. Maybe he wouldn't be sick
after all, now that he could breathe something besides
the other guys' sweat. He looked back over his shoulder and saw Felton sitting on a crate near the TV,
leaning forward over his potbelly, as if he were going
to stick his head right into that other little room, the
grainy black-and-white one on the other side of the
screen, where now the blonde with the dead eyes had
her butt up in the air, the pale flesh slapped by the
stomach of the man pumping behind her.

"Yeah, these are really hot—" Felton's face was red
and damp, with a couple of the greased black strands
that he usually combed over his bald spot now dangling along the soft angle of his chin. "I get 'em from
some guy up in Vancouver. He gets 'em from someplace . . . I don't know; Sweden, maybe. Pretty good
stuff, huh?"

Felton looked around at the teenagers for confirmation. Hoping for it; pathetic with his wobbly face, the eyes made small and piggish by the swaddling jowls. Trying too hard, as he always did.

Larry turned back toward the door, feeling sick in a different way.

Another team member stood leaning in the doorway, finishing off a beer. For a moment, Dennie's eyes caught Larry's, then slid toward Felton; a thin smile showed Dennie's contempt for the old fuck, with his dirty tapes and beer and kissing up to the footballers. As if he could be one of them, be buddies with them. Larry could remember what Dennie had said, the first time he'd gone along to one of the parties at the drive-in, when he'd asked Dennie who this Felton guy was. *Just some old homo. Don't worry about him grabbing your ass—he just wants to sniff your jockstrap a little.* Dennie's gaze came back to Larry—*See? What'd I tell you?*—then he turned, pitching the empty beer can out into the darkness. He let out a gassy belch as he sauntered outside.

Larry followed him. The night air chilled the sweat that had seeped through the shirt under his jacket.

"That stupid old fuck." Dennie stopped a couple yards away from the building. It had been the snack bar and projection booth back when the drive-in had still been showing movies; Larry remembered coming here with his mom and dad. Dennie dug in the side pocket of his jacket, rooting around under the big letter M, his hand finally coming out with a cigarette. "As if anybody cared about his dirty movies."

That was true; Larry could look back through the doorway, the light spilling out across the asphalt, and see that it was only Felton and a couple of the grosser guys on the team, like that second-string center with the big slobbering laugh, who were paying much attention to what the stringy blonde and the man were doing to each other. The other footballers were working through Felton's cases of beer and talking shit with one another or their girlfriends. Leaning back against the office's walls or sitting on the cardboard boxes of videotapes, not the dirty ones but the ones Felton sold at the swap meet every weekend; not caring whether they buckled open the plastic cases holding the tapes, Felton being too chickenshit to tell them to move their butts.

The voices and the laughter thinned out in the night air, floating over the empty asphalt, a whisper echo bouncing back from the pockmarked white screen looming over the far end of the drive-in.

"Catch you later." The cigarette waggled in Dennie's mouth as he talked, a spark dropping across the front of his jacket. "Gotta take a leak."

Larry watched him walking away, one hand already fumbling at the top of his fly. Dennie stopped by one of the cars parked in a ring around the snack bar. One of the other guys on the team lifted his head to look out the driver's-side window, his girlfriend pushing herself up from the seat on one elbow, holding the loose band of her bra against her breasts. The voice drifted back, annoyed: "Hey, asshole—you're pissing on my tires—"

Dennie smiled and flipped the guy off, the upraised finger caught in the cigarette's glow.

The guy in the car settled down, grumbling. Dennie had the weight advantage over him, over anybody on the team. A pissed-on tire wasn't worth getting your brains knocked out.

Larry leaned back against the snack-bar building, out of the light falling from the doorway. By his feet, an exhaust hose from a little Honda generator puffed away—that was the only electricity old Felton had in the place. The smell of the exhaust drifted up to him. He didn't feel sick any longer; all he'd needed was air. Now he wished he had another beer.

The flashlight beam swept over the ground, from left to right and back again. Behind it, Taylor walked, picking his way through the rocks and dry, scrubby brush. He knew his way up the low rise of the hill—he'd come this way dozens of times, always in the dark. The prints of his shoes were still there in the dust, from the last time. As he came to the top of the hill, he switched off the flashlight, so no one in the distance on the other side would be able to spot him.

He could hear them better now. He'd been able to hear them even before he'd unlocked the door of the intake unit and stepped outside. The voices, the laughing and roaring of car engines, had grown louder as he'd walked the damp grass toward the perimeter fence. Now, standing at the crest of the hill, the noise washed right up against his chest and into his face, as though he'd waded into some ocean choked with floating trash. That's what the voices sounded like, if they could have been grabbed hold of and squeezed down inside his fist. Taylor stood looking down, listening and rubbing the cold metal of the flashlight in his palm.

On the other side of the hills was the old drive-in, circled by a narrow access road and a chain-link fence. Once the fence had been made of tall boards, nailed together without a gap between them, to keep people from parking outside and seeing the movies for free, doing without the sound tracks, just watching the giant faces on the big screen. When the drive-in had been shut down for the last time, the board fence sagged and fell apart, until the fire department made the owners drag the lumber away and put up the new fence. That had been years ago.

From up here, the drive-in always looked like a forest to him, one that had been strip-logged, leaving nothing but short stumps, the land scraped bare around them. He'd seen that once, when he'd been driving around up north. Enough light spilled from the open doorway at the side of the old snack-bar building to show the rows of metal poles from which the speakers had hung, waiting for cars to drive up and windows to roll down. About half the poles had no speakers hanging on them at all; they'd been ripped off by the kids. Just the wires remained, dangling to the cracked and gouged asphalt.

The footballers had parked their cars in a loose circle around the snack-bar building. As Taylor watched, a couple more turned off the road running in front of the drive-in, speeding down the drive-in's entry lane, then cutting across the humps and valleys of the asphalt, headlights bouncing up and down as they went. Heading for the party—just past midnight when Taylor had left the hall to go on his nightly perimeter check, and the kids sometimes didn't really get going until nearly two A.M. The noises from the party would just get louder. As he stood there, he heard glass shattering—probably bottles, maybe one of the windows at the front of the snack bar—followed by more raucous laughter.

Taylor caught the flashlight's head as he struck it into his palm. Those little shits down there . . . He turned, letting the party noise wash against his shoulders, and strode away, heading back through the dark to the juvenile hall.

Repken looked up from what he was reading when he heard the side door opening. He didn't bother taking his feet off the desktop behind the intake-unit counter, just tilted his head back to raise his eyes from the *People* magazine in his lap. It was Taylor coming in, pulling his key from the lock and shoving it into his pocket, the lanyard dangling from his belt. Taylor was okay; Repken had been nodding out between Michael Jackson's chimpanzee and some blond TV star graduating from the Betty Ford Clinic. Taylor had that pissed-off look on his face; there'd be at least enough action, of one kind or another, to help get through another slice of the graveyard shift, ease the clock down to seven A.M. and going-home time.

He laid the magazine beside his feet as Taylor crossed through the dayroom to the counter. He didn't even have to ask what was going on, what it was that had yanked Taylor's chain while he'd been out doing his nightly prowl around the hall's fence.

"Those jerk kids . . ." Taylor didn't bother with the rest of the sentence, one that Repken had already heard enough times: . . . *are at it again.* The same thing, at least two nights every week, sometimes three or four once the football season was over and they weren't worn out from practices and the games.

They weren't even particularly bad tonight; there had been lots of nights when the parties at the old drive-in were lots louder, the shouting and laughing, and the boom-box thumps and car engines revving, all of it coming across the dark athletic fields around the juvenile hall and right inside the building. When it got that loud, it'd wake up the kids inside the hall, the distant hilarity getting them all on the same rowdy wavelength; they'd start pounding on the metal doors of their rooms—you weren't supposed to call them "cells"; you weren't supposed to put what were technically children into "cells"—and shouting and ripping up their bedding. They'd have to spend the whole shift, at least until four in the morning or so, when the footballers' party started to fade, just quieting the hall's

living units down. That was *really* the shits—that was
worth getting pissed off about. But on a relatively quiet
night like this, when all the little felons and car thieves
were still snoozing away . . . If Repken had been in
charge on the night shift, rather than Taylor, he'd have
let it slide.

Taylor reached over the counter, knocking Repken's
shoes aside to reach the phone. He picked the phone
up and set it down facing himself, then dialed. Leaning against the counter, he waited for somebody to
answer.

Somebody did—Repken heard the muffled ringing
cut off, then somebody going *Mutter-mutter* at the
other end.

"Yeah, this is the night duty officer over at the juvenile hall." Taylor turned around, holding the phone
to his ear. He kept his voice dead level. "Look, I was
just out by our rear fence—there's a bunch of kids over
at the old drive-in." He paused. *Mutter.* "Yeah, it's
the same bunch; I'm pretty sure. Look, it's audible all
the way over here. That constitutes a disturbance as
far as we're concerned. You're going to have to send
somebody over there to break it up." *Mutter, mutter.*
"Yeah, right. Okay, thanks."

He took the phone from his ear, and carefully—the
phone's base was cracked from where he'd slammed it
once before—set it down.

Repken scratched the side of his face with the rolled-
up *People.* "I don't know why you bother. The cops
never do anything . . ."

Taylor set the phone back on the desktop. He picked
up the intake unit's logbook, flipped it open, and began writing up the incident, glancing up at the dayroom's wall clock to get the time right. Just past one
A.M.

He closed the book on the pen. "Yeah, well . . .

we'll see about that." He turned and looked out the bank of windows filled with night, listening to the distant noise.

It was better to be invisible. To be so quiet, not even breathing, until no one could see you. Steven could do that. If he tried hard enough, he wasn't even there, there was no one in the back seat of the car at all. There were just two eyes watching, seeing everything.

He could see that his sister's boyfriend was angry. Just from the way Mick drove, the way his shoulders were bunched up inside his jacket, the same jacket that all the football players wore. Every once in a while, Steven saw Mick's eyes, narrowed down to mean little slits, in the rearview mirror, glaring back at him, or where he'd be if he was really there in the back seat. *Invisible* . . . Steven looked out the side window and watched the blue pools under the streetlights sliding past.

"So how come we always gotta bring him along?" Mick's voice was sour, as though he had some thick wad rolled up on his tongue to spit outside. He took one hand from the steering wheel and pointed over his shoulder with his thumb. "Huh?"

That was why Mick was angry. Not just because they'd had to stop and get something to eat—there hadn't been anything in the house, and Steven's mother hadn't gone to the store the way she'd said she was going to. She had fallen asleep on the couch instead, and both Steven and his sister Kris had known better than to try to wake her. Better to let her go on sleeping. He had enough of his own money to get a hamburger at the Burger King, eating it at one of the little benches outside while Mick and Kris took theirs back to the car. Until Mick had honked the horn and had shouted for him to get this butt inside the car, it was time to go. They were already late getting out to the party.

But it wasn't just that. He knew, even before Mick had said anything. Mick was angry about having to drag around his girlfriend's ten-year-old brother.

Steven watched his sister smiling at Mick. Her eyes looked lazy, half-shut. He knew they'd been drinking when they'd been at the Burger King—that was why they'd gone back to the car to eat, so nobody would see them emptying the little bottle of Bacardi into their Cokes. The restaurant manager had already chased off Mick and his buddies a couple of times for hanging around the parking lot and doing stuff like that.

Kris reached over, her arm drifting loosely, as though underwater. He could tell she was really plastered, already. She toyed with a curl of Mick's hair, winding it around her finger. "Because—" Her smile widened. "Because he's my little chaperon." She turned her head, looking over the back of the seat. "Aren't you?"

Invisible . . . Steven looked at her smiling at him, smelled the sweet tang of the alcohol on her breath, like their mother's. He wasn't really there; Kris was smiling at nothing. He looked out the side window, at the shapes moving past in the dark, in and out of the pools of light.

"Aren't you, huh?" She said it through clenched teeth, the smile turned into something mean and hard. From the corner of his eye, Steven saw the point of her finger, the sharp curved edge of her nail. His sister reached across the back of her seat and jabbed her finger at him, catching him on the cheek. He batted her hand away, a quick reflex, and felt his stomach churn up a red wave of fury, which he had to swallow, pushing it down in his throat. She had already seen him, made him be there in her boyfriend's car, trapped, and if he said anything, shouted at her to leave him alone, it would only make it worse. She was bored and playful—Steven knew how she got—and he'd be the handiest thing to have fun with. As usual.

He shouldn't have knocked her hand away, he shouldn't have reacted at all. Steven turned back to the window beside him, staring out at the dark. He wasn't inside Mick's car; he was out there, in the night, watching and listening.

He could hear his sister still talking. She had lost interest in him, and had turned back around to Mick.

"Mom thinks you won't try anything with him around." She laid her arm along the back of the seat, her hand rubbing Mick's shoulder, fingers kneading through his varsity jacket. "That's how she's keeping me a virgin."

Mick glanced at her. "Yeah, right . . ." Voice sour, still pissed off. "Shit." He reached and snapped on the radio, turning it up so the music hammered at them, filling the car.

Steven looked at the two of them, then back at the dark outside. Things, the streets and the buildings, stopped moving past; the red glare of the traffic light Mick had stopped at washed along the ground. Then it snaked upward, as though it were alive, over the grille and across the hood of another car that had pulled up and stopped at the light in the next lane. Steven watched the other car, black and low, like a hole that had been cut out in the night that let a deeper black show through. He couldn't see the driver through the dark glass, just a shape behind the wheel. Underneath the radio's whining clatter he could hear the low murmur of the other car's engine, soft as it waited.

Kris was still talking. Far off, another place. "So anyway, the stupid bitch really started ragging on me, like she told me it was the third time I'd been late to

her class, and I just go, you know, like Fuck you, I
don't have to listen to a word you say—''

"Yeah, sure . . ." Mick drummed his fingers along
the top of the steering wheel, waiting for the light to
change.

Outside, in the night, the other car's door opened.
Steven watched as the driver stepped out onto the
street.

"I did!" Kris' voice shrilled up a notch. "That's
just what I told her!"

If there had been other cars pulled up at the intersection, with their headlights coming across from the
other side, he might have been able to see the driver's
face. But there was just Mick's car and the other one,
side by side, their lights falling into darkness, showing
nothing. Mick and Kris didn't even see the driver as
he stepped around the back of the other car's dark
shape and walked toward them. Steven saw, and
watched, holding his breath so that he was silent and
invisible again.

The driver walked up to Mick's door and reached
for the handle.

"Hey—" Mick jerked around, startled by the door
being yanked open, the night spilling inside the car.
"What the—"

The driver's arm swung in an arc down to Mick's
face. The blow rocked Mick back against the seat,
snapping his head around. In the distance, Steven
heard Kris screaming as the bright drops of blood
spattered across her face. Mick's eyes, astonished,
goggled at her, the blood welling from beneath the flap
of skin torn from his jaw. The red seeped around the
teeth showing through. Mick's own scream sobbed up
in his throat as he raised his hands, cringing against
Kris beside him. The driver's arm lifted, Mick's blood
a wet patch across the back of his hand, and swung

down again, the blow a curve that Steven saw hanging
in space, solid and hard, the moment of its impact
reeling out with no end to it. . . .

Then the car was silent, the screaming, Mick's and
Kris', snapped away. Into the same nothing as before.
The light turned green and Mick hit the accelerator.
He looked back at Steven in the rearview mirror. No
blood, just the same broad face, the little mean eyes.
Beside him, Kris picked at one of her stick-on finger-
nails; she looked bored.

"What the hell you staring at?" Mick's eyes glared
from the mirror.

Steven didn't say anything. He turned and looked
back through the side window, at the other car still
sitting at the intersection. The driver, with the face he
couldn't see, still sat behind the wheel, a dark shape
in the darkness. He hadn't gotten out of the car, come
around to Mick's door, and done all that. The arc, the
backhand blow, still frozen in its moment inside Steven. The driver had just sat there, waiting.

He could hear Mick grumbling. "Fuckin' weird
kid . . ."

The other car didn't move. It drew back into darkness, the headlights dwindling to points, until he
couldn't see it any longer, his cheek pressed against
the cold window glass. He went on looking, long after
the night had filled in the hole where it had been.

2

Larry watched Mick's car pull around, a big parading loop across the drive-in's asphalt, the headlights swinging up and down as it bumped over the hills and valleys. A big Chevy, a family-type car that Mick's old man had let him have, rather than trading it in when they'd bought a new one. Mick slammed on the brakes a couple of inches from the nearest in the ring of cars around the snack bar, the Chevy rocking back and forth on its squashy suspension. Larry leaned back against the side of the building, sipping at the beer he was nursing to get through the rest of the night.

Mick got out of the car. His girlfriend, that stupid Kris, still sat there, putting on lipstick and checking herself out in the mirror, as though she were about to make her entrance at some friggin' prom dance, instead of the usual beer and horsing-around session. She thought she was hot shit, because she'd latched on to—at least for a little while—the captain of the team. Both of them thought they were hot shit; Larry figured they made a good match.

The party had moved outside, bored with old Felton's dirty videotapes. Only Felton and that slobby second-string center, and a couple of the scrubs, were still in there, watching a different blonde with the same dead eyes fingering her own bald crotch. As Mick came sauntering over, one of the guys threw him a beer.

Mick caught it with both hands low by his hip, like a pass bulleting into the end zone. He popped it open and took a long pull, tilting his head back. Already there was a little group forming around him, his teammates doing no more than shifting position or turning around from other conversations, the motions showing the new gravity pull in their midst.

Dennie had had a couple over the line and was working on another, pouring the beer in on top of all the rest he'd drunk. He stood right by the doorway to Felton's office, where he could get at the cases easily. Larry had seen him like that before—it happened at every party—where Dennie got to the point where all he did was drink, one after the other, as fast as he could. He didn't even look as though he were enjoying himself, sweating red-faced and breathing hard, the way he did when he was ramming his shoulder into the sledge out on the practice field on a hot afternoon.

He hadn't even seen Mick come driving up, or get out of the car and come ambling over, a smile on his face. Larry watched as Mick came up behind Dennie. When Dennie raised his beer to his mouth, guzzling noisily, Mick's smile grew wider; he smacked Dennie's elbow with his hand, a good hard jolt. Dennie's head snapped back as the can hit his nose and mouth, the beer splashing out in a foaming gush, dribbling down Dennie's mouth and onto the front of his T-shirt.

Dennie whirled around, the beer can already dropped, his fists coming up. His eyes had been red before—now Larry, standing yards away, saw them narrow with anger. That lasted only a second, all it took for Dennie to see who had been messing with him. The anger faded, replaced with a silly-ass smile, mirroring the sharper-edged one on Mick's face. Mick could pull shit like that and get away with it; he blocked a pretend punch from Dennie with his forearm, then feinted one back before handing Dennie his half-empty can of beer and reaching past him to get a fresh one. Larry turned away from watching them. He'd seen all of their little buddy moves before; these parties were like some kind of funky time warp out of a science-fiction magazine, where the same shit happened over and over, with nobody ever escaping.

Some of the girlfriends had collected in a knot to one side. Kris had finally managed to make it out of the car, going over there to talk with the little pack. Larry thought it was funny that they all hated each other so much—scheming on each other's boyfriends, out of pure malice or a desire to move up in some complicated rating scheme, or talking shit about whichever one of them wasn't there at the moment— yet they all smiled at each other and said Hi in two syllables whenever one of them showed up. Like they were just fucking overjoyed to see Kris.

Larry rubbed the beer can against his face as he watched them, though it had warmed to the same temperature as his skin. He knew he'd gotten to the point where the beer was ebbing out of his brain cells, leaving him tired and cooled-out. That was the best time for watching people and the stupid shit they did, just floating above them, as though you were facedown in the ocean and they were scuttling around in the rocks and crevices below.

Most of the others didn't know how to be cool, though; how to just relax and feel the slow motion crawl of their thoughts inside their heads. They had to get hyper and do shit. As Larry watched, two of his teammates, a tackle called McNuldy and some beefy punk whose name he could never remember, went strolling up to the side of Mick's car, beers in hand. There was somebody in there, slumped down in the back seat, staring straight ahead, ignoring McNuldy and the other guy when they rapped on the window.

"Hey, Kris!" The side of beef—that's what he looked like, with his big raw face—called over to the girls. "You brought that little turd along, huh?" He pointed with his thumb to the car's window.

Kris looked over and made a disgusted face. "Yeah—I had to."

McNuldy stepped back as the other guy jerked open the car door. He leaned inside, a leering smile spreading over his face. "Hey, kid, ready for a little party? You look like you could use it."

The kid, on the small side even for a ten-year-old, glanced up at the footballer. The kid—what was his name? Larry couldn't remember—shot a look of pure simmering hatred at the figure looming over him. He didn't look like a kid, with that kind of face. The two footballers, on the other hand, looked like babies who'd been puffed up and made big, with big booming laughs to match.

McNuldy reached past the other guy and grabbed hold of the kid's shirt. He dragged the kid to the edge of the car seat, his hamlike fist bunching up enough of the shirt to pull it out of the kid's jeans, showing his pink stomach. The kid pushed futilely with both hands at McNuldy's forearm.

"Come on—it's party time." McNuldy and the other guy grinned at the kid's efforts to pull free. "You know how to party, don't you, kid? You start like this—" McNuldy brought his beer around and shoved it in the kid's face, squashing the kid's nose against the top of the can as he tilted it. The kid spluttered, the beer pouring over his cheeks and down his neck, wetting the shirt in McNuldy's fist.

Larry heard the laughing grow louder. He looked around and saw that they were all laughing, everyone at the party. Something, a little spark in the boredom that had set in. Mick and Dennie over by the doorway, Dennie's guffaw, practically doubling over, his face growing even redder, and Mick's smile lifting to show the teeth at one corner of his mouth; and Kris, the kid's own sister, shrieking along with the other girlfriends. The sound of all their laughing, the voices shouting, battered against Larry, filling his head, until he felt it pushing against his skull from inside. Part of him wanted to laugh, too, join in, to be there with the rest of them. He looked at the kid with the beer running down his chin, and felt his own mouth tighten, the lips drawing back. Then the laughter came out, from his own mouth.

McNuldy looked over his shoulder, grinning, drinking in everyone else's hilarity. That gave the kid his chance: twisting around, he managed to knock the footballer's grip free of his shirt. McNuldy, taken by surprise, stumbled back a step. The kid grabbed the door's inside handle and pulled. An inch short of slamming shut, the door was grabbed by McNuldy. A couple of seconds of tug-of-war, the kid bracing his feet against the car's floor and both skinny arms straining at the handle, and the footballer getting pissed off. Then the kid suddenly let go, the door flew open, and McNuldy landed on his butt.

The laughing went louder. McNuldy was drunk enough that for a second or two, as he sprawled backward on the asphalt, he still had a stupid grin on his face; then he realized that everyone was laughing at him now. Even his buddy who had gone over to Mick's car with him, just to torment the little kid—the guy was practically choking, eyes squeezing out tears as he leaned against the car's rear fender, holding his arms against his gut.

The grin drained off McNuldy's face. He scrambled

to his feet, jaw jutting forward. The kid had made a fool of him—that was why they were all laughing. He reached for the door's handle, but it was already swinging open, pushing him back. Kris' little brother slid out and ran, brushing past McNuldy's laughing buddy.

"You little shit!" McNuldy grabbed for the kid, but was too slow; the kid was already out of his reach, sprinting into the dark beyond the ring of cars. "Come back here, goddamn it!" McNuldy scooped up his beer from the ground and threw it after the kid; the can bounced hollowly on the asphalt, beyond where anyone could see.

Larry wiped his eyes, his own laughter dying inside him. Now, that had been funny, seeing that big tub of shit knocked on his can by a skinny little ten-year-old. He drew in a deep breath, feeling still a little sick at the base of his throat. Maybe if he'd drunk more, he wouldn't have remembered what had started him laughing.

He looked out across the drive-in's empty field, to where the kid had gone running off. The kid was out there, still running in the dark.

His breath burned inside him, and his ribs ached where he had collided with one of the speaker poles. He'd been running blind, legs and pulse pumping, and he hadn't seen the pole, one of those that had been bent over at nearly a forty-five-degree angle; it had caught him right in the side, sending him skidding onto one knee and his hands, a burst of red light behind his eyes. Dizzy when he scrambled back to his feet, he'd taken off running again. The only thing he'd been able to see in the dark was the chain-link fence at the drive-in's far edge. He ran toward that, putting

as much distance as he could between him and the
footballers' party.

Steven slowed, pulling in gulps of breath, when the
fence was a couple of yards away. He stopped, turning
to look behind him. The palms of his hands stung as
he pressed them against his jeans, head lowered as he
panted.

He could see the cars silhouetted by the light from
the snack bar's open doorway. The shadows stretched
across the asphalt. Plus some of the footballers, his
sister's friends, standing around and talking; this far
away, he couldn't hear any of their voices, only the
muted thump of music from one of their tape players.
Nobody was coming after him—he'd managed to disappear, to become nothing again, invisible in the dark.
They'd have to go back to their other games now.

There was just the rest of the night to get through,
until it was time to go home. Steven limped over to
one of the speaker poles, holding the edge of his ribs.
Now that he wasn't running, he could feel the pain of
the impact, a dull throb in time to his heartbeat. He
probed with his fingertips, wondering if maybe he'd
broken something. The memory of the arm he'd broken when he'd been seven was still clear, a piece of
time that he could take out and look at, everything still
bright as the lights in the hospital emergency room.
Even the part where the doctor, a young-looking black
woman—Steven's mom had called her black, though
she'd looked brown to him, like coffee with cream—
with bright-red frames to her glasses, had taken him
to a little room by himself, the smell of the cast's drying plaster tickling his nose and the metal strut sticking out like a piece underneath a folding table. The
lady doctor had asked him how he'd gotten his arm
broken, and he'd told her just what his mom had told
him to say, even after the doctor had asked him was

he *sure* for the third time, her voice soft but insistent. That was the one part he couldn't remember now, what his mom had told him to say. When they'd come out of the little room, the lady doctor had looked hard at his mom, but hadn't said anything to her.

It didn't feel like anything was broken. Steven pushed his fingertips harder against his bottom rib. The thought of it being broken, a sharp, jagged edge floating around and puncturing his stomach, or sticking out like a bicycle spoke, made a picture in his mind that wouldn't go away. It's just bruised—he told himself that, and took his hand away from his side. Bruises always went away, eventually.

He sat down on the asphalt, leaning back against a speaker pole. His breath had slowed to normal, and the ache in his side was slowly ebbing away. That was all right—he'd gotten off light, compared to a couple weeks ago, when they'd caught him and thrown him around, up in the air, and he'd landed with a scraping jolt to the side of his head. When he touched his ear, there had been blood all over his hand, and for a moment he'd wondered, in a numb dizziness, his head still ringing, whether his ear had been torn all the way off. He'd actually picked up himself up onto his hands and knees and started looking for it, while their laughter washed over him from miles away. Kris had told their mom some story when they'd gone back home, about how he'd gotten so banged up—the blood had dried to a black crust on his ear and down his neck— and she had just shrugged, barely open eyes still on the TV, and told him to be more goddamn careful. He couldn't remember any of the stories, no matter who told them, even if he told them; there was just a hole there afterward.

What really hurt was that they had seen him. The footballers, Kris' boyfriend and all his buddies—he hadn't been able to make himself invisible, nothing at all, just an empty space where he could watch and listen from. No matter how hard he tried, how quiet he stayed, every breath slowly whispered out and drawn back in . . . they always found him. Somebody always did.

He laid his arms on his knees, resting his chin on the sleeve of his jacket. He looked back toward the party, the shadows wavering back and forth. Maybe they had forgotten him, at least for a while. Out here in the dark, he could watch and wait, and spot any of them coming his way, before they could catch him again.

The palms of his hands stung where he'd fallen on them. He turned one hand up to his face, brushing the specks of dirt off against his chin. All he had to do was wait.

Silence around him—those other noises, the laughter and the music, were far away. Steven raised his head; there was another sound, from behind him. He heard the low murmur of a car's engine, a bass note barely audible in the still night air. He turned his head, looking over his shoulder.

The car's headlights, two bright spots against the dark—that was all he could see at first. Down the fenced-off lane that led into the drive-in, where it opened onto the road outside; the headlights hung there, motionless. The engine sound, something Steven felt more in his stomach than heard, drifted across the asphalt to him. He twisted around from where he sat, leaning forward to see better. There was a dark shape out there, behind the headlights' glare. The car, black against black—he couldn't see inside, it was too far away and somehow filled with the darkness, a piece of it. But there would have to be somebody inside it.

He knew who was inside the car. Sitting behind the wheel, and waiting. He'd seen the car before.

Steven turned away, pressing his spine back against the cold metal of the speaker pole. Even when he closed his eyes, he could still hear it out there, the engine murmuring its slow patience. The driver could wait, too. There was all night to wait.

People had started to leave. Once the beer ran out— most of the guys who were by themselves, without girlfriends, took off, after ambling back from taking a piss at the far corner of the drive-in. No point in sticking around; it was just as boring here as anywhere else. Even old Felton had fallen asleep, tanked out on his own beer, slumped in a folding chair inside his office, the screen of the television turned to gray dancing snow, the last dirty tape he'd put on run all the way through.

"Come on." One of the other guys nudged Larry's shoulder. "Let's go get something to eat."

He was sitting on the ground, back against the wall of the snack-bar building. A shake of his head as he looked up at his teammate. "Naw—" He rubbed his face; it felt stiff, as though the alcohol ebbing out of his system had taken something with it. "I'm gonna head on home. I'm feeling kinda bushed."

"Suit yourself." The guys started heading over to their cars. "Catch you later."

"Yeah, right—later." Soon as his head cleared a little more, he'd push himself upright and get in his car—his folks' car; they let him have it whenever he wanted, though—and go home, hit the sack. He didn't feel drunk; he hadn't hit that point all night. Just tired and sick. He felt stupid, disgusted with himself, coming to these parties. Every goddamn week, night after night. They weren't even parties, just a bunch of high-school jocks soaking up some aging football groupie's free beer. Because there wasn't shit else to do. He had already set it down in his heart that when he graduated next year, he was going to get out of this dump, if he had to join the fucking army to do it.

He looked over toward the cars. Mick and his girl-friend Kris were there, horsing around. She sat on the edge of the back seat, with Mick leaning on top of the open door. With her little brother out of there—where did the kid go off to hide?—they could do what they wanted. Though they did it, Larry knew, whether the kid was around or not. A favorite topic with the other girls, what Kris would do, practically right out in pub-lic; they chalked it up to her wanting to stay latched on to Mick, at the top of their little social ladder. You got points for laying the quarterback.

Mick and Kris were finishing off a couple of beers, ones he must have had stashed in the trunk of his car. He said something and she laughed, loud and sloppy, head tilted back so her back teeth showed. Mick threw away his empty can and pushed her farther back into the car, climbing in after her, then reaching over and pulling the door shut.

The back of Mick's head bobbed up in sight, then disappeared below the level of the window. Larry looked away, and out across the empty drive-in. He could still hear them laughing inside the car.

The car was gone. Steven raised his head and looked over his shoulder. He'd fallen asleep—he didn't know for how long; maybe only a couple of minutes—and the car, the black one out by the drive-in's entrance, had disappeared. He blinked and rubbed his eyes, hard enough to draw a pulse of light from inside his head.

When he took his hand away, he saw again the empty road, the space where the car had been.

Quiet now—the noise, the laughing and shouting from the party, had ebbed away. As though the night had flowed in across the asphalt, a dark tide covering up the things that had been visible for a little while, the signs of life. Dark and quiet; that was the way it ought to be, the way it would be for a long time.

Steven pushed himself up from the ground, pinpricks climbing up the back of his leg. He held on to the speaker pole and shook his foot to get the blood flowing in it again. Looking across the drive-in, he saw a few cars still parked around the snack-bar building. The footballers' party had died down to the last few stragglers; some of them, he knew from the times before, were so drunk that they would be sleeping it off right there.

He couldn't tell if Mick's car was still there. It was hard to make out the Chevy this far away, in the dark. Maybe Mick and his sister had gone off and left him there; maybe they had called for him while he'd been asleep and he hadn't heard them, their shouts drifting across the emptiness. They wouldn't have bothered to go around looking for him, blundering around where they couldn't see; they'd have laughed and said To hell with it—since they hadn't wanted him around in the first place.

The light still spilled from the open doorway at the side of the snack bar. That gave him something to head toward as he walked across the empty drive-in, the pinpricks just a tingle around his ankle now. Part of him hoped that they had gone and left him; if they weren't there, then he was free, at least for a little while. He wouldn't have to endure all the little torments that his sister and her boyfriend could cook up. To be lost, a million miles away—that was even better than being invisible. He'd pay for it when he got back home, though.

He saw Mick's car at last. It didn't look as if anybody was there inside it. Slowly, stretching the distance out, he walked on toward it.

3

"Jesus fucking Christ . . ." Felton mumbled the words aloud. His mouth tasted as if some dead thing were rotting under his tongue. He shook his head, the last dregs of sleep rolling in a heavy slurry across his brain. He spat, but the foul taste remained.

The screen of the television simmered with gray dots. Out of habit, he reached over and punched the EJECT button on the tape machine. It whirred and ground out a half-inch of black plastic. As he put the cassette back into its case, he glanced at the grainy black-and-white label on top. It looked like two women, heads in each other's crotches, but he couldn't be sure. He couldn't even remember seeing any of the tape; he must've crashed out right after he'd hit the PLAY button.

He wondered if any of the team were still around, or if they'd all split by now. Pushing his sleeve back from his watch, he saw that it was nearly three in the morning. There were probably some of them still hanging around, even though the beer was all gone— the floor of the office was littered with empty cans, the bare concrete shiny-wet where some had spilled. The sight triggered a twinge deep inside his gut, and he realized he had to take a piss. Just lucky it hadn't happened while he'd been passed out—he hated that, waking up still half-drunk and finding the front of his trousers wet and chilled by the night air, the stink of his own urine rising to his nostrils. Whenever it had happened before, his self-disgust had been enough for him to go without drinking for nearly a week.

He pushed himself out of the chair and shambled to the door. There were a half-dozen cars still out there, the last of this night's party. The ache in his bladder sharpened; he didn't bother trying to see which of the footballers were still around, but stepped out into the dark and started walking toward the fence in back. That was where the kids all went to, making their little trips during the night; he ground his teeth together, wincing and walking faster.

"I don't see anything going on." Harrelson swung the patrol car's searchlight across the entrance of the drive-in. The wide beam swept across the asphalt beyond the fence, the chain link's shadows stretching out into the dark. "Seems pretty quiet to me."

Pineda looked across the front seat of the car at his partner. This stupid fuck—it took an effort just to keep from yelling at the guy. What he really wanted to do was pull his big flashlight out of the loop on his belt, and just beat some sense through Harrelson's thick skull. Instead, he kept his voice level. "Maybe that's because we're about two hours late responding to this call."

Harrelson shrugged. "Can't be everywhere at once."

You stupid sonuvabitch—Pineda closed his eyes and let a couple of slow, careful breaths go in and out. Take it easy, he told himself. As he did a dozen times, at least, every shift he pulled with Harrelson. The guy was as bad as that fat little fucker at the drive-in: they both were in love with these goddamn punks. Just because they were on the high school's piss-ant little football team. Fucking pathetic—careful; Pineda held down his temper—the way Harrelson let them get away with anything. These football punks could murder somebody, there could be a call over the patrol car's radio that they were dead bodies all over the drive-in and these dickheads were dancing around in their numbered uniforms and pads, waving machine guns, and Harrelson would *still* fiddle-fuck around for a couple of hours, cruising some neighborhood way over on the other side of town where some old granny had gotten her basement window broken two fucking weeks ago . . . Then hanging out at a doughnut shop, for Christ's sake, a fucking Winchell's, like some goddamn cartoon or something, everybody's mental picture of lazy, fat, do-nothing cops drinking stale coffee and wheezing old jokes over the jelly-filleds and maple bars . . .

Cool it. Pineda swallowed the sour wad that had grown in his throat, just thinking about this shit. Just hang on, be cool—Harrelson was already skating on thin ice back at headquarters. There was already a stack of citizen's complaints—Pineda had seen the file, his buddy the division chief's secretary having pulled it out and shown him—about this little love affair between Harrelson and the varsity squad. The trick from here on, Pineda knew, was to stay cool, let Harrelson hang himself, and make sure that none of the shit in which Harrelson was about to land splashed out and got on him.

He opened his eyes and gazed out through the windshield, not looking over at Harrelson. "Tell you what . . ." Voice level and flat. Under control. "Let's just go on in there, and check this one out. Okay? Because I'm not going to sign off on this one unless we do. And then somebody on the morning shift will have to drag their asses out here and take a look. And every-

body will ask how come we didn't take care of it."
He turned toward Harrelson. "Okay by you?"

Harrelson brushed powdered sugar from his fingertips; he rolled down the top of the paper bag and
stowed it behind his seat. Pineda rolled his eyes upward—doughnuts, for Christ's sake! The guy was a
fucking *joke!* Then Harrelson wiped his mouth with
the back of his hand. "Yeah, sure. If that'll make you
happy." He dropped the patrol car back into gear and
one-handed the wheel around.

Yeah, it'll make me happy. You dumb sack of shit.
Pineda said nothing aloud, keeping the words like a
roll of spit on top of his tongue. It'll make me happy
when they can your ass, and I get assigned to something besides baby-sitting Mister Wide-Fucking-World-
of-Sports.

He leaned back in the seat, gazing out through the
windshield, watching to see if any of the little high-
school jerk-offs were still hanging around. If they knew
what was good for them, they wouldn't be. Their asses
are *mine*—Pineda nodded to himself, thinking about
it.

Felton worked his zipper back up. Taking a piss like
that, when your bladder felt as big around and tight as
a friggin' basketball, was nearly as satisfying as getting drunk in the first place. He even felt slightly more
clearheaded, as though he had drained a couple of pints
of stale beer right out of his skull, where it had been
sloshing around behind his eyes. Time to go home and
get some sleep—he could come back and clean the place
up, sweep the beer cans and all the rest of the kids' shit
into a pile, get the drive-in ready for the weekend swap
meet, later on when the sun was up.

He turned, hearing footsteps crunching across the
gravel on the other side of the fence. A couple of

cops—he recognized them from before—walked across the narrow access road that ran alongside the drive-in. Their black-and-white was parked several yards away, the gumball lights and chrome siren on top now dark and silent.

The short leaner-looking one stopped at the fence. He stopped at the fence, raising the flashlight in his hand, the beam darting right into Felton's eyes, making a quick throb of pain bounce off the back of his skull.

"Felton," the short cop shouted from behind the flashlight's glare. "Get your ass over here!"

The guy was a real prick—Felton couldn't figure why they'd put a Mexican on the police force, unless it was some sort of equal-opportunity program, and the feds *wanted* everybody to have to put up with pushy little taco-benders. The other cop was okay, though; he'd keep this short shit from giving him too much hassle. Felton pulled the metal tag on his zipper up to the top of his fly and ambled over to the fence.

The cop lowered the flashlight as Felton approached. "Party tonight?" Sarcastic, but no smile.

Felton shrugged. He didn't give a shit what the cop said.

The cop leaned a little closer to the chain-link mesh. "We've been getting some complaints about you and your little boy-scout troop over there." The flashlight beam flicked over toward the snack-bar building, across the empty asphalt field.

Felton made a face, as though he were rolling up the sour taste in his mouth, getting ready to spit. "Aww, man—those fuckin' old biddies. Why don't you just tell them to mind their own goddamn business?"

That pushed the short cop's button. He went red-faced, yelling. "I'm telling *you*, asshole! I don't care if you've got the whole goddamn varsity football team hanging around out here—I'll be glad to take every one of those little punks down to juvie and book 'em—''

The other cop stepped forward—he'd been hanging back, just watching—and grabbed his partner's arm. "Back off. I'll take care of this."

For a moment, it looked as though the short cop was going to cock his arm back, fist balled up, and unload on his partner. That would've been something to see—the two cops going at it, rolling around on the gravel road, pounding away at each other's faces. Felton watched in silence, all the yelling and shit aching inside his head.

The short cop glared at his partner, biting his lip before the words inside could get out. Then he walked a couple feet away, keeping his back to them.

The other cop—Harrelson, that was his name; Felton remembered now—crooked his finger, signaling Felton closer to the fence. So they could just talk, instead of all this shouting.

"Look . . ." The cop seemed apologetic. They both knew this was horseshit. "I've told you before. You're gonna have to tell the guys to hold it down out here." Voice low, reasonable and cool. "I mean—they should have a good time, they've earned it, but they're just gonna have to—"

He didn't get to finish. The other cop, the short one, came storming back up to the fence. Shouting, his spittle flying through the chain-link mesh into Felton's face.

"You giving those little bastards beer again?" The cop's voice even shriller than before—Felton winced, as though it were a nail being scraped across a chalkboard inside his head. "You are, aren't you? I can haul your ass in right now—providing alcohol to minors. Any business licenses you got, you can wipe your ass

with 'em after that, fucker. You won't be holding any
more swap meets out here, I can guarantee you that—''

The one named Harrelson was bigger; he grabbed
his shouting partner by both arms, pushing him back
from the fence by sheer weight. When he let go, the
short cop staggered back a couple of feet, his eyes
furious.

Harrelson faced the other cop down, his broad-
shouldered bulk standing in front of the fence. "Get
back in the car." He sounded pissed. "I said I'd take
care of this, didn't I? So just stay out of my way."

The other cop glared at Harrelson for a moment
longer—Felton wondered dizzily if he should hit the
deck; the guy had a fuckin' gun on his hip, for Christ's
sake. And a Mexican like that—they were all hot-
tempered, weren't they?—maybe he was about to pop
off a few rounds, settle the discussion that way.

Then the cop, still looking pissed, turned and
walked away, back toward the black-and-white.

Harrelson turned around, gazing through the fence
at Felton. The little confrontation with his partner had
left him pumped up, breathing hard. A bit of the
friendly tone he'd had before was gone now. Felton
nodded, listening to the cop. Two sensible guys out in
the night, the stars and sinking moon blue on their
faces and hands.

"Don't worry about that asshole." Harrelson kept
his voice level. "I'll take care of him. But I want you
to think about what I said. Okay? Just keep it cool out
here. That's all you gotta do."

"Yeah, okay . . ." Felton gave another nod of his
head. "I'll tell the guys." Tell them what?—he still
didn't know. They hadn't done shit; that's why they
came out here, in the middle of nowhere, so they could
horse around, let off a little steam, without bothering
anybody. If people would just give 'em a fucking

break, instead of getting so tight-ass about it all the time . . .

He couldn't say that to the cop, of course; not out loud, at least. But he knew the cop was thinking it, too—he was just doing his job, coming out here and talking like this. People did these things because they had to, and then everything went back to the way it was before.

The cop was already walking back to the patrol car, where his partner leaned against its fender, watching the whole scene with a sour expression.

"I'll tell them," Felton called after the cop, louder so the other one would hear as well. "I'll take care of it."

It was all bullshit. There was no way he was going to get on the team's ass about making too much noise. Whoever had been doing all the complaining, they could just go fuck themselves, thought Felton. He started back toward the snack-bar building, trudging through the dark.

They were in the car, Steven knew; he could see them in there. Just under the level of the side windows—they'd be all around each other, his sister Kris on the bottom, knees drawn up to fit on the back seat, and Mick on top of her, his jeans pulled down in front, the top of his butt showing white, the same cold paleness as her thighs spread and clasped around him.

He stood a few yards away from Mick's car, wondering what to do. They were in there, but he couldn't hear them whispering or laughing, or anything else. And he couldn't see them moving, Mick raising his head, arching his back as he straightened his thick, heavy arms. Everything was all still inside the car.

Steven hugged his arms around himself, trying to rub the blood into warmth beneath his own thin jacket.

He felt cold and tired—falling asleep out there, his back against the speaker pole, hadn't made it any better. It had made it worse, dreaming about that black car out on the road . . . He'd been dreaming, he knew that now; there had never been anything out there except the layers of darkness, one after the other, all the way around the world.

And it was late now; he couldn't tell how late, but he knew they usually went home before this. The party had broken up, all over except for some of the footballers still hanging around—Steven could see them, dark shapes leaning against the outside of the snack bar, talking to each other in low voices, as if the weight of the night had pressed down upon their shoulders, quieting them, all the fun gone until the next time; a couple of them sat with their backs against the building, forearms on their knees, hands dangling loose, their heads nodding downward in sleep. They were just drunk, Steven knew. The whole point of the party for some of them—ones without girlfriends, who didn't have someone like his sister Kris, the way Mick did—was to just pour as much beer down into their stomachs, as fast as they could. As many of the high-school girls as were around for the parties, there were never as many as there were guys. It just worked that way.

Maybe Mick and Kris had fallen asleep, lying there inside the car. After they had finished what they had been doing. There'd be trouble if they went home this late, and his and Kris' mom was awake. Sometimes she woke up, way in the middle of the night, getting up off the couch where she'd been lying with the blue light of the television, and the laughing, banging noise of it washing over her, like the waves of a tide that kept coming in, filling the room to its corners when all the lights had been switched off. He was the one who would switch them off, but he knew his mom hated to wake up in the dark, hated to know that she'd fallen asleep, not watching the TV at all; so he left that on. Then, hours later sometimes, he'd hear her getting up and stumbling around, muttering *Shit* between her clenched teeth as she knocked over the bottle next to the couch. She'd be in her own bed, still dressed in the same clothes she'd had on the day before, lying on her back and breathing openmouthed, shallow and fast, when he got up in the morning. The TV would still be on, with the bright chatter and big faces of some show like *Good Morning America*, and he could hear them talking—shouting, it sounded like, turned up so loud—as he got dressed and fixed his breakfast.

Thinking about that, about his mom waking up and stumbling around the dark house, and realizing that he and Kris weren't home, and how late it was—that made him worried. He rubbed against the chill in his arms, trying to think of what to do. She'd be so mad—she'd fly right at both him and Kris, yelling and stuff. Which was all right for Kris—she could just yell back and then go off someplace with Mick, the way she'd done before. And that would leave Steven there—because there was no place else to go, there was just home and nothing else. Without Kris around, he'd catch the full force of their mom's anger. The thought made him feel hollow under his stomach, sick and miserable, as though he wanted to throw up but there was nothing there, just the knowing of what was going to happen.

Maybe there was still time—he could always hope that. Maybe his mom would still be asleep; sometimes she didn't get up from the couch at all, but was still there in the morning. It all depended.

He'd have to go wake them up. Kris and Mick— she'd get all pissed off, of course, but still, that'd be better. Than the other, what would happen if they didn't get on home pretty soon. Kris was still pretty much of a lightweight when it came to getting mad. More of a sulker and snapper, rather than a pure screaming fury. He could put up with whatever she did. All he had to do was stay quiet, go invisible, not be there at all—just let all of Kris' sharp words, her razor voice, go right over the top of his head. He couldn't do that with his mom. She could always find him, wherever he hid, no matter how far down in the silence and waiting.

He looked over to see if any of Mick's football buddies had spotted him. There were only a few of them, maybe six or seven; he could hear a little knot of them talking, over by the snack-bar building, their voices murmuring in the dark, their hands dug deep into the pockets of their varsity jackets against the night's cold. Nobody looked around toward him. That was a relief; maybe they had forgotten all about him. He walked over to Mick's car, making each step silent.

The window was cold as he put his fingertips against it. He leaned close to the glass, his breath making two small ovals of fog against it as he peered inside the car. So dark in there, even the light of the stars shut out, that he couldn't see anything. It took a moment before he could make out the two shapes inside, his sister and Mick lying together on the back seat. They didn't move, except for their breathing, slow and deep, in time with each other, the curve of Kris' ribs lifting against Mick's hand. Her T-shirt was pushed up under her arm, Mick's fingers spread across her small breast; a little circle, black in the darkness, showed between two of his knuckles. All the light seemed to come from her skin, so pale it looked blue, the glow of white beneath the whispering lights of an empty parking lot.

Mick's flesh was darker, netted with the black of his hair; the hard bone of his hip showed where the corner of his unzipped jeans folded back. His skin gray against Kris' white, shiny from sweat and another wetness—the muscle underneath was still clenched, as though straining even as he slept.

Steven drew back from the car window. He clenched his fist and raised it to rap on the glass: Before he could move, he knew somebody was behind him. He turned and tried to crouch down, away from the other, but it was too late. A hand grabbed the collar of his jacket, bunching it into a fist and jerking him away from Mick's car. The collar of his T-shirt pressed tight across his throat as his feet dangled free of the ground.

One of the footballers, the one he knew was called Dennie, lifted him higher in the air, dangling from the fist like a rock at the side of his face. Dennie jutted his own broad face close, grinning.

"What're ya looking at, you little asshole?" Dennie shouted into Steven's ear. "Huh? What's so fucking interesting?"

Steven flailed about, his elbows striking Dennie in the chest. "Nothing!" Dennie's grip held him fast, the bunched T-shirt and jacket tight enough to choke his shout. "Let me go!"

Dennie's smile pressed closer, right into his face; he could smell the beer on his breath. "You dirty little shit—" The smile widened, showing wet teeth. "Looking at your own sister—"

"I wasn't—" There were others looking at him now; he saw their faces as he dangled from Dennie's grip, the toes of his shoes brushing helplessly against the asphalt. His yelling had drawn the attention of the footballers that had been hanging around the snackbar building, their faces breaking into smiles like Dennie's. The party wasn't over yet; there was still some fun to be had. They hadn't forgotten him. And in the car, Mick and his sister Kris were awake—maybe they had never been asleep at all—and had sat up, pushing themselves up from the back seat, so they could see what was going on. He could already hear their laughter, muffled behind the glass. His sister threw her head back and laughed, wrapping her arms around Mick, hugging him tight, the two of them laughing until their eyes were squeezed shut.

"I wasn't watching anything!" Steven twisted in Dennie's grasp. He tried to slide loose, out of his shirt and jacket, but Dennie had them bunched too tight in his fist, pulling Steven's shoulders back in a bow, the T-shirt riding up like a tourniquet across his ribs. "I wasn't—"

He could see Dennie look past him, exchanging a smiling glance with Mick in the car. Then the laughing faces of the other footballers stepped back, making way as Dennie carried him dangling toward the snackbar building and the open doorway with the light spilling out.

Dennie pushed him down onto the floor, jamming his face against one of the televisions in the little room. Steven's cheek smeared flat against the screen's glass, the black-and-white snow dazzling in his eyes. He could see Dennie fumbling with his other hand at the tape player sitting on a box next to the television; Dennie pulled out a tape from the machine and threw it away, clattering against the shoes of one of the other guys who had crowded in to watch. Without looking to see what it was, Dennie picked up another tape and shoved it into the machine's slot, then punched the PLAY button.

Steven pushed against the television, but Dennie pressed him back, the big fist right at the nape of his neck. The snow on the television's screen disappeared, replaced by gray shapes that intertwined with each other; it took him a moment to realize that they were people, naked and clambering onto each other. This close, they had looked like one organism, something you'd see writhing at the bottom of a rock pool at the edge of the ocean, multilegged and formless.

"That what you like?" Dennie was shouting behind him, over the wet noises and moans leaking from the television's speaker. "Huh? You like that?"

The laughing filled the room. Steven squeezed his eyes shut, but the gray light slid under, shadows seeping into one another.

"Maybe you're tired of watching." Dennie shouted louder, over the laughter and the television noise. "You're such a horny little fuck—maybe you want the real thing. Huh? That what you want?"

The cold glass of the television screen wasn't against his face anymore. He felt himself falling, jerked back by Dennie's grip. His breath burst out of him as he landed on the room's concrete floor, a red wave coursing along his spine. He gasped, the pain filling his mouth. His eyes opened, and he saw Dennie reaching down for him. He couldn't move to get away.

A girl was in the room, laughing with the rest of them. Not his sister, but one of the other girlfriends. She laughed and spilled the beer she'd been drinking, dribbling it across her T-shirt, as Dennie pulled Steven up and pushed his face into her breasts.

"You like that? Huh?"

The girl laughed harder, a drunken bray above Steven's head, as she stumbled back against the wall, Dennie pushing Steven against her.

"Nice, huh?" Dennie pulled Steven back; he was still gulping, trying to get back the wind that had been knocked from him. Dennie stooped down, his face close to Steven's, the grin wide and loose. "Did that give you a hard-on? Huh? Why don't we see if ya got it up—or maybe you don't like girls. Maybe you're a little homo or something.''

He felt Dennie's hand fumbling at the fly of his jeans, pulling the belt buckle loose. With a sudden rush of panic, he balled his fist and swung it into Dennie's face. The blow was hard enough to snap Dennie's head around. He lost his balance and fell backward, Steven's shoulder sliding out of his grip.

Run—he heard the one word inside his head, his own voice level and calm, miles away but somehow right inside as well. If he could just get out, out of the little room with the laughing faces, away and into the dark outside—then he could just run, and go on running, where they could never find him. Where no one ever could.

It was already too late. Before he could move, a hand grabbed his arm. Dennie, a red patch across the side of his face, lifted Steven up, the hard fingers digging their hold into his arm. Then Steven felt himself falling backward, the room and the faces spinning around him.

He crashed into a stack of cardboard boxes against the wall, scattering videotapes over the floor. Dazed, Steven couldn't move, as though his arms and legs had been knocked clear of his body. He could just look up and see Dennie looming over him, reaching down for him again.

4

Taylor watched the cop coming back from the fence, where he'd been talking with the fat jerk who ran the drive-in. The cop was pretty hefty, too, but in a different way. The drive-in guy looked as if he'd always been fat, as if there were nothing to him but fat; you could poke your finger into him like the Pillsbury Dough-Boy, and if you poked hard enough, probably go all the way through him and out the other side. Under the cop's sagging gut, however, you could still see muscle: big arms, big shoulders, everything growing slack and migrating to the ass, which was becoming the widest part of him.

Some aging jock, figured Taylor. Same team, same high school, a long time ago. It explained a lot.

They couldn't see him, the fat cop and his partner leaning against the fender of the patrol car; he'd come walking slowly down the slope of the hill, the flashlight in his hand switched off. And had stopped yards away in the darkness, the stiff dry weeds brushing against his knees, where he could watch and listen to the little scene going on at the drive-in's fence. A lot of yelling, all of it from the fat cop's partner. That had brought a wry smile to Taylor's face—at least he wasn't the only one around here who'd had enough shit from these punks hanging around the drive-in.

Beyond the fence, the drive-in's manager was wobbling back toward the distant snack-bar building, the little impromptu conference with the police over. Taylor hadn't been able to hear what had been said, once the cop who'd gotten so ˙pissed off had been chased away, but he could guess. Business as usual.

He wanted to talk to the two cops before they took off. The flashlight's switch clicked under the slight motion of his thumb. He swung the beam up and shone it right on the two men, a slanting oval of light glaring off the white door of the patrol car.

Startled, the cops jerked around, staring up at the hillside bordering the drive-in's access road. Taylor lowered the flashlight as he walked down the hill and stepped onto the gravel road.

They recognized him from times that they had brought kids into the the juvenile hall to be booked. And from the complaints phoned into the police headquarters, about the footballers' parties out at the drive-in—they knew he was the one behind all that. The big cop—Taylor had never bothered to remember his name—nodded slowly, giving a sour little grimace of recognition as Taylor walked toward the patrol car.

"You sure took care of that problem." The sarcasm was just as sour in Taylor's mouth. "Didn't you?"

The cop pulled open the driver's-side door and glared across the top of it at Taylor. The other one watched, his gaze going back and forth from Taylor to his partner.

"All right, fella. You just listen to me." The big cop's anger simmered behind his eyes. "I don't want to hear any more shit from you—got me? I'm tired of you making a big fucking stink about something that's none of your business."

From the corner of his eye, Taylor saw the cop's partner shake his head and look down at the ground alongside the patrol car, as if he were embarrassed by the whole scene. Taylor felt sorry for the guy—the poor bastard couldn't do shit, while his loudmouthed partner dug a hole big enough for both of them. Running the juvenile hall on the night shift made him part of the county's probation department; the cops were city employees, but even so, there was supposed to be some pretense of all being on the same side, doing their bit in the trenches of the local war on crime. Instead of spouting off like this, the way you wouldn't even do to some slob civilian, Joe Fucking Average on the street. Taylor turned his gaze back into the big cop's eyes, waiting for his red-faced spiel to reach its end.

"Those kids are more important than you." The cop's jowls shook as he jabbed a blunt finger toward Taylor. "Get that through your head. They're the *team*, for Christ's sake—and if they need to blow off a little steam once in a while, there's nothing you're gonna be able to do to stop 'em. Got it?"

You big fucking cornball—Taylor couldn't believe this guy. *The team*, the words spoken with actual reverence; as if the cop had said Hey, we can't give that guy a parking ticket—that's *the pope*. And you were just supposed to genuflect or something. The other cop let out a sigh—Taylor could hear him, leaning against the patrol car with both hands, head down—and radiated silent words along the line of Hey, *don't look at me; I gotta ride with the guy, isn't that bad enough?*

The big cop, satisfied with his speech, maneuvered himself behind the wheel. Taylor stepped forward and grabbed the edge of the door before the cop could slam it shut.

"So that's it, huh?" Taylor's own anger tightened his voice. "You're not going to do jackshit about—"

The cop knocked Taylor's hand away from the door and pulled it shut. The little red eyes, just slits now, glared out through the window at him.

Taylor raised his fist. Before he could hit the glass, the clang of metal on metal sounded a few feet away. The other cop looked over the roof at the patrol car's rear fender. On the ground beside the wheel, a dented can rolled in the dirt, beer foaming out the top.

It must've been lobbed over the drive-in's fence—Taylor looked around from the patrol car and saw, in the distance across the access road, the figure on the other side of the chain-link mesh. One of the kids, complete with varsity jacket, his hands in its pockets, pushing it down low on his hips. The footballer rocked back and forth, heel and toe, grinning at the adults on the other side of the fence. The kid knew who Taylor was, too. His grin grew wider as he took one hand from his jacket pocket, raised it, and gave Taylor the finger. Then he turned and walked away, slow and nonchalant, away from the fence and back toward the snack-bar building.

Taylor heard the patrol car's side window being rolled down. He looked around and saw the cop leaning his elbow on the chrome sill. The cop's face was no longer so red; he'd managed to simmer down, pull his act together.

"Look—why don't you just lay off?" The cop made an effort to sound reasonable. "Just about every goddamn night you're phoning in some complaint about these kids. And we're getting sick and tired of it. It doesn't do any good for you to keep making a fuss. Do we come over there to the hall and try to tell you guys how to run things?" He waited for an answer and got none, Taylor continuing to gaze at him in silence. "You know we don't. So why don't you just get off our backs about this small shit? These kids aren't hurting anybody."

The other cop shot Taylor a look of combined ex-

asperation and apology, before he opened the door on
his side and got in.

"Just mind your own business. All right?" The big
cop started up the patrol car's engine and dropped it
into gear. The rear wheels spit gravel as the car pulled
away.

For a moment, Taylor looked at the patrol car's rear
lights heading down the access road. At his feet, the
beer can continued to gurgle, spreading a dark stain
across the ground. He rubbed the curve of the flashlight's head against one palm, the cold metal pressing
into his skin. He stood in the dark, listening and
watching.

This is all bullshit, thought Larry. All these guys
thought they were such big fuckers—they'd been getting their asses kicked all season long out on the football field, and now they were terrorizing some stupid
little ten-year-old kid. As though the kid were respon-
sible for them getting their faces shoved into the mud
and grass by every other school in the district.

From where he stood in the doorway of Felton's office, Larry could see the kid, that snippy bitch Kris'
little brother, sprawled across the cardboard boxes and
videotapes in the corner. Dennie had tossed the kid
there, the way you'd backhand a cat that had scratched
you. The kid looked as if he'd had the wind knocked
out of him, gulping for air, not moving but staring up
with scared-rabbit eyes as Dennie loomed over him,
reaching down to grab him with one big hand. The big
pile of shit.

Larry shouldered his way through the other guys
standing around in a circle, watching and laughing.
They were piles of shit, too—the sound of their bray-
ing and guffawing tightened a knot inside his stomach
as he shoved his way past.

He grabbed hold of Dennie's shoulder. And pulled—
Dennie wasn't expecting anything from behind him; it
was enough to spin him around, facing Larry.

"Let him go, Dennie." He dropped his hands by
his side, loose and ready, as Dennie straightened up
and faced him.

Dennie smiled, incredulous. "What?"

He didn't know why he'd done it, why he'd come
shoving his way in, into the middle of everyone's fun,
and had pulled Dennie off the kid. Dennie had fifty
pounds on him—it looked more like a hundred, for
Christ's sake, all of it muscle, when Dennie smiled
mean like that, his eyes looking at something smaller,
something that had gotten in his way. Larry had seen
that look, through the face guard of Dennie's helmet,
in practice when Dennie had a clear shot at dumping
some of his teammates on their butts. And laughing
about it afterward.

And what did this stupid kid mean, anyway? Just
some little punk who should've been home in bed . . .
But then they all should've been home in bed, instead
of out there drinking some football groupie's free beer
and making noise.

Larry looked straight into Dennie's eyes, pushed
smaller by the grin below. It just hadn't seemed like
fun anymore. That was why he'd done it.

"Come on." Everyone else had stopped laughing;
Larry felt them watching, the weight against his shoulder blades. "Just let him go, for Christ's sake . . ."

Dennie did a comic double-take, dropping his jaw
open. "You're . . . telling *me* . . ." As if it were the
most amazing thing he'd ever heard. He pointed with
his thumb at Larry—*Can you believe it?*—as his gaze
traveled past, on toward the doorway.

Larry glanced over his own shoulder. Mick stood in
the room's doorway, his shirt still unbuttoned under

his varsity jacket. He leaned against the doorframe, watching, the little smile on his face, smarter than Dennie's, but just as mean. He waited to see what was going to happen.

Silence, measured in heartbeats; Larry felt them up in his throat, the heat spreading across his face. He turned back around to Dennie's smile.

Then he was pushed against Dennie, the two of them rocked back a couple of feet by something that shoved past their legs.

The kid—nobody had been watching him. Long enough for him to get his breath back, and scramble to his feet from the boxes in the corner. Making his break—Larry pushed himself away from the front of Dennie's jacket, and saw the kid dart past the legs of the other guys, faster than any of them could grab hold. Even Mick, standing in the doorway, was taken by surprise. The kid shoved past him and was gone, running into the darkness outside.

"There—you happy now?" The smile had gone from Dennie's face. He had caught himself with one hand against the wall; he regained his balance, his beer-reddened eyes glaring at Larry. His broad shoulder brushed against Larry's chest as he headed for the door.

Larry didn't say anything. He just watched as the rest of the guys made their way outside. The party was over now.

He ran. He didn't care where to; he ran in the darkness, across the empty asphalt field, past the rows of speaker poles standing like the remains of dead trees in the night. Until he couldn't hear anything behind him, back where the light spilled from the little room's doorway; until all he could hear was his own breath and pounding heart.

Steven slowed down, then stopped. He turned and bent over, rubbing the stitch in his side; it felt like a knife under his ribs. The night had turned cold enough that he could see his own breath, panting out silver in the dim starlight. In the distance, he could see figures, tiny silhouettes crossing in front of the light from the snack-bar building. The cough of a car engine starting up, then another; headlights came on and swung across the drive-in as the cars moved away. Steven crouched down for a moment, afraid the beams would sweep across the asphalt and find him. But they turned and moved away, growing smaller as the cars headed for the lane that took them out to the street.

His breath slowed, leaving a thick salt taste under his tongue. The fear ebbed away, too; he was safe out here. Always, as long as he could remember, being scared meant running, or wanting to run, to somewhere he could see all around him, a great empty space in all directions. It didn't matter if it was dark. Dark was better, even, because it meant he could hide, become *really* invisible, not just pretending and wishing he were. The worst was to be in somewhere, a room with walls, a corner that he could crouch in and try to make himself small, smaller, but never small enough. Rooms with doors he could never reach, never get outside and run, doors that might as well have been a million miles away because there was somebody standing there, somebody bigger, like his mom or his sister or one of her friends. If you could get away, you had a chance.

When the fear dwindled away, there was nothing left inside. Steven walked slowly, to nowhere. He was glad he'd gotten away, that he was here in the dark and quiet rather than back there, in the little room with the laughter battering at him. He didn't feel angry at them, though; not anymore. A long time ago, before he'd known better, great hot tears of shame and rage had scalded his cheeks. But he'd learned; it only made things worse if you cried where they could see you, where they still had you trapped in the corner of a little room. They only laughed harder, or got madder and madder, shouting at him in a voice that wasn't his mother's any longer, but some shrill thing that tore at his ears with blows more furious than her hands could give.

And crying where no one could see you—that had ended, too, when he'd learned that it was better to feel nothing, to be empty inside. As long as you were crying, you were still there; you weren't a million miles away, you weren't invisible. Better to swallow everything, to force it down your throat, no matter how big and sharp and choking it was, down into the dark hole inside, under your stomach. Where no one could see.

He reached the fence. The chain link felt cold against the crooks of his fingers as he reached out and held it, a soft metallic creak in the stiff wire when he squeezed. In a little while, he'd let himself start thinking about what to do now, about making the long walk home, along the empty roads and streets. There was traffic zooming along the distant freeway overpass, a constant river with lights that thinned and quieted this late, but never stopped. All those people were going somewhere else, where there were lights and noise. But here there'd be nobody; he could walk all the way home and maybe see three or four cars total, winding their way past the rows of houses and apartment buildings, all the windows dark.

In a little while, he'd think about that, and start walking. He knew he wasn't going to be going home with his sister Kris, in Mick's car, not after what had happened. This had been a bad night. Usually he managed to stay out of trouble—*invisible*—when he had to come along to his sister and her friends' parties. Usually nothing happened, and all he had to do was sit out in the dark and wait until it was over and it was time to go home. Sit, and sleep a little, the noise and the laughter sliding in and out of his dreaming.

Something he'd dreamed tonight . . . He remembered it. A black car, a piece of the night . . . waiting and watching, just out there where he could barely see it, black against black . . .

"Hey—" A shout came out of the night.

Steven looked up, startled, the skin drawing tight across his shoulders. A man's voice; he looked through the chain-link fence and saw on the other side, along the narrow road, a black silhouette against the slope of the hill. The shape of a man, looking toward him— he could feel the points of the man's gaze, though he couldn't see the eyes or anything else, just darkness.

He pushed himself away from the fence and started running. Behind him, the man shouted again.

"Hey—come back—"

The words barely touched his ears, blocked by the wind of his running and the pump of his blood. He kept running, not looking back, heading for the drive-in's distant gate.

Taylor watched the kid running away, a small form disappearing into the darkness on the other side of the fence. Not a teenager—maybe ten or eleven, he figured. Small enough, with a pale, thin face, to be even a nine-year-old. That thin face had looked older, though, the way kids did sometimes, like old men who had been shrunk down to a child's size again, the wrinkles smoothed away, the gray skin made pink and white again. But the eyes stayed old, and wary, watching you all the time from some place way back at the end of the tunnel inside, where you or anyone else couldn't get to them. Taylor had seen kids like that before, over at the dependent children's ward next to the juvenile hall—the two buildings shared the same medical and kitchen facilities, so there was always a certain amount of traffic back and forth. The battered children—those who hadn't been hurt badly enough to go to the hospital, or worse, the county morgue—were brought in to be checked out by the nurse, while the cops hauled away the parents, or the mother's boyfriend, or whoever looked guilty enough to go for a little ride downtown. If the kids were brought in on the graveyard shift, and Taylor wasn't out making his rounds of the living units or doing his nightly perimeter check, he'd go to the medical unit and read the arresting officers' reports on the nurse's desk. He'd read enough of the cop's flat descriptions—"observed injuries"—that they no longer evoked a knife in his gut, but instead a hollow, empty feeling that was worse. Numbness; you got used to it, you got used to seeing ten-year-olds with dead eyes, nine-year-olds, five- and four-year-olds. All they'd learned was to watch and wait, from that place inside where they couldn't be hurt, at least not bad enough to die.

And if you worked at the hall long enough—Taylor had put in twelve oozed-by years—you could see the same kids again later, when they were older and the cops brought them in for whatever trouble they'd finally learned to engineer for themselves. They didn't need their stupid parents or mom's boyfriend anymore; they could bruise themselves with a needle just as well. And at least it would be in their own hands. The eyes stayed the same, though, the tunnels behind the dead gaze maybe longer, the child in the darkness inside just that much farther away.

It wasn't a good thing to think about, standing on an empty gravel road in the hours creeping to morning. The kid Taylor had spotted, who'd put his mind in that grim, well-worn track, had disappeared completely now, running off into the dark. He figured he must've scared the kid, startled him with a big adult voice booming out of nowhere like that. So the kid had just taken off, God knows where. What had he been doing out here this late, anyway? Maybe something to do with the older kids, those football punks bashing away at the drive-in's center.

Hard to tell. And nothing he could do about it, anyway. That was what you learned when you got to be all grown-up, and an adult. You could read the arresting officers' reports all night long while the nurse in the examining room measured and counted the bruises and swabbed the dark blood crust from the small ears with a cotton wad dipped in alcohol, you could do that but you couldn't erase the reports, in triplicate with the bottom yellow copy for the permanent files. Everything was permanent—you learned that, eventually.

He turned away, back toward the hillside on the other side of the road. Slowly, the flashlight switched off and dangling in his hand, he made his way up through the dry weeds, and back toward the juvenile hall.

"Hey—I got an idea." Kris pushed close to Mick, sliding her hand inside his jacket and trailing her fingertips across his ribs. He didn't even look at her, but took another pull at his beer, the last of the ones he'd brought along. She brought her mouth close to his ear, lowering her voice. "Why don't we go back to my house? So we can be comfortable. And alone."

That was the advantage of her stupid little brother having run off. Privacy. Not that there was anything Steven ever said or did that got in the way of her doing what she wanted. He was just such a fucking comedown, was all; even with him just being somewhere else in the house, with the door of her bedroom shut and the radio on to cover her and Mick's noise and giggles, still you always knew he was out there, in his own room or sitting up watching the television beside their mom snoring away. With his stupid little face. Just looking and never saying anything—Mick hated the little geek just being anywhere nearby; Steven got on his nerves, put him in a bad mood. Even though dragging her kid brother along made all sorts of nice things possible, cooled out all the hassles their mom would otherwise make . . . Kris had explained it all to Mick at least a dozen times, but he still didn't care, he just wanted the little twerp to vanish. She had to be extra nice to him, do the things he liked, to get through the sullen barrier her brother's presence produced in him. Sometimes it took *hours*.

Tonight was different, though; she could tell that Mick was thinking the same thing. Steven had disappeared all on his own—or at least she could tell their mom he had. It wasn't her fault the little sonuvabitch couldn't take some tiny bit of teasing without getting all freaked out about it and hightailing it off into the dark where they wouldn't have been able to find him even if they'd tried. So it wasn't really lying to tell their mom that she and Mick *had* gone looking for Steven, calling his name and everything . . . but he must've been hiding. All teary-eyed and snuffling to himself, the crybaby. Just because the guys on the team had had a little fun with him; they hadn't hurt him or anything. Though she wouldn't have minded if they had—if her little brother wound up in the hospital for a couple weeks, like he deserved just for being his snot-nosed self, then there'd be a lot more privacy for her.

But tonight would do, for starters. Kris snuggled in

closer to Mick's side, looking up at him and waiting for him to say something.

Mick took another pull at his beer. "What about your mom?"

Kris felt the sneer move across her own face. "You kidding? Even if she wakes up at all, she'll be so pissed off about Steven splitting on us, she won't give a fuck what we do."

He didn't need much convincing. The empty beer can bounced across the asphalt. Then Mick smiled at her and pulled open the car door.

5

He couldn't find the way out. When he'd started to run, the man's voice shouting after him, he'd plunged into the dark with no thought of where he was going. Just to get away, just to run until whatever scared him was far behind.

Steven stopped running, leaning forward, hands on knees, to catch his breath. Silent and dark here, in a corner of the drive-in's empty field; he looked and saw the speaker poles, curving in their ranks across the asphalt, narrow lines of black against the night. Around to the other side, a few yards away, was the fence. He gulped down another stinging breath, then walked over and started to climb, his fingers gripping the chain-link mesh. When he reached the top, he swung his legs over and dropped onto the gravel road.

Brushing the dirt from the knees of his jeans, Steven walked alongside the chain link. Now he knew where he was—from on top of the fence he'd glimpsed the distant blue glow of the streetlights on the main road. Once he got there, it was easy enough to find the rest of his way home. An hour's walk, maybe. In the dark, his shoes crunched in the loose gravel.

Out on the road, he headed toward town, the drive-in's screen looming behind him, a pockmarked white square covering up the stars and moon. All he had to do now was walk, and he'd be home, and maybe everything would be all right. Maybe his mom would still be asleep. It was something to hope for, at least.

He heard the car's noise, the sound of its engine, from behind him. At the same time, the road lit up with the rounded edges of its headlights' beams, pushing the dark back, out of his reach. He stopped and looked around, but he already knew who it was.

Past the glare of the headlights, Mick's car came down the street toward him. Shielding his eyes, Steven could see the silhouettes of the two figures inside, Mick behind the wheel and Kris beside him.

They hadn't come looking for him, he knew that. They were heading home, the party at the drive-in over. So now they'd spotted him.

They would stop and pick him up, too—he knew that. Not because Kris wanted to, or cared whether he was left wandering around in the middle of the night. But just because she knew how to make the least trouble for herself. If their mom found out—if he told her—that they had seen him on the street and had driven right by, leaving him there in the middle of the night, if their mom heard that, then there'd be all kinds of trouble, yelling and stuff. It wouldn't be worth it to Kris; it'd be better if she brought him home with her, same as when they'd left.

He even knew what they'd be saying, inside the car. As though it were inside his head, he could hear his sister's voice, in that disgusted, bitter tone she had. As soon as she saw him up ahead, caught in the headlights' beam—*Christ, there's the little shit now.* She'd sigh, she already had, her shoulders slumping. *Guess we'd better pick him up.* Beside her, Mick would grunt, had grunted, everything had happened already; Mick was already steering the car over to the side of the road, pulling up where Steven stood waiting, watching. He could see their faces now, behind the windshield.

Mick leaned across, in front of Kris, and pointed with his thumb toward the back seat. "Get in." He pulled himself back upright, squeezing the steering wheel in his big hands.

Steven climbed into the back seat. Before he could close the door, Mick jerked the car away from the curb, the tires squealing.

Over the top of the front seat, Kris gave him a dirty look. "I thought we were rid of you . . ."

He said nothing. It was just what he'd have to put up with, that was all. At least their mom wouldn't hit the roof about him running off from them. If she was awake when they got back home . . . It was better to put up with Kris and all her little remarks than to take that chance.

Out the side window, the dark street rolled by, broken by the blue pools of light beneath the streetlamps. Steven kept his face turned to the window, watching the empty night.

It wasn't empty. He knew it as soon as he heard the sound of the other car.

The black car, the one he'd seen before, roared up in the lane next to them. The low murmur of its engine, which had traveled through the earth and up into the pit of Steven's stomach, now shrieked, climbing in pitch and volume, cutting through the windows of Mick's car and filling the interior.

"What the fuck—" Startled, shoulders hunched up inside his jacket, Mick jerked around, staring at the black shape alongside.

The driver inside the other car, just as Steven had seen him before: a black shape inside blackness, faceless, not even eyes. But he felt the driver's gaze as the silhouette behind the wheel turned and looked straight at him.

Then another sound, twisting inside the black car's roar. Steven knew it was his sister screaming. He didn't turn away from the side window, but he knew Mick was scrabbling at the steering wheel, turning it in desperate panic as the black car lunged ahead and cut in front of them.

Steven raised his arms in front of his face as he felt himself hurtling up from the seat and hitting the door with his shoulder. Mick's car bounced over the curb and slammed to a stop, the corner of one bumper digging into a slope of earth beyond the road's edge. For a moment, the car tottered, suspension creaking, close to rolling over; then it settled back with a jarring thump.

His sister's scream had changed to a whimper of pain. He saw her fall back against the front seat, a net of blood streaming across her face; the windshield had blood on it, too, at the center of a cobweb of broken glass. Mick touched his mouth and then looked at his hand, his eyes dazed as they stared at the wet red smeared across his palm. The blood looped in thick dark spit along the rim of the steering wheel.

All they could see was their own blood. But Steven could see past them, through the thousand still pieces of the shattered windshield. The other car, the black one that had detached from the night and become real, realer than anything else—it had stopped a couple yards beyond Mick's car. The low murmur of its engine thickened the air, growing solid in Steven's throat. As he watched, the car's door opened—no light came on inside; the dark stayed unbroken. The driver got out, sliding from behind the black car's steering wheel. He walked toward Mick's car.

Through the cobwebbed windshield, Steven saw the

figure, faceless in the dark, stop at the side of Mick's car. Mick saw the driver now, too; he looked up. The blood streaming around the fingers pressed to his mouth; a little whimpering noise, like that Kris made beside him, escaped from Mick's throat.

Then the car filled with pieces of light, exploding across the front seat. Steven flinched, raising his hand; against his palm, the tiny fragments of the windshield sparked and stung like insects, a flurry that was gone and past in a second. He opened his eyes and saw the pieces of glass around the rim of the windshield dangling and dropping like ice, silvered by the headlights of the black car in the distance. The driver's hands and forearms were dotted with the glass shards, embedded in the knuckles of the fists that had thrust through the web of fracture lines.

The driver leaned through where the windshield had been, where now there were just the last bits of broken glass falling with the sound of small bells across the dashboard. The driver's hands opened from battering fists, the fingers spreading wide, then closing around Mick's throat. The blood bubbled at Mick's lips, the scream inside his throat choked off by the driver's fingers pressing deep into the flesh, thumbs digging into the corded windpipe.

Steven pressed himself against the back seat, watching, seeing everything. His sister was screaming now, crouching against the door on her side, her hands up to her face as if to protect herself.

The driver straightened, pulling Mick out of the car, his belly dragging across the jagged edges of glass along the bottom of the windshield's rim. Mick's hands clutched at the driver's wrists, his fingers scrabbling to break loose the grip tightening on his throat.

Steven's hands fumbled at the door latch at his side, his own fingers closing on the metal handle. Then he

stopped, the metal cold inside his hand. He could open
the door, get out and run; nothing was stopping him.
But the voice that had told him before to do that, that
he always heard inside . . . it was silent. Nothing but
emptiness, silent and waiting. Silence that he could
stay inside, and watch. His hand drew back from the
door handle.

Outside the car, he saw the driver toss Mick down
on the road. Mick lay where he fell, his arms out-
stretched. The blood welled from his open mouth and
made a dark pool around the back of his head. The
driver stepped back; his dark face turned to the car
again. Steven felt the eyes he couldn't see, the gaze
narrowing across the distance. The driver stepped over
one of Mick's hands and walked toward the car.

Some glass remained in the windshield frame on the
passenger's side. The black car's driver swept it loose
with the back of his hand. Kris' scream went higher,
with a breaking sob as the glass pieces scattered across
her. She curled into a trembling ball on top of the seat,
her hands clutching into her hair, forearms covering
her face. The driver reached in and grabbed her by the
wrist. With the same easy strength he pulled her out
across the dashboard.

Slowly, Steven pushed himself forward from the
seat. He raised himself, hands clutching the back of
the seat in front of him. So he could see.

The driver had dragged Kris to the front of the car.
The headlights cut across his chest, leaving his face in
darkness, as he threw Kris against the radiator grille.
The blow dazed her, a red bruise from one of the
grille's chrome bars spreading over her face. Blood
trickled from her nose and over her lower lip.

Her face grew brighter, a white spot against the
night, as the driver dragged her in front of one of the
headlights. Inches away from it, the light's glare eras-

ing all her features, leaving only the bright mark of
the blood on her skin. The driver's hand clenched tight
in her hair, drawing her head back, her throat drawing
tight beneath her tilted chin.

With one sharp thrust, the driver slammed her face
into the headlight. The light burst with an electric
crackle, sparks coursing over Kris' forehead and along
the driver's forearm. Steven could hear his sister's
moan, the last bit of her awareness ebbing away in
pain. The darkness folded back around her, the headlight extinguished. The driver opened his hand, fling-
ing her away. She crumpled onto the road, facedown,
a darker stain spreading and pulling her tangled hair
into the wet.

In the road beyond, Mick had pushed himself up to
his hands and knees. His face crusted with blood, he
looked toward his car. He saw, but didn't understand—
Steven knew that, looking at Mick from the back seat,
out through the space where the windshield had been.
He doesn't know—he suddenly felt sorry for Mick, a
little twinge of feeling that was extinguished when he
saw the driver turn away from the front of the car. The
dark figure strode toward Mick.

Mick didn't see the driver coming toward him—he
was looking at Kris, his dazed eyes staring at her
crumpled body, the pool of blood widening to her
shoulders. The sight of her, lying motionless like that,
a broken doll thrown away, brought fear into Mick's
face. Everything became real to him now. The blood
bubbled at his mouth, a little whimpering sound, as
he looked up and cringed from the driver only a few
yards away.

The fear broke through the hold on Mick. He scrambled to his feet and started to run. Steven saw him in
the headlights of the car, stumbling toward the edge
of the beams' reach.

The driver didn't run after Mick. He walked unhurriedly to the black car and got in. The murmur of its engine whined higher as he dropped it into gear. Gravel spat from under the black car's wheels as it swung about, headlights sweeping across the road, and picked up speed.

Mick had already reached the safety of the dark when the black car's headlights caught him, sending his shadow writhing in front. Still running, panic making his strides clumsy and erratic—he looked over his shoulder into the sudden glare. Even at this distance, Steven could hear him scream, a sound wrenched out of his lungs and hanging in the night air.

A little bit of Mick's brain still worked, a particle not yet frozen by fear. Enough for him to break suddenly, as though he were on the football field, eluding one last tackle bearing down on him. He had been running down the middle of the road—he turned and ran to the side, trying to reach someplace where the black car couldn't follow.

Mick ran headlong into a chain-link fence, a newer one than that around the drive-in, the metal still bright and unrusted, taut rather than sagging between the poles holding it up. A parking lot on the other side, herringbone lines surrounding a set of commercial buildings. The scene lit up in the glare of the black car's headlights, a shadow mesh widening across the asphalt, Mick's shadow lengthening at the center.

The car had swung wide to the other side of the road, so it could come at him full-on, pinning Mick between the bright wedges of its lights. The driver gunned the engine and the car surged forward, over the low curb and the narrow strip of sidewalk. Mick jerked around, flattening himself against the fence. He shrank back, spreading his hands as if to protect himself from the car's rush. A small cry of terror and shock burst from him as the car rammed the upper edge of its hood into his gut.

Mick bent in two, his palms sliding across the black metal. The fence bowed behind him as the car's engine growled lower, pressing its grille on into Mick's spine. Face contorted, Mick pushed himself back into the fence, his varsity jacket squeezed into diamond shapes by the chain-link mesh. His ribs snapped with the sound of dry kindling.

Something wet, looking black in the night, seeped through the back of Mick's jacket, seeping around the fence's wire. Then the seams split open, nylon threads ripping apart stitch by stitch. The blood pulsed out, shining on the crisscrossed metal.

The car backed up, and Mick's body, a broken puppet, slid to the ground.

Steven had lifted himself onto the front seat, until his head brushed the ceiling of Mick's car. Watching, and seeing everything; though it had happened far down the street, as far as Mick could run before the black car had caught up with him, the crushing of Mick's spine into the fence had been completely visible to him. Every last detail—when the black car, with its faceless driver inside, had rolled forward, collapsing Mick's rib cage, the sounds of the bones breaking had been as sharp and quick as twigs cracked close to his ear.

And closer—right here at this car, in the beam of one headlight—Steven could look down and see his sister's body, twisted about itself, face downward in a spreading puddle.

It happened—the thought moved slowly inside his own head, like something uncoiling inside his brow. The very first time he'd seen the black car, when it had pulled up alongside Mick's car, he'd known.

Something was going to happen. That was what it was there for. They hadn't seen it, they'd been too stupid to see it. Until it was too late.

The sound of the black car's engine drew him back. He looked and saw it swerving back from the fence. The headlights came around to glare straight across the distance at him. It drove forward, heading back to Mick's car.

The black car stopped a few yards away, the engine growl dying to a low tremble in the night air. As Steven watched, crouching behind the front seat, the driver's dark figure pushed open the door and got out.

No place to run, even if he'd been able to move. Steven remained frozen in place, kneeling on the back seat.

A hand reached for the door handle; the metal inside slid and parted, and the door swung open. Steven shrank back against the other side.

"Steven . . ." The driver's voice, low and soft; a whisper coming out of the darkness around the car.

He'd known that the driver would know his name. The driver had to—everything had happened just the way he'd known it would. But Steven didn't know what would happen next; that was what scared him, pushed him back against the other door, away from the hand reaching slowly into the car.

The door handle slid into his fingers. Steven quickly jerked it down, his weight pushing the door open. He tumbled out onto the road, his shoulder and the corner of his forehead jarring against the rough surface. The little voice inside had woken up, speaking its one word. *Run* . . . He scrambled to his feet and broke away from the car.

Only one stride, and he fell again, the palms of his hands scraping and stinging against the road. Something had caught and tripped him. He looked and saw

Kris stretched out alongside where he'd fallen, her face still turned down into the shiny wet pool that mired her dark hair. One of her outflung hands had clutched his ankle, locked onto it, the fingers squeezing through the sock and into the thin flesh around the bone. A cry welled up and stuck in his throat as he scooted backward, hands shoving against the road, kicking to dislodge his sister's hand. It held on tighter, pinning him to the spot.

A deeper night suddenly fell across him. He looked up and saw the driver standing above him. The face, all shadow, regarded him. The hand reached down toward Steven.

The voice, low, even kind. "Steven . . . don't be afraid . . ."

All he could see now was the driver, the dark figure blotting out all the rest of the night. Steven fell backward, and the darkness was there to catch him.

6

He could hear the voice coming out of the blackness. All around him—he'd fallen into it, and there'd been no bottom, just the slow falling and the dwindling away of all the world outside his head. Where there were cars and a white thing that had been his sister, that had once had a face, crumpled on the road.

Faceless. The dark took away faces, made them into dark things that you only felt looking at you—

He turned slowly inside the dark, floating; a bed, an ocean all black and warm, welling up across his face.

—Looking at you, reaching a hand down into the darkness in which you were falling, the face with no eyes, just the darkness, the voice soft and gentle, whispering your name—

"Hey . . . hey, kid . . ."

But the voice had changed; it was different. Steven scowled in his drifting sleep, as though a mosquito had buzzed its sharp, discordant note in his ear. Why would it have changed? That didn't make any sense. The driver had his voice, his one voice, that whisper sliding soft in the still night air.

"Hey, come on . . . You with me?"

Not soft and low-pitched, like the murmur of the black car's engine, waiting with its headlights cutting two sharp-edged swathes out of the dark. This voice had a needling, worried tone to it. So it couldn't be the driver.

At the same time, Steven felt something holding him by one shoulder, shaking him, his head lolling back and forth. Pushing away the darkness, drawing him back up from it.

He opened his eyes. White light pulsed and washed over him; his eyes stung from the sudden glare. It ebbed back as his eyes adjusted, and he saw shining white porcelain and chrome pipes, faucets and handles. Sinks; four of them in a row, with mirrors above each one. The floor was white, too, and the walls, the same square shining tiles covering them, broken only by a round metal drain, black slots in chrome, right in the center of the room's floor.

Steven looked down and saw his hands beside himself, lying palms downward on a wooden bench. The darkness in which he'd been floating had turned into thick, worn-smooth planks. They smelled damp, overlaid with the sharp bite of chlorine, like the Comet cleanser his mom kept under the kitchen sink.

"You okay?" The hand didn't shake him again, but held on to his shoulder.

He didn't say anything. Just looked around, at the bright tile walls flooded with light from the fluorescent panels overhead, the smells of hot water and disinfectant stinging with each slow breath he took.

A face lowered in front of his gaze. The man who'd shaken him awake, bending down to look more closely at him. Narrow, with thinning hair and a sandy-red mustache—just a face, with eyes and everything else.

"You just sit here awhile—okay?" The man let go of Steven's shoulder and stepped back from the bench. "I'm gonna take care of a little business, and then I'll be back and we'll check you in. Is that cool?" The man smiled as if he'd managed to tell a joke. "You just sit tight." He turned and walked out of the white-lit room.

Steven raised his head, looking behind himself. Above the wooden bench, the wall was set with windows, crisscrossed with wires inside the glass. Through the windows he could see another room, larger, with a dark corridor branching off one side. The man stood at a tall counter, reaching behind it to pick up a telephone.

He was somewhere, Steven realized. Different. He could feel the night, the darkness still outside this little pocket of light. He'd just have to wait and find out.

Taylor was out at the far end of the living units when Repken called him from Receiving. Hassling around with the cops and the party going on over at the drive-in had thrown his schedule off: he usually tried to make his rounds through the living units earlier on, around one A.M. or a little later. Now it was past four, over halfway through the shift, and he was just finishing up.

On top of the cops and party business had been a little ruckus over in Unit F; that had eaten up time as well. Some dopey sixteen-year-old car thief had decided it was a good night to do wolf imitations, baying at the moon through the security grille of his window. Taylor knew you had to nip that sort of thing in the bud, before the little jerk got all the other kids in the unit awake and making trouble, kicking at their locked steel doors and screaming their heads off. That kind of nonsense could spread from one living unit to the next, all the way down the line, until the whole juvenile hall was rocking and rolling. Nothing but noise, but it made for a long night. With the staff from Units D and E called over for backup, Taylor had popped open the door and talked some sense into the howler kid. It helped make his point to have a couple of "soft

ties'' in his hands that he could peel the rubber band
from around and unreel in front of the kid's face. The
kid was enough of a juvenile-hall veteran—his probation department file was nearly an inch thick—to know
what the long, skinny strips of padded cloth meant.
They meant the kid getting spread-eagled on his bed,
the ties knotted at his wrists and ankles, good and
tight, and the loose ends pulled up sharp around the
bed frame's four corners. *Because*—Taylor had told the
kid—*we don't want you hurting yourself.* Which was
bullshit; he knew it, the kid knew it, everyone knew
it. But the kid also knew that the staff were going to
pile on him and strap him down, and leave him that
way for a nice long time, if he didn't knock it off with
the wolf shit.

Reason had prevailed. The kid wasn't looking for
major action, just a little fun. And attention—he'd gotten that, and now he was ready to go to sleep, like a
good boy. Lights out in the little room, door locked
down again, and good night. Taylor's backups wandered back to their own units, returning to their portable typewriters or college texts or general boredom,
whatever they brought in with them to get through the
long hours of the graveyard shift, all the way to their
seven A.M. quitting time, when the day staff would
come mumphing in, half-awake and clutching the big
styrofoam cups of coffee from the Seven-Eleven near
the freeway off-ramp.

Taylor had told the various staff involved not to
bother writing up a special incident report on dealing
with the kid; as long as they hadn't actually needed to
use the soft ties on him, it was all minor enough to
forget hassling with paperwork. The kid was already
snoring away as he'd continued on his rounds.

"I take it you finally got the party crowd chased
away." Willis out in Unit K had his feet up on the

desk behind the counter, crowding his typewriter and stacks of paper to one side. He folded the book he'd been reading over his stomach and flicked gray ash from the end of a sour-smelling cigar.

Taylor grunted as he leafed through the unit's logbook. "Yeah—finally." Unit K was at the end of the juvenile hall's L-shaped building, closest to the perimeter fence and the hills on the other side. It caught the most of whatever ruckus came drifting across from the abandoned drive-in. "No thanks to our heroic boys in blue."

A shrug from Willis, behind a gray cloud of exhaled smoke—he'd developed the ability to ignore the footballers' noise. An aura of cynical calm, like a jaded Buddha, radiated from him. More than once he'd advised Taylor that he shouldn't get worked up over a bunch of asshole teenagers. Sooner or later, they'd all get dragged into the hall and then their lily-white pampered asses would be in line for all sorts of butt-kicking payback action. If not here, then somewhere else when they were older and not shielded by their privileged high-school-hero status. If they pulled some of the same shit when they were adults, they'd find out—in jail, rather than a candy-ass hotel like the juvenile hall—just how grim payback could get.

The phone rang. Willis had to swivel his feet off the desk and sit up in order to get to it. "Unit K. Huh? Yeah, he's here." He held the phone across the counter to Taylor. "Receiving wants to talk to you."

Repken's weedy voice came over the line. "We got an intake here, that Midford P.D. just brought in. I thought you might want to take a look at him before I processed him on through."

Taylor leaned back against the counter, the phone to his ear. "Why? What's so special about him?"

"Well . . . he was kind of, um, unconscious when

I checked him out just now.'' The words squeezed through Repken's embarrassment.

The information pulled Taylor upright. "He was *what?*"

"You know . . . like passed out . . ."

"Jesus . . . fucking . . . *Christ.*" Taylor knew that Willis was staring at him, wondering what was going on. "The medical unit accepted this kid, and he was *unconscious?* How the hell—"

Repken's voice moved up in pitch, the words faster. "Well, he wasn't really all the way unconscious when they first brought him in; just kinda groggy, you know? And the nurse really didn't get to see him, 'cause she was out on her break, and we got that new girl up at the reception desk—those Midford police just walked all over her, dumped the kid and the paperwork off before she knew what was going on—"

"Yeah, right; forget it. Look, I'll be right there. Don't move the kid, okay?" He dropped the phone back in its cradle, then hurriedly signed off his rounds in the Unit K logbook.

"Take it easy," Willis called after him as he unlocked the unit's exterior door and stepped out into the dark.

All I goddamn well need—Taylor jammed the key ring on its leather lanyard back into his pocket as he strode across the damp grass. To make his night complete: some kid who's had his skull fractured like an Easter egg by some dumb cop's nightstick, dying of a cerebral hemorrhage on a bench in the receiving unit shower room. In his twelve years at the hall, he'd been through a death-in-custody only once—a suicide, hanging himself with a ripped-up sheet in Unit B—and that'd been enough to last him for good. The paperwork on that kind of incident went on, literally, for months. And if you didn't wind up in court testifying in front of some judge looking at you as if you were some kind of Auschwitz child molester who'd somehow gotten on the county payroll, then you'd gotten off lucky.

The Midford police were exactly the sort of clowns to pull a stunt like this. Taylor and the night nurse had already had some real dust-ups with the Midford cops, over their trying to dump off kids at the hall who should've been taken straight to the emergency room at the county hospital. Kids with broken arms, or overdose cases that were so far along they were turning blue. The cops preferred unloading them at the hall, if they could get away with it, because the paperwork involved was less than what the hospital ER demanded. And they didn't have to hang around while the doctors and interns worked away, keeping some little felon breathing—the cops could split, and go back to hanging out at some doughnut shop.

Striding past the baseball cages—cutting across the hall's athletic field was the shortest route to Receiving—Taylor swore under his breath. The Midford cops were probably already munching through a load of jelly-filleds, swilling stale coffee, and laughing their heads off about slipping this one past. Unconscious, for Christ's sake. The kid's brain could be swelling up like a sponge in a bucket. *And on my shift*—that was what really pissed Taylor off.

It might even have been the same cops, the ones who'd come out to the drive-in. The juvenile hall was a county facility, taking in kids from all over, but it was officially inside Midford city limits. As well as the drive-in—the whole territory around this end of the low scrubby hills and dry riverbed was part of Midford. There had been some jurisdictional hassles between the county probation department and the Midford police, about whose authority was final on the juvenile-hall grounds—could a duty officer such as Taylor, for example, order the cops to strip off their guns and stow them in the lockboxes up by the reception desk, when they brought in a kid? It had gone all the way to the state supreme court, who'd come down against the Midford police. They'd had a bad attitude about cooperating with the juvenile-hall staff ever since.

Repken was standing by the receiving unit counter; he looked around at Taylor as he unlocked the door and stepped into the unit's dayroom. "I called the nurse." Repken nodded toward the windows of the shower room. "She said to bring him down as soon as we could—"

"Yeah, right—" Taylor picked the booking sheet off the counter and glanced at it. The kid's name was Steven; it helped to know that, to be able to call him by name, if a response had to be coaxed out of him. "Let me take a look at him first."

The kid sat on the shower-room bench, shoulders slumped, gazing at the drain in the center of the floor. Taylor hadn't read far enough on the booking sheet to get the kid's age; he was taken aback for a moment when he saw how young this one was. Ten, at the oldest—usually, any kid who'd put up enough of a fight with the cops to get popped over the skull would be fifteen or older. Or if it was drugs pushing them off the cliff edge into unconsciousness—they usually didn't get them quite so brain-fried until they were of high-school age.

Taylor bent down in front of the kid. "Hey, Steven . . ." He kept his voice low and smooth, not wanting to startle the kid. "That's your name, isn't it?"

The kid looked up, and Taylor recognized him. From just a brief sighting, at a distance of yards, out in the dark. A couple of hours ago—he'd seen the kid's pinched face and somber eyes through the fence around the drive-in, before the kid had gotten scared and run away, disappearing where his gaze couldn't follow.

Those eyes looked back at him now—whatever had made the kid run away was still there, buried in the smaller darkness inside. The kid didn't say anything.

At least the kid was awake and alert. Taylor reached out a hand and brushed the kid's hair back from his forehead. A good-sized bruise, reaching down one side, almost to his cheekbone—the kid had come within inches of collecting a real shiner for himself. A small crust of dried blood right at the hairline. Taylor picked up the kid's hands and turned them over. They were scraped bright pink, with a few deeper red scratches running parallel toward the wrists.

Easy enough to figure out: the kid had taken a header when he'd been running in the dark. Tripped over something and gone flying, catching himself on his hands, but not quick enough to save him from getting a good crack on the head. That was what had knocked him dazed, not a whack from a cop's stick. The Midford P.D. was off the hook for this one, at least. The nurse would check him out, make sure he didn't have a mild concussion. Taylor doubted it; the kid's eyes followed his movements with careful, guarded observation.

The kid might even have been running away from him—Taylor knew that. Scared him off into the night. Where you could run into all sorts of things.

Taylor stood up. "You were out at the drive-in, weren't you? A little while ago?"

The kid lifted his head, regarding the adult in front of him. He shrugged, the silence wrapped around him unbroken.

"Come on—you were or you weren't. Just say yes or no." Taylor waited.

The kid looked away, over to a corner of the shower room. "Yeah." A small voice, barely audible.

"What were you doing out there?"

"Nothing—" A defensive spark in the word, and louder. Then sullenly: "I wasn't doing anything."

Taylor sighed, exasperated. "Come on." He stepped toward the door, then turned and waited. After a moment, the kid stood up from the bench and followed him.

Repken was sitting behind the counter, visibly less nervous now that somebody else had taken over. He watched as Taylor picked up the booking sheet again and read it all the way through. The kid stood next to him, waiting, face expressionless.

"What a crock of shit." Taylor slapped the paper down on the counter. " 'Violation of curfew'—they brought him in here on a candy-ass charge like that? Christ, I don't even remember the last time I saw a kid busted for curfew. And he's got no previous record on him? Why the hell didn't they just take him home? That's the usual procedure."

The angry barrage shrank Repken back in his chair. He pointed to the booking slip. "Well, look . . . I mean—the kid wouldn't give them his address or phone number."

Those lines on the slip, right under the kid's name, were blank. Taylor reached behind the counter and picked up a plastic bag, heavy with its contents. The kid's personal belongings, stashed together for safe-keeping: belt, the coins and things that had been in his pockets. And a wallet, a thin plastic one, embossed to look like leather. Taylor opened the bag and fished the wallet out.

"Christ, it's right here." Taylor's voice curled with disgust as he held the open wallet out to Repken. A transparent sleeve held an ID card, the kind the local

schools handed out to all the students. "Those assholes didn't even bother to look." He stuffed the wallet back into the plastic bag, then turned around and
looked at the kid.

"Okay, Steven—" He glanced again at the name on
the booking slip. "Welsky—that your name?"

The kid had been staring off toward the dayroom
windows, at the night wrapped around the building.
He jerked his gaze back toward Taylor, as if startled
at hearing his own name.

Taylor kept his voice low and calming. "All right,
Steven. Do you know where you're at?" He waited for
an answer, even a shrug of the shoulders, but didn't
get one. "This is the juvenile hall. It's no big deal.
We'll get you home soon as we can—okay?"

Nothing. Still silent, the kid looked back at him.

There was plenty of time. Some of the night staff,
with an easy one like this, would have slammed him
through the intake procedure, gotten him showered and
into a change of the hall's faded jeans and T-shirt, and
stuffed him into one of Receiving's little rooms, before
the kid had a chance to blink. The conviction being
that the probation department didn't pay them enough
to hold some little dink's hand, make sure his tender
psyche didn't get bruised. Let the day staff handle all
that business; that was what they got paid more for.
Taylor liked to make a certain distinction, though, re-
serving the hard-guy stuff for the ones who really deserved it, the older, lippy punks who came in with
attitudes three feet thick. If you came down hard on
everyone, including wide-eyed squirts like this one,
then it took the specialness out of chopping some real
turkey down to the size necessary for the smooth
meshing of the probation department's machinery. He
hadn't lasted this long at the job without finding the
small satisfactions to be had.

"I got to ask you some stuff." Taylor leaned one elbow on the counter, easy. "And you can just tell me, okay? You don't have to worry about it—it's not like telling the police stuff you think might get you into trouble. We don't give a shit here—the sooner you're out of here, the less work for us. You understand?"

Finally, a response. The kid nodded.

"There some reason you weren't quite with us there for a while?"

The kid frowned, not understanding.

"Come on—I mean the way you sort of zoned out over there. Did you take something you shouldn't have?" Always a possibility—the kid's breath didn't smell of alcohol, but that still left a wide range of shit. "Like pills, or something?"

"No." Barely audible, the kid shaking his head.

Taylor believed him. The kid's silence was from being scared about something, not the weight of chemicals. "You got any medical problems? Like epileptic, or something? Maybe you take insulin, or something?" If that was the problem, the kid would recognize the words.

Another shake of the head.

"How'd you get that bump?"

The kid's hand darted up and touched the bruise at the side of his face. Slowly, the hand lowered. "I was running. And I fell down."

He waited, but there was no further explanation. *I fell down*—that was all he was going to get. Taylor wanted to ask another question—*What were you scared of?*—but instead: "Why were you running?"

A shrug. "I don't know."

"What were you doing out there at the drive-in?"

Not even a shrug this time. The kid lapsed back into his silence, far inside himself.

The kid apparently didn't recognize him, didn't remember seeing him beyond the drive-in's fence. Where Taylor had shouted across to the kid, startling him. *Running from me*—that was the explanation. Which explained nothing. It wasn't the reason for the fright that was still there, locked at the far end of the kid's silence, where the deep tunnels of the child's gaze led. Where no one could follow, even if you already knew what was down there. Taylor knew; he'd already seen it, from a long time before.

Those things weren't worth thinking about. He reached his hand out toward the kid's brow. "Let me take another look at you." He tilted the kid's head back, the way he had before. He pushed the kid's eyebrow up with his thumb, opening the eye wide. Nothing—this one wasn't on anything. Nothing but the dark at the center. Taylor could see his own tiny reflection there, his own face looking back at him from the darkness inside. That brought a wry nonsmile to one corner of his own mouth.

He dropped his hand from the kid's brow. He picked up the wallet from the counter and flipped it open, holding it out. "This your home phone number?"

The kid nodded.

Taylor picked up the telephone from the desk and set it on the counter, right between himself and the kid. He glanced at the number inside the wallet, then started dialing.

7

He had never been in a place like this before. The strangeness of it, this brightly lit pocket inside the night, the fluorescent panels overhead softly humming, wrapped around Steven, as though the air itself inside the big space was somehow different from other air.

And the people who worked here—the one who'd been asking him all the questions, who seemed to be getting mad about something all the time, and the other one—they must be part of this little world. When everybody else was asleep, or doing things out there in the dark, they were here in the bright light, doing whatever they did, the things adults did to make money. Like sailors, out on the sea, in their ships; you could lie on your bed with the lights out, and think about it, and know they were out there, someplace different from you.

There were others here, too, though—just not awake. Steven knew they were there, even without seeing or hearing them. Sleeping—behind the doors that lined the dark hallways on either side of this bright space. The way you can tell there are people around you, just by feeling something in the air. They must be kids, he figured. Because of this being the juvenile hall. Older kids than him, as old even as his sister and her friends . . . ones who'd gotten in trouble . . .

His sister . . . Steven shut his eyes tight, blocking out the bright light, pushing away the big room and the voices of the two men, the one loud and mad, the other squeaking like he was guilty about something. Until they were far away, and he was by himself again, in the darkness inside his head. If he just stayed quiet, didn't let them in . . .

They'd want to know about Kris. That's what they'd ask him, eventually, he knew; what had happened to her. And to Mick. Did they know already? He'd managed to stay silent with the policemen, the ones who'd found him out on the road, where he'd been lying with the earth tilting crazily under him and his head throbbing, a bright stab of pain poking at the corner of his head and a sticky black wetness on his fingertips when he'd touched it. They hadn't known, they hadn't found her yet. Where the driver of the black car had left her, and Mick.

He could remember the policemen finding him, and picking him up—carefully, because they didn't know how badly he might be hurt—and putting him in their car, with the screen that separated the front seat from the back and the radio that clicked and talked and they talked back to. He'd still been so woozy then, his head aching from where he'd hit when he'd fallen, that he hadn't even been sure if that part had been real, if he were really riding somewhere in the back of a police car.

Then he remembered waking up again, a little at a time, as though his dreaming hadn't let go of him and he still wasn't sure if he was sitting on a bench in a bright room or not, with a line of sinks and tile that went up the walls, and a smell of steam and wet soap. And somebody shaking him, trying to get him to wake up, to be in that bright room. Instead of in the dark behind his eyelids, where the driver, a dark shape with no face, was still reaching his hand toward him, speaking his name in a low, soft voice . . .

That'd been real. Everything else seemed just pretend—he had to make an effort to even play the game a little bit, like when the man had taken him out to the bigger room and asked him all those questions, and looked in his eyes as if trying to see the black car and the driver and his sister's and Mick's bodies sprawled out on the road, leaking wet black pools around themselves and not moving, not ever again. . . . All of that was in there, inside himself; that was why he had to keep quiet. They'd all find out soon enough.

Just stay quiet. That was all he had to do. To keep all of them outside. *I don't need them*—he'd been scared when it'd happened, when the black car had come out of the dark and its driver had taken his sister and Mick, and had done those things to them. The things they couldn't stop, that left them all broken and still. It had happened so fast; that was what had scared him. But now it was over, locked away inside him, and all he had to do was stay quiet.

Steven stood beside the counter in the big room, waiting. For whatever was going to happen next. The man who'd been asking him all the questions was now dialing a number on the telephone. The man leaned against the counter, waiting for somebody to answer. Steven could hear, faintly, the far-off ringing sound.

The ringing stopped. A little voice, inside the phone held to the man's ear, said something that Steven couldn't make out.

"Yes, is this the Welsky residence?" The man's voice took on a different tone, all official-sounding. A mumbled reply from the other end. "Yes, I know; I apologize for calling at this hour. But this is the county juvenile hall—we've got a young man here, named Steven. Is this Steven's mother I'm talking to?'' The man waited, listening to the voice inside the phone. "I see; you're his sister. Could you hold a minute?" He covered the bottom part of the phone with his hand and turned toward Steven. "You do have a sister?"

Steven frowned, wondering what the man was trying to do. By asking something like that—was it some kind of a joke? Maybe they all knew already, they'd always known what had happened out on the road, what the driver had done, and now they were going to make fun of him. Teasing him, by pretending it hadn't happened. The bright overhead lights pressed down on him, the glare suddenly dazzling him and making the room swim in his eyes.

The light receded a bit, and Steven realized that the man was holding the phone out to him. Slowly, he took it and held it to his ear.

He heard his sister's voice. Annoyed: "Hey, what is this shit, anyway?"

His sister; he couldn't believe it. Steven held the phone with both hands, pressing it close. "Kris . . . Kris, is that you?"

"Oh, for Christ's sake." Her disgust thickened. She sounded as though she'd been drinking a lot. "Who the fuck else do you think it'd be?"

It couldn't be. The other place, the dark place, that had been real—the road and the still figures lying on it, the pools that looked shiny and black spreading around them, her hair trailing in the sticky wetness. Everything had been real; it was still there inside his head, where he could remember it, turn it over and look at it. But now . . .

He could only whisper. "Are you . . . okay?" The words sounded foolish to him, as though he were talking to a ghost, one he couldn't even see.

Her exasperated voice needled his ear. "Why shouldn't I be okay?"

"I thought . . . something had happened . . ."

Steven heard his own voice dwindling away, falling inside himself. It didn't make sense. *I saw it. I saw everything.* It was all still there, in the darkness. He knew that if he closed his eyes, he'd see it again, he'd see the driver, the face hidden in shadow, reaching toward him, whispering his name. Telling him not to be afraid.

He wasn't afraid now. Something hollow opened up inside him, big enough to swallow the darkness, leaving him in the bright room, standing there and nowhere else.

The man took the telephone from his hands. Steven listened to him talking.

"All right, Kris—that's your name, right?—look, Kris, is your mother there?"

Steven touched the bruise at the side of his face, then the crust of blood up by his hairline. It didn't hurt. It only felt numb.

The kid had zoned out on him again. Just standing there, as though hearing his sister's voice had left him dazed. Taylor had taken the phone back, to make sure the necessary business got taken care of. Sometimes it worked that way, with him having to do all the talking.

"Hello—you still there?" He hadn't gotten an answer to his question; there had only been some muffled laughter and talking from the other end of the line. "I said, is your mother there? I'd like to speak to her, if I could."

The girl's voice came back on, with a bored, wisecracking tone. "She can't come to the phone . . . right now." That brought a laugh from somebody there with her.

Taylor ran the tip of his tongue across his incisors, nodding to himself. This wasn't the first time he'd run into shit like this. The big laugh, one sibling scoring points off the fuckups of another one. His own family, his brother and sister, hadn't been much different from that, when he'd been a kid. Everybody he knew, it'd been just the same for them as well. It made you wonder where they got those families on TV.

He let his voice go hard, cutting out all the polite official crap. "Okay, now you just listen up. Just shut up and listen. If your mother isn't there, I want you to get word to her, or leave some kind of message for her, that Steven's here at the hall. You got me? I'll be calling back in a few hours—"

"Fuck off, pig." A sharp click sounded as the phone at the other end was slammed down.

Taylor looked at the dead phone in his hand, then set it down in its cradle. He turned toward the kid. "Looks like you're here for the rest of the night."

The kid shrugged. He didn't seem to care one way or the other.

She had put Mick's T-shirt on when she'd padded out of her bedroom to answer the phone. He was standing behind her now, just wearing his jeans; he slapped her on the butt, just below the bottom of the shirt. Kris turned around in the circle of his arm, his hand sliding up to her waist, and watched him tilt back the half-full bottle of supermarket vodka they'd found beside the sofa.

Mick was really swacked, pouring that stuff on top of all the beer he'd already had. He almost lost his balance, pulling them both against the counter that separated the kitchen from the living room. Kris caught the telephone before it got shoved off to the floor. Nothing else, none of the noise they'd made, talking and giggling, had woken her mother, but she didn't want to take any chances.

They'd had a lot of luck already, the kind she liked. First, her stupid little brother running off like that at the drive-in, so they didn't have to drag him along with them back home. Even if they had spotted Steven out on the street, walking along in his stupid mopey way— Christ, the sight of his sad-sack little face irritated the piss out of her!—she would've told Mick to just zoom right past him, leaving him in their dust, rather than picking him up. That at least would've given them a little time in relative privacy back here, before Steven had come dragging his butt up to the front door.

But this was even better—the stupid little twerp had managed to get himself picked up by the police. For once, the cops had done something right, and dumped him off at the juvenile hall. She'd never been in juvie, but some of her friends had told her how it worked. Steven wouldn't be home again until maybe nine or ten A.M.

Too bad they weren't going to just lock him up for good, keep him there until he was eighteen or so. And keep him out of her hair—she was tired of this "chaperon" bullshit. Fucking nuisance, is all he was.

That wasn't going to happen, but still . . . She and Mick had a nice big lump of time now, hours and hours. The sun could come up on them in her bedroom, right through the curtains. That'd be nice, like they were married or living together already, in their own place, away from her mother and all these hassles. . . .

She snuggled up closer to Mick, pressing one tit through the thin T-shirt cotton and against his warm, sweat-smelling chest. A glance to the side, across the room, and she saw her mother still lying on the sofa, mouth open, snoring soft and wet at the back of her throat. One hand still flopped down to the floor, palm upward, by where the vodka bottle had been. The blue light of the television washed over her, the shadows from the screen moving like slow ocean currents.

"Come on." Kris took Mick's hand and led him, grinning, toward the hallway, and her bedroom at the end of it. "We don't have to worry about anybody snooping around now."

"You know—this is such bullshit." Taylor slapped the kid's wallet against his own open palm.

Repken looked up at him. Taylor was shaking his head slowly, one corner of his mouth twisted in disgust.

"This is, man. This really is." He looked as if he'd come to a decision, somewhere inside himself. Still holding the wallet, Taylor reached across the counter with his other hand and picked up the plastic bag and the inventory sheet Repken had started to fill out.

"What're you doing?" Surprised, Repken watched as Taylor tore the inventory sheet in half, then into quarters; he stuffed the ragged pieces into his shirt pocket.

Taylor ignored him. He handed the plastic bag, dangling with its contents, to the kid standing beside him. "Here—" After a moment, the kid reached and took the bag.

"Hey . . ." Repken's protest sounded anxious. He half-stood from his chair, as though he were going to swarm over the the counter and snatch the kid's things back. "Why'd you—"

"I'm taking this kid to his home." Taylor spoke quietly, unexcited, as if it were normal procedure. "It'll take me about fifteen, twenty minutes. Big deal. I'll drop him off and be right back." He pointed with his thumb to the corridors surrounding the dayroom. "This kid doesn't belong in a place like this. Not for some candy-ass curfew violation."

Repken went wide-eyed in disbelief. "Yeah, but—he's already booked—"

Taylor reached over the counter and picked up a loose-leaf binder, lying next to the Receiving log. He laid it open on the counter and flipped to the last paper in it. With one quick motion, he tore out the booking slip that Repken had inserted a couple of minutes before.

"Not now he isn't." Taylor crumpled the booking slip into a ball in his fist. "He was never here at all. Was he?"

"Jeez . . ." Repken shook his head dubiously. "Okay, man—it's your ass . . ."

The kid had opened the bag and was looking into it, as though he'd never seen the contents before. "Come on—" Taylor nudged him. "Put your belt on. Let's get out of here."

Nothing made the kid smile; the same guarded expression, or lack of any, stayed on his face. He reached into the bag and took out the belt, then threaded it through the loops of his jeans.

Taylor had gone around the end of the counter, to fish his car keys out of the drawer where he'd left them. "If anybody asks—" He straightened back up, rattling the key ring in his hand. "Just tell 'em I'm making another perimeter check. We had a lot of disturbances out there tonight." Taylor didn't wait for a reply, but started down the corridor, with the kid following him, stuffing his wallet into his pocket.

Crossing the parking lot at the front of the hall, Taylor sorted his car key from the others. The vapor lights overhead silvered his hands as he unlocked the passenger-side door and pulled it open.

He got in on the other side, sliding behind the wheel. The kid hadn't gotten in yet, but was still standing outside the car.

"Get in." He made a little motion, curling his fingers. The kid wasn't even looking at him, but staring off, looking someplace out in the darkness. "Come on, come on."

The kid finally looked around at him, then climbed into the car. He sat staring straight ahead through the windshield.

For a moment, Taylor drummed his fingers on the top curve of the steering wheel. Then he fished out a crumpled ball of paper from his jacket pocket. He held up the booking slip he'd torn out of the Receiving binder and wadded up. It caught the light sliding through the car; the kid turned his head and looked at the ball of paper.

"You know—" Taylor's voice sounded loud inside the car's small space. "I didn't just bend the rules. I broke 'em. Don't even ask me why I bothered. I just figured you didn't belong in there. Okay? Besides which—nobody's likely to make a big stink about it. It's not as if you're some friggin' mass murderer." He put the key into the ignition and started it up. "Anyway—if anybody ever asks, you tell 'em your mom came down here and picked you up. Agreed?"

The kid glanced from the paper ball to Taylor, then nodded.

It was like pulling teeth—Taylor gave up. "Hey, that's okay. No need to thank me." He threw the booking slip into the other trash around the car's back seat, then reached for the gear shift.

A glum little voice spoke up: "Thanks." The kid was looking straight ahead again.

Taylor dropped the car into reverse. "Don't mention it."

Before he could back up, the kid spoke again. With the same hesitant voice that Taylor had to strain to hear. "Uh . . . you know . . . you don't have to drive me home. I can walk from here." The kid reached for the door handle, but drew his hand back when he saw Taylor's warning look.

"Sure," said Taylor. "At five in the morning, I should let you go wandering off in the dark. With my luck, the cops who brought you in would catch you again, and then my ass really would be grass. No, thanks—you get the whole ride, and no arguments about it. Okay?"

The kid nodded, resigned, and settled back in the seat.

Taylor glanced over his own shoulder as he backed the car out of the space.

The man from the juvenile hall didn't know. Steven didn't know, either; he didn't understand how different things could be real at the same time.

He'd seen what the driver had done, when he'd gotten out of the black car, and had come and dragged Kris and Mick out onto the road. The driver had left them there, the soft, broken things he had turned them into; they didn't move, not anymore, but had just wept dark, shining pools around themselves.

But then Kris was alive, too; alive now. She had spoken to him on the telephone, and he'd even been able to tell that Mick was there with her, laughing. That couldn't be real, too, if the other Kris—the broken thing bleeding on the road—if that was real.

The hollow space inside him opened wider, as if it had scooped out all his insides, made him empty, with a knot lodged in his throat to hold the emptiness in.

Steven watched the streets roll past, the lights moving in darkness, the man from the juvenile hall beside him. Driving him home. He closed his eyes. *I dreamed it.* The words, the thought, had been sliding around in there, inside his head, at the limit of the dark. Where he could keep it for a little while, not wanting to see it, to speak the words to himself. *I dreamed it.* Everything—the broken things leaking onto the road, the black car, the driver with his shadowed nonface striding toward him, reaching his hand out, whispering his name . . . Like a TV show; you saw it, but it didn't happen. Not really. The bump on his head—without touching it, he could feel it, the bruise warm at the side of his face, the stiff crust of blood at his forehead—he'd gotten that when he'd fallen down, when he'd been running away. And maybe he'd knocked something loose inside; that was how people wound up believing in stuff that'd never happened. The dreams get knocked loose, and you see them and think they're real.

The juvenile hall, where he'd woken up—that'd been real. With its bright lights and the murmur you could barely hear, of people sleeping while the others, the ones who ran the place, were up doing things through the night. Like sailors on that little ship going along in the sea.

Like the man driving him home. Steven glanced over at him. The man drove, working the car's easy way through the empty streets. He was doing him a favor—Steven knew that. The other guy at the juvenile hall hadn't wanted to let him go, had wanted to keep him there, the way the rules said. The thing was, the man driving the car only thought he was doing him a favor. It wouldn't have been so bad to stay at the juvenile hall—that would've delayed going home and all the trouble that he was going to run into there, his mom and everything.

Plus, if they locked you up—it was like a jail, wasn't it? With bars and stuff on the windows, even though the bit of it that Steven had seen had looked more like the waiting room of the public health clinic he'd gone to with his mom a couple of times—if they locked you up, then you were safe. Safe from stuff that was *out there*, out in the darkness.

In that big, hollow space inside him, which seemed bigger than he was, there were two little things that had moved, turning in on themselves, when he'd whispered *I dreamed it* so softly to himself. One was that he didn't have to be scared now; at least not scared of the black car and its driver, the figure with its face all made of darkness. That wasn't real. Or if it was, it was only in his head.

And if that wasn't real, if it hadn't happened, the way he'd seen it happen—then the other thing moved inside him. The thing he'd felt when he was no longer scared.

Disappointment.

The kid stayed quiet the whole way. When Taylor looked over at him, he was gazing straight ahead, sunk in his own thoughts. He looked like the sort of kid who'd have big deep broody spells; Taylor had been the same way at that age. The kid's silence made him a little uneasy, turning his own gaze back toward the road ahead. Uneasy because it reminded him of that time so long ago, now locked away beneath his grownup comings and goings. You stayed busy so you didn't have to remember.

He tried to make a little conversation. Then he saw the kid turn around on the seat, looking behind the car as it went down the street; the kid's hands gripped the top of the seat as he peered intently into the dark.

"What's the matter—you miss the place already?" A joke; Taylor tried to put a laugh in his voice. "You want to go back?"

The kid looked around at him, startled, eyes wide. He'd been completely absorbed in whatever he'd seen out there, behind them. Or what he'd been looking for. He shook his head, slowly turning back around, sliding down onto the seat. "No . . . no, I thought . . ." His mumbled words died away. "I thought I saw something . . ."

"Yeah? Like what?"

No reply. The kid slumped down in the seat, going back inside himself.

Taylor looked up at the rearview mirror. He saw nothing, just the empty street unreeling behind. Then, several blocks away: a pair of headlights swung around, two small dots of light, holes punched in the dark.

No big deal. Other people drove on the street; the time was at that point of switching from *very late* to *very early,* when people with long commutes to their jobs had to get out and hit the freeways.

Taylor reached up and turned the mirror to get a better look at the other car. It stayed behind, trailing at the same speed. A gas station's bright pool of light spilled across the road—when the other car rolled through that, Taylor saw it better. Some late-model American jobbie—the glimpse was so quick that he didn't recognize the make—or maybe one of the flashier foreign ones, where they'd put their minds to getting down the low-slung, big-engined look of Detroit iron. Whoever the driver was, he took some care in his wheels—the car shone like polished obsidian, the gas station's lights dazzling off the sleek black flanks.

He had to look back to his own driving for a moment. A traffic light flicked to yellow ahead. As he slowed, Taylor glanced back up the mirror. The black car was gone, turned down one of the other streets. He didn't see where; even the red glow of its taillights had vanished.

Alone on the empty street again, Taylor waited for the light to change.

He knew where the kid lived. When Taylor had read the address inside the kid's wallet, he'd recognized the neighborhood. It wasn't that far from his own apartment, on the other side of Midford's original, Korean War–era shopping center. The juvenile hall got a lot of business from the area.

Taylor slowed the car down, looking for the numbers by the front doors. Most of the houses had fallen into a dilapidated state, with rusting screen doors hanging lopsided from broken hinges, and rain gutters sagging broken-spined from roofs with gaps of missing slates. Broken windows with flattened cardboard boxes taped over the shard-rimmed frames. Kids' toys, headless dolls and broken Big Wheels, abandoned in the lawns' ragged grass. A quarter of the driveways were filled with cars that looked as if they had crawled there to die, their tires leaked flat, the crevices of the rust-spotted hoods filled with dry leaves.

He pulled over to the curb and killed the engine. The house didn't look any better than the ones around it; he hadn't expected it to. He glanced over at the kid. "This it?"

The kid nodded.

"Come on, then." He got out of the car and headed up the drive to the house's front door. After a moment, he heard the car's other door open, then shut, and the kid following after him.

Taylor rang the doorbell. He could hear it inside, the noise barely dimmed by the window glass and thin curtains to the side. Nobody answered. He pushed the button again, and waited. The kid, standing next to him, looked up at him, then turned the knob and pushed open the door—it hadn't been locked.

Now he followed. The kid walked into the center of the living room. Taylor stopped just inside the door, looking around.

He'd known it would look this way. The living room was lit by the shifting glow of a television and an overhead kitchen light on the other side of a counter at the side. The air smelled musty, as though no windows had been opened in years, the breath of the people who lived there bottled up and lifeless. A stack of newspapers, high enough for the ones on the bottom to have begun yellowing, tottered against one wall, ready to collapse at any moment. The counter that marked off the kitchen area was cluttered with dirty glasses and the trays of TV dinners, grease dried to a mottled skin over the aluminum foil.

The room was empty, except for the kid standing in the middle of the floor. By the sofa, a cigarette pack and an overflowing ashtray—Taylor could see the faint haze of smoke thinning out above.

A woman appeared at the hallway leading off the back of the living room. Grumpy and hung-over-looking, a thin bathrobe wrapped around her—for a moment, she didn't see Taylor standing by the door as she shuffled toward the sofa. Then her red-rimmed eyes focused on the kid.

"What the fuck're *you* doin'?" She lifted her head, her squint finally taking in Taylor. "Who the hell are you?" She pushed her tangled hair back from her eyes with one hand as she sat down and reached for the cigarette pack.

The kid had said nothing. Taylor stepped forward from the door. He could smell the woman's breath from a yard away—not just booze and stale cigarette smoke, but something sourer, as if she had just come back from being sick, kneeling by the toilet bowl.

"Are you Mrs. Welsky?"

"Yeah—so?" The woman dug a lighter from the pocket of her robe. "What's the problem?" She seemed undisturbed about strangers who spoke with official-sounding voices, standing in her living room at five in the morning.

He swallowed the taste that had collected in his mouth. "My name's Taylor, Mrs. Welsky. I'm the night duty officer at the county juvenile hall. Your son Steven was brought in to the hall a little while ago. Nothing major—just curfew violation. We thought it best to handle it informally, and just brought him home. We figured that saves everybody a lot of trouble."

The woman lit up with a shaking hand, and snapped the lighter shut. She glared at Taylor. "Yeah, well, thanks a lot. If he did like he was supposed to, and didn't go running off and getting into trouble, you wouldn't have had to come around here bothering us, would you?"

She got up unsteadily from the sofa. The cigarette dangled in her mouth as she stepped forward, past Taylor. She drew back her arm, the floppy sleeve sliding to show the loose skin above her elbow; she backhanded the kid across the side of the face, hard enough to stagger him away a few steps before he caught his balance.

. Taylor had known that was going to happen, too. The same way he'd known just how the house was going to look inside, how it would smell, the sour breath of the kid's mother—it had all been right inside his head, a track that all of them were moving along, all the way to its end. He'd known, but there was no way he could stop it. There was no point in trying.

The kid wasn't surprised, either. He took the slap without crying, without saying anything. Except for the red mark surging up on his face, below the bruise he'd already had, she might just as well have slapped a department-store mannequin. The dead eyes looked back at her without changing expression.

"There you are—" Another voice, a girl's, from the hallway.

Taylor recognized it, from hearing it on the phone. He turned and saw a teenager standing in the hallway. She glared across the room at Steven.

"Where the hell did you run off to?" The girl's voice screeched like her mother's, minus the tobacco gravel. "We looked all over for you! We kept looking and looking—and now the cops pick you up, God knows where." She turned toward her mother. "See, I told you he was doing shit like this. How come I gotta look after him all the time? Huh?"

The mother flopped back in the couch with an expression of weary martyrdom. "Kris, honey—come on—I got enough problems with him already. . . ."

A crock of shit . . . and Taylor had managed to walk right into it, even though he'd seen it coming, had fucking *known* how it'd be. You stupid bastard—he closed his eyes for a moment, grinding his teeth together. This is what he got for being a do-gooder. The main reason he'd always stuck to nights at the hall, rather than going days, was that he didn't want anything to do with these kids' loathsome families. A couple of times he'd filled in on the day shift, monitoring the twice-weekly visiting hours, he'd had his fill, till he was choking on it, of screaming drunk parents, or just plain bat-fuck crazy ones, who all should've been shot before they'd ever been allowed to have kids. Listening to these people talk to their children—"talk" used loosely—was like watching a parade of lizards. You could look in their eyes and see nothing but the bright glitter of unhesitating cruelty; something that should have been locked behind glass.

And here was this poor kid's sister—she was one in training. Standing there in a T-shirt that barely covered her ass; she already looked like a hard piece. The same lizard brain had been grafted in above a pair of magazine-quality legs. They didn't do anything for Taylor; the contradiction brought a tightening nausea up in his throat.

He turned back toward the mother. "I suppose that if I were to tell you that your daughter's a lying little bitch, you wouldn't believe me, would you?"

No good reason for saying it—he didn't even know whether the girl had gone looking for her little brother or not. He just couldn't imagine anything coming out of her mouth except lies.

The woman's fury came ripping through the room at him, her saw-edged voice cutting the air. "Get out of here. What the hell do you mean, coming in people's homes—saying shit like that? I'll have you fired, you sonuvabitch—" Her trembling rage spilled ashes down the front of her robe.

His disgust had finally reached its limit. Taylor sighed as he looked at the kid. The red slap mark had started to fade from the kid's cheek. "Well—take care of yourself. Okay?"

The mask slipped for a moment; the kid gave him a wry, oddly adult-seeming smile. As if he could taste the irony of advice like that, in a place like this.

The kid nodded. "Yeah, sure." In his soft voice.

Taylor turned and walked toward the front door, the weight of the mother's and the daughter's narrow gazes targeted on his back, heavy enough to feel.

Mick was sitting up in the bed when Kris came back. She slammed the bedroom door behind her. She looked mad enough to spit.

He reached down under the blanket to scratch himself. "What the hell was that all about?" He'd heard all the yelling and shit coming down the hallway, but hadn't been able to make out the words.

Kris slid under the covers, pressing herself close to him. She laid a finger across his lips. Her anger was already fading back to playfulness. "Shh—keep it quiet; my mom came to, finally." She nodded her head toward the window. The sound of someone walking down the driveway came through to them. "That was some asshole from the juvenile hall. Bringing my stupid kid brother back home."

Raising himself up, Mick turned and pulled back the corner of the curtains beside the bed. There was some grim-looking dude out there, heading for a car at the curb. Mick got a good look at him as the man went around to the driver's side and got in.

"Hey, I know that fucker." Mick went on looking through the little corner of the window. "I've had a couple run-ins with him. He's the sonuvabitch who's always calling the cops down on us."

Kris rubbed his neck, tracing the curve of his ear with one finger. She could see a smile forming on his face.

Mick nodded slowly. His voice went down, almost to a whisper. "I even know where he lives . . ."

Part Two

Morning After

8

As Taylor came walking up to his apartment building, a folded newspaper hit the concrete behind him. The paper skidded and clipped his heel; he turned and saw a rust-dappled Volkswagen heading down the street, an arm with another newspaper cocked out the window. He picked the paper up and added it to the thin stack of mail he had gotten from his box over by the manager's office.

He felt tired, ready to pull the lightproof curtains in his apartment shut, tune in some university radio station murmuring classical music to shut out the daytime traffic noise, and crash out. The night staff at the hall was about evenly divided between those who slept right after they got off work, and those who saved it for the late afternoon and evening. And then there were always a few sorry bastards who tried to go without sleep altogether, as if the long dark hours from midnight on were just something they could add to their normal lives, without making any adjustments to pay for them. Those types always wound up burning out in a few months—Taylor had come across them more than once while making his nightly rounds through the living units. Not even being sneaky about it; he always tried to make as much noise as he could, clomping down the hallways between the units, even whistling, for Christ's sake, if he thought anybody needed extra

warning to pull their act together, to get their heads
up off the desks and the books they'd fallen asleep
over, to blink themselves awake and wipe the spit from
the corners of the mouth. Taylor figured it was only
fair, as falling asleep was just about the only way
somebody could get fired from the hall's night shift.
Stay awake, cruising through the long, slow nights until the day staff showed up, and you could have the job
forever. If you wanted it . . .

Some of the night guys had been heading over to the
Denny's by the freeway for breakfast—they knew the
restaurant manager well enough to get him to open up
the bar for them at that hour—but Taylor had begged
off. It hadn't been the hassling with the footballers and
the cops out by the drive-in that had made him so
tired—weary, actually, down into his bones—but the
whole business of dropping that Welsky kid off at his
crummy home. Crummy home, crummy alcohol-
soaked mother. A dismal glimpse into that place where
the kids locked up in the juvenile hall came from, before they turned into the messes the county's taxpayers
paid people like Taylor to sweep up and stow away in
neat little cubicles for a while. It took him a while to
pull back on his insulating cynical armor, which had
allowed him to go on pulling shifts at the hall for
twelve years, after something like that. It was just
something you didn't think about, that you locked inside your head and forgot about, even though you always knew it was still there. That was why he'd never
left the graveyard shift and gone days—he could deal
with the kids easily enough, especially since they spent
most of their time asleep. It was everything around
them that griped his ass.

The grass in the apartment building's central courtyard was wet with dew. Snails had crawled out during
the night, leaving silvery trails across the doorstep of

Taylor's apartment. He already had his key out before he realized that the door was already unlocked and standing ajar. He pushed it open with the end of the folded newspaper.

A woman's arm appeared in the opening, her hand holding a half-gallon carton of milk.

"Milkman's here," came the playful voice from inside.

Anne stepped back as Taylor came into the apartment. He closed the door behind him and gave her a one-handed hug. When he let go of her, she carried the milk carton over to the kitchen area.

"I remembered you were out of milk from last night." She set the carton down on the counter, and began pulling some other things from a brown paper sack. "And coffee—so I brought some over. Really, you ought to try going to a supermarket once in a while. You'd starve to death if it weren't for me."

Taylor slung the newspaper onto the dinette table and walked into the living room, rubbing the stiff pain in the small of his back. He half-listened to Anne; her nagging was just pretend, not the real thing. She saved the hard-edged stuff for her husband—their slowly crumbling marriage had become a war of attrition, small nicks and other bloodlettings. None of which interfered with their operating a small data-processing business together, and raising an eight-year-old son. Anne had a repertoire of anecdotes about her husband's girlfriends, which she related to Taylor with a certain grim amusement. The high point of the litany was one number who had gotten drunk enough to throw up all over the front seat of some Mercedes her husband had just gone into heavy hock for; the smell never had come out of the glove-leather seats.

He didn't know if he wanted her here now, though. He'd never regretted giving her a key to the apart-

ment—mornings, between the hour he got home from
the hall and she had to leave to go groom some bank's
database printouts, were their regular times together.
That, and the evenings her husband took the boy to
soccer practice. Taylor just wasn't in the mood, for
her or anything. Weary unto death—that was what it
felt like. Or the absence of feeling.

The mail was all bills and other bullshit. He stood
in the middle of the living room, between the stuffed
bookshelves and the desk with the battered Royal manual on it, ripping the ends of the envelopes open with
his thumb. Ed McMahon wanted to give him a million
dollars. He crumpled the smiling face into a ball and
dropped it into the trash can by the desk.

He recognized the handwriting on the last envelope.
When he opened it, he found a photograph of a smiling girl. A school photo. He turned the picture over.
In the same handwriting: To DADDY—LOVE, KAREN.
He looked at the photo for a moment, then set it on
the desk, propped against a framed photo of the same
girl. His daughter. Her mother and stepfather—her new
father, thought Taylor—had actually sent the framed
picture to him a couple of years ago as a Christmas
present. They liked doing civilized shit like that. Karen
still had the same smile as before, but she was wearing
her hair different—the teenage fashion of a fancy braid
to one side had hit the far-off land of Minnesota. He
had to take a moment to calculate whether she had
started high school yet. No, that would be next year,
even if her mother and stepfather had managed to get
her skipped ahead a grade.

"You're welcome."

He turned around and saw Anne leaning against the
wall that cut off the kitchen area, her arms folded and
watching him. It took another moment for him to remember—the milk, schmuck. And the coffee. He nod-

ded his head. "Right—thanks for bringing that stuff over. I appreciate it." He looked out the window, his view of a parking lot that was slowly beginning to fill as the morning wore on. "I'm just kind of tired, I guess."

Anne came up behind him and rubbed his shoulders. "Something going on down at the hall? You're a little late getting home."

A few months back, there had been some hassle between the probation department and the employees association, something to do with the number of part-timers the department was hiring—they were cheaper, being cut out of the county's medical-insurance package. Taylor had had to sit in on some early-morning committee meetings before it had finally gotten resolved.

He shook his head. "Naw—just more of the usual bullshit."

Anne laid her head on his shoulder. "When are you going to quit that place? It just drives you nuts."

A shrug. "It's okay." Then a smile. "Gives me plenty of time to work on my book." With the toe of his shoe, he tapped a briefcase sitting beside the desk.

She pushed herself away from him. "That's not a book. That's an excuse." They both knew he hadn't taken the briefcase, containing the manuscript and his notes, to work on at the hall in weeks.

He watched as she walked over to a chair by the dinette table and picked up her coat and purse. "So what's the latest between you and Richard, then?" Immediately, he knew he shouldn't have said it. But the crack about the book had stung him.

She gave him a rueful smile. Touché. "Yeah, well—we all have our problems, don't we?" She glanced at the wedding ring on her finger. "When you got a kid to raise, you put up with a lot of things."

A nod from him. "Yeah, I guess I put up with a lot of shit when I was married, too."

Carrying her purse and coat, she walked over to Taylor and gave him a kiss on the cheek. "Gotta go."

He snagged her around the waist. "Why don't you go in late this morning?" He still felt tired, but not so bad that he couldn't deal with company.

She leaned back in his embrace. "I went in late last morning. And the morning before that."

"So why disappoint 'em? Give 'em something to talk about." Besides Anne's husband, the business had two data-entry operators, a pair of women who regarded life in the office as a great unfolding soap opera. The one time Taylor had come down there to pick Anne up for lunch, she'd reported to him the next morning that the gossip and giggling quotient had gone up by a factor of ten.

Anne peeled his arm away from her waist. "Go to bed." She started putting on her coat. "Alone."

Outside the apartment, she turned around as he leaned against the doorway. "See you when you get off work?"

She shook her head. "I don't know. If they don't cancel Danny's soccer practice." She shrugged. "Maybe later tonight."

Taylor watched her heading out to the front of the building and her car at the curb. She didn't look back as her heels clicked against the sidewalk.

He flopped down on the sofa, legs splayed out in front of him. For a while, he angled his head back to look out the window, watching the salesgirls at the shopping center heading to their jobs, and the shadows slowly drawing back under the lampposts in the parking lot.

* * *

Mick was at the wheel. With his buddies—team-mates—beside him and in the seat behind, splitting a six-pack among themselves. When they'd driven up and parked the car, a ways along the street from the apartment building, they'd been all pumped up, like for a big game, ready to do the deed right then. But he'd had a feeling—that was why he was the captain; because he *knew*—and had made them all wait. Cool it, while he scoped out the situation.

Sure enough, some prissy-looking broad had come clickety-clicking out of the apartment building, out to her car. Later than when people usually left for work, and things quieted down. If the bunch of them had been making their play then, they would have run right into her. Which would've been definitely uncool.

Now it was time. Mick felt the easy certainty down in his belly, warm and loose, like when you fired one off and you were still standing up in the pocket, safe behind your blockers, and you could see the ball spiraling on its way like it was wired to a model-train track in the sky. Lately, that had happened more often on the practice field than during a game, but it was still a good feeling. The right feeling. The right time.

"Okay—" He nodded, then tossed back the last of his own beer and dropped the can out the window. He turned, reaching over the top of the seat. "Give me your knife."

Dennie was sitting in the back. He smiled at Mick, then dug inside his varsity jacket and came up with his clasp knife. A nice big one, big even in Dennie's hand—he slapped the knife into Mick's palm. Mick gave him a smile in return as he carefully folded the blade open. Shiny metal caught the morning sun.

One of the other guys sitting in back had a burlap sack nestled between his feet. With something inside it; something alive and moving. The thing inside the

sack was scared, and wanted to get out. It gave a little
mewling sound, frightened and pathetic. The footballer holding the top of the sack bunched in his fist
poked with his other hand at the thing inside; it hissed
and thrashed, catching the teenager's finger with a claw
poked through the burlap. The footballer looked at the
drop of blood welling up on the side of his finger, then
gave the sack a hard punch that produced a yowl from
the contents.

Mick tested the knife's blade, scraping the edge
across his thumb. Then he reached over the back of
the seat and took the sack from his buddy.

Taylor woke up when he heard the pounding against
the front door. Hammer blows, banging through the
apartment loud enough to make the window glass
shimmer—his eyes jerked wide open to sunlight pouring in. He'd fallen asleep on the living-room sofa, one
shoulder slumped down into the angle of the uphol-
stered arm. Dreaming nothing, just straight out of it—
for a moment, confused, he thought the hammering
was the dream, something pumped up from nightmare
adrenaline. Then it stopped, and he heard feet running
away outside, and laughter fading into distance.

The other sound hit him then, and he was pulled
completely awake, the last tatters of sleep snatched
away. A yowling screech, as sharp-pointed as a knife.
Fear and pain spiraling upward, right at his door. The
sound, an animal cry, pulsed through the apartment's
air and into the center of his skull.

"Jesus Christ—" Taylor pushed himself up from the
couch and ran to the door. The sound was already
dying down into something softer, a bubbling wet
moan, as he reached for the knob. Red splattered
across his chest as he pulled the door open.

It took a second to realize what the thing was. It

moved, and bled; the dark fur was matted and shiny with its own blood. The nail, a big industrial one, that pinned the creature to the door, protruded from beneath its neck; the mouth with its sharp points of teeth gaped open, more red welling up with its strangling breath. A cat, its front paw scrabbling weakly, hopelessly at the the wood of the door—Taylor's gut clenched at the sight of the animal's agony, dangling at eye level.

The cat's belly had been slit open, from its breast-bone to the hind legs. The mottled pink coils of its intestines oozed outward, the weight of the other organs squeezing down from above. It was dying, but not fast enough; the eyes in the small distorted face were crazy, protruding from the skull. Its breath came in quick panting now, the lungs straining against the blood froth-ing over its jaws.

"Shit . . ." The nausea clotted in Taylor's throat. He stepped outside the apartment and pulled the door shut, the cat's blood running in rivulets down to the sidewalk. He turned away and strode toward the little room at the end of the building where the gardener kept his tools.

Mrs. Ortiz, the building manager, spotted him as he was coming back with the shovel. All the noise had drawn her out, in her faded housecoat. She waved a cigarette in her hand as she called across the courtyard. "What's wrong? What's going on?"

He walked quickly back toward his apartment. "Nothing, Mrs. Ortiz." Shouting over his shoulder. "Just don't worry about it. I'll take care of it."

She caught sight of the cat pinned to the door, and turned pale. She scurried back into her own apartment and slammed the door shut.

It was still alive, writhing slowly, its innards droop-ing lower, bluish-gray sacks, smooth and trembling. Taylor lifted the shovel up and placed the edge of its blade against the cat's neck, just below the nail. He gritted his teeth together and gave a quick push; the cat jerked, the front paws drawing smeared circles in the blood. Another push, harder this time. The cat's body dropped to the sidewalk. It twitched for a moment, then lay still.

He was able to use the edge of the shovel to pry out the nail. The cat's head, eyes open but blind now, fell with a soft wet sound upon the carcass below.

Taylor pushed the shovel blade into the grass at the edge of the sidewalk and leaned upon the end of the handle. He let his breath slow, swallowing the sick taste in his mouth. He'd been moving fast, on autopilot, the noise of the dying cat pushing him into motion. Without thinking; now that came, with anger ticking higher with each pulse. *Some goddamn little bastards.* It pissed him off. He knew it had been kids— teenagers—and he had a good idea which ones.

He lifted his head. The apartment's front door looked like a table from a slaughterhouse, lifted into place and hinges fitted on. The mess at the foot of the door was even worse. He had some cleaning up to do.

After the little body had been scraped into a plastic garbage bag, and the door and sidewalk hosed off, he carried the shovel back to the gardener's storage room. As he set the shovel inside, he felt somebody watching him.

Beyond the rear of the apartment building, the alley to the covered parking spaces opened onto the street. Taylor turned his head and saw a car parked there. With faces inside, looking at him. And smiling.

One of them leaned out from the driver's side window. Taylor had seen him before, out at the drive-in. One of the footballers. The teenager's grin grew even wider—Taylor could hear the laughter of the others.

The kid behind the wheel had something wadded up

in his hand. He pitched it toward Taylor; the object unfolded and fell in the middle of the street. Then the car's engine revved up, the tires squealing as it peeled away from the curb.

Taylor closed the storage-room door. He walked out to the middle of the street and picked up the thing the teenager had thrown. A burlap sack draped over his hand. The rough cloth was heavy, sodden with blood.

9

The trash can weighed a lot. Because it hadn't been emptied in a long time; it had just sat in its corner in the kitchen, the stuff in it getting jammed down harder and harder, cans and milk cartons and the flat packages of TV dinners. And things that weighed a lot just by themselves, like the empty bottles. The can weighed so much that Steven had to lean back, balancing it against his chest as he carried it by the two handles on the sides. It smelled bad—the last few days had been hot—and a trickle of something wet oozed over the rim and onto his bare forearm.

He carried the can out to the side of the house and dumped it into the bigger container, the one the trashmen came and emptied whenever somebody remembered to haul it out to the curb. It was better if he just took care of it himself, but sometimes the big container was too heavy for him and he needed his sister's help, or more rarely his mother's, to manage it. A couple of times when he'd tried it on his own, he'd fucked up pretty bad, one time gouging out a strip of grass from the neighbor's lawn with the bottom edge of the container, the other time losing his grip and spilling the trash and garbage all over the driveway. Both times, there'd been trouble, yelling and stuff that he'd just had to hunker down beneath, like rain beating against his shoulders. There wasn't anything you could do about it, you just had to wait until it was over.

The trash can's contents slammed noisily into the big container, with the loud clatter of bottles breaking; a squadron of flies buzzed upward. The bottles were his mother's, the ones she emptied. Supermarket varieties—the plain-wrap labels, white with a blue strip, held slivers of glass together where they had crashed. There had been a time—Steven remembered it, so it couldn't have been too long ago—when his mother had bought better stuff, bottles with real labels with real names on them, like you saw ads in magazines for, that showed people smiling and laughing when they drank it. She'd also been more careful about the bottles back in that time, whenever it had been; she'd taken them out to the trash container herself, wrapped up in a paper bag with the top folded down tight so they wouldn't rattle and clink. Steven supposed she didn't care now.

He heard her voice then, shouting from inside the house. "Steven! Get your ass in here!" Carefully, so as not to make any more noise—maybe he had woken her up with the crash of the bottles, and that was why she sounded mad—he set the lid back on the big container and went inside.

She glared at him as he set the trash can down in its corner. Her cosmetics were spread out in front of her on the counter; sitting on one of the stools, she'd already started the process, layering on the makeup and lipstick and eye shadow. Only on her worst days, the ones where she never got out of bed, did she omit this part of her waking-up rituals.

The false eyelash in the tweezers she held looked like a bug, something with rows of black legs. She dropped the tweezers by her cup of black coffee, the small metal bit clinking on the linoleum. With a look of fury on her face, she slid off the stool and snatched open the door of the refrigerator.

"Look at this!" Her face had gone white with trembling rage, making the edges of the makeup on her cheeks even sharper. "There's not a goddamn thing to eat in this house—didn't I tell you to get your goddamn ass down to the store?" She slammed the refrigerator shut.

Steven stayed by the trash can. "You didn't give me any money."

The explanation did nothing to simmer her down. She was still glaring at him as she shot her hand out for her purse, scattering a couple of the small make-up bottles across the counter. It took a moment of rummaging around—that made her madder, hissing something under her breath—before she dug out a wadded-up bill. She threw it at him. "There. And I want the change back—every goddamn penny of it. Understand?"

He picked the money up from the the floor. It was a ten-dollar bill. He folded it back up and tucked it into the pocket of his jeans.

Taylor took Anne's advice. The business with the cat had wired him up, every muscle clenched, but he'd still managed to fall into a restless sleep. When he finally woke up—later than was his usual habit, and with a bad taste thick on his tongue—he'd slogged into the kitchen and found nothing to eat. Unless he wanted to live on coffee. Both the half-loaf of bread in a drawer and a substantial piece of Gruyère in the fridge had grown two-toned spots. He stood for a while holding a can of asparagus, the only thing he'd found in the cupboards, wondering what the hell good it was. He didn't even remember buying it.

He showered and dressed and headed, as Anne had

needled him, to the supermarket. It was one of the advantages of working nights—you got to take care of your survival errands when everybody else, except for the dying breed of confirmed housewives, was at work. Though he wouldn't be beating them by much today; it was already nearly four P.M.

It was walking distance to the supermarket, tucked in one corner of the shopping-center complex. He drove over anyway, to avoid lugging the groceries back. The afternoon sun slammed into his face as he got out of the car and crossed the parking lot. Taylor didn't know why he put off this kind of thing until he was down to starvation level, other than sheer laziness. The laziness of someone who'd become a bachelor again, inching toward forty, with an apartment full of books and other insulating shit. Between that and the isolation of working at the hall—a little world to itself—he thought that he might have lost his capacity for dealing with people. That connection, to the bigger world, had started to slip after the divorce. Now the thought of going into a supermarket, say around six, when it would be crowded—it filled him with distaste. Wouldn't even have done it, but just driven out to some fast-food place where he could stay in his car and just deal with a squawking metal box and the girl at the window.

The automatic doors of the supermarket hissed aside as he stepped up to them. The cool air washed over him as he strode toward the aisles, to get what he wanted and out of there before it got any more crowded.

He came out with a single bag riding in his arms. He set it on the car's fender as he fished his keys out of his pocket and unlocked the rear door. When he stowed the bag on the seat and slammed the door shut, he heard something else. A little ways off—the voices of kids shouting. Young kids, not like the teenagers

who'd paid him a visit that morning. He straightened
up and turned, shading his eyes to see where the shouting came from.

Steven hadn't been paying attention, except to the
deep, wordless thoughts inside his own head, so they'd
been able to catch him. Usually he could feel when
somebody was around, somebody looking for him, and
he could slip past them, sneaking out a different way
or just staying someplace safe, like in the store, until
they got bored and went away. But he'd forgotten, he
hadn't been careful enough—he hadn't even known
they were there, all around him, until he'd practically
bumped into the chest of the biggest one.

His arms were full with the bag he'd carried out of
the supermarket. He looked across the top of it, and
up into the face of the bigger kid. Bigger, lots bigger,
even if the kid was only a couple of years older than
him. Steven didn't even know the kid's name, but he
knew who he was. The kid brother of one of his sister's friends; the kid even looked like a scaled-down
version of a footballer, all bulked up and with the same
broad, grinning face. Grinning at him, as the kid's
buddies circled around—Steven saw them out of the
corner of his eye—and cut off any escape route.

The big kid's mouth twisted in a sneer. "Going to
the store for your mommy, huh?" He snatched the
grocery bag out of Steven's arms. The other kids
laughed—there were at least six of them; he could feel
the two standing right behind him, crowding him into
the big kid's reach. The big kid looked into the sack.
"Knowing your mom—you probably got a couple six-
packs in here."

They all laughed again at that, harder. Steven said
nothing, but let the words and the laughter sink into
someplace inside himself.

"Shit." The big kid dropped the bag, straight down; it split open on the asphalt. "Your old lady sends you to the store for junk like this?" He picked up a carton of eggs from the bag. "You oughta take better care of it, then, stupid." A couple of the eggs in the carton were already cracked, oozing snotlike from their shells. The big kid picked out one of the others, and smiled as he cradled it in his hand. He shoved it against Steven's chest, hand flattening as he pushed it harder. The egg crunched, the insides spurting through the shell fragments. Smile even wider, the big kid wiped his palm across the front of Steven's shirt, smearing the runny white and yolk.

The push of the big kid's hand had knocked Steven a step back, up against the other kids behind him. They shoved him forward, and he almost tripped over the split-open grocery bag.

Or he would have, if he had really been there. But he was already gone, a million miles away, far inside where they couldn't reach him. It was like watching it on TV: there was a kid who looked like him, surrounded by other kids, the victim in the little shrinking circle. He didn't care what happened—they could do whatever they wanted. As long as he was invisible, or better than that, not there at all. That was what he'd learned to do.

The mess from the crushed egg seeped through Steven's shirt. One of the other kids bent down and picked up a bottle of syrup from the bag. He laughed as he held the bottle up. "Maybe they put the booze in here for him." It wasn't even a good joke, but the other kids went on laughing.

The big kid took the syrup bottle and unscrewed the cap. He sniffed at the opening. "Nahh . . ." He shook his head. "Just more crap."

Like something you see on TV, the funny bit where

somebody pours something wet and gooey over some-body else's head, and they just stand there as it runs all over them, right down to their shoes; they just stand there looking funny, because that's the joke. The big kid knew the joke, everybody does; he grinned wider and wider as he lifted the syrup bottle up above Steven's head and tilted it.

In a sudden burst, Steven's hand flew up and knocked away the bottle. That was a mistake, because he wasn't even there—only, he was there, standing in the middle of the ring of kids, a knot of fear and anger inside his stomach. His hand knocked the syrup bottle out of the big kid's grip, and it went flying, a thin brown stream reeling out of it and splattering the big kid's shirt.

Delight filled the big kid's face. That was what he'd really been hoping for—to have Steven make a move, show that he was there, that he knew how in deep he was.

"Oh, you wanna take a swing, huh? Come on—" He thumped Steven in the chest. "Come on, you little shit, take a swing."

That was how it worked, how the little rituals moved from one stage to the next. Steven already knew everything else that was to come. Knocking the big kid's hand away, making a move—it was like some ticket the big kid had been waiting for, that he knew he was going to get. So he could double up his fists and move to the next level.

A couple more shoves backed Steven up, stumbling to keep from falling. The kids behind him moved away, over to the side; he found himself suddenly hitting a wall, his shoulder blades scraping against rough brick. The big kid, and his little circle of buddies, had backed Steven into the alleylike space running behind the supermarket, where the trucks went to the loading dock. Away from the parking lot—now nobody would see, or if they did, it would just look like a pack of kids, doing whatever kids concerned themselves with; nobody would see him at the center of the group, back against the wall.

The big kid took another shot at him, his fist right into Steven's shoulder. He felt the back of his head snap against the brick wall. If he just stood there and took it, didn't cringe or raise his arms to shield his face . . . if he didn't fall down into the angle of the wall and the asphalt, where they could start kicking him . . .

He braced himself, looking into the big kid's smile and waiting for the next punch.

Taylor had recognized the kid, just before the others had crowded around him, blocking their victim off from anybody's view, anyone who might be just passing by, in and out of the store. He had stepped around the rear of his car and seen the thin face, with its frozen stoic mask, the reactions to everything that happened bottled up inside. The weariness he'd felt before washed over him again—he turned back to the car, pulling open the door to get in. He stopped, head down, his hand gripping the top of the door.

It didn't matter to him. It wasn't his business; his job, his shift. If schoolyard bully crap like this was going on—because he knew that was what it was, the wolf pack of kids with some lippy little thug as their leader, standing a full head taller than their prey—if that was what was happening out here in the real world outside the juvenile hall, it wasn't his concern. Shit like this was happening all the time. It was the nature of reality, especially for a little sad sack like that Welsky kid. One of life's victims. Bullies were like wolves or any other predatory animal—they all had a finely

tuned sense of just what they could attack and get away
with it. You didn't see these schoolyard thugs picking
a fight with anybody who was likely to hand their asses
straight back to them. Or anybody who was on the
inside track, with that golden-boy glow around them
that meant they were going to be student-body presi-
dents or the like in a few years. Taylor knew, the same
way everybody does, down in their hearts, that schools
tolerated bullies for the simple reason that there were
always those sorry kids that teachers didn't care for,
because they were drags, they made you feel guilty
because you couldn't do anything for them, or they
reminded you of what your own wretched childhood
had been like—so the teachers were just as happy to
have them shoved around and humiliated and beaten
back down into the ground where they belonged,
creeping around out of sight, where you didn't have to
look at them. Invisible. If the bullies, those enforcers
of the teachers' secret wishes, could only have gone
all the way, actually killed and eaten their victims,
crunching the bones up in their mouths . . . That
would've been perfect. Inside, in the dark places, a
little bit of the loathing and rage might have died. They
might have let go and forgotten, at last.

It all went spinning through Taylor's head, like a
cassette tape on FAST FORWARD. One he'd heard so
many times that it was no longer necessary to do anything except look at the label to know everything that
was on it. The kind of stuff that he knew, everybody
knew, but if you spoke it out loud you sounded like
somebody still holding grudges from fourth grade.
People were just supposed to grow up and stow this
stuff away, not brood about it when you were pushing
forty.

The group of kids, the pack with their victim, had
moved into a space beside the supermarket, backing

the kid up with their collective force; the pack wanted their victim left to them, undisturbed. If they really lit into him out in front of the store, some adult do-gooder might interfere, spoil their fun.

Not my job. The whole world wasn't Taylor's job. He had his car keys out, slipping the bits of cold metal through his fingers. All he had to do was go back to the car, get in, and drive away.

"Jesus fucking Christ." He muttered the words as he shoved the keys back into his pocket and headed for the alley beside the store.

The pack of kids didn't see him coming—they were all too intent on the game they had circled around, the game with its back to the wall. Taylor strode up and grabbed the shoulder of the the biggest kid; he caught the kid just as as he was cocking his fist back for another punch. The kid lost his balance as Taylor pulled him sharply back, then shoved him to one side. The other kids stopped laughing and goggled at him.

"Knock it off—" They backed away as he barked at them, the circle loosening. He motioned to the Welsky kid, standing against the wall, watching him with no expression. "Come on."

He turned around and, without taking a single step, nearly collided with someone bigger. Bigger than the kids standing around in the alley, bigger than himself. Taylor took a step backward and looked up into a smiling face, the image of the kid who'd been doing all the taunting and punching, but now older.

And wearing a high-school varsity jacket—even without that, Taylor would've been able to recognize him. He'd seen this one, not just out at the drive-in, from a distance, but up close. This one had had his ass dragged into the juvenile hall a couple of times.

The teenager looked like a fucking gorilla, if gorillas were as mean as ignorant people thought, and were proud of being big and mean. Taylor couldn't remember the guy's name, but he could recall—vividly—the hassle they'd had with the turkey when they'd had him at the hall. The footballer had decided he didn't have to go along with all the bullshit formalities of the intake process, didn't have to do anything any candy-ass juvie staff told him to. And then he'd started swinging, and Taylor had had to call in backup from every living unit in the building, to pile on to the kid like a wild bull at the rodeo, and sort him out. Taylor hadn't even bothered trying to get him into soft ties, but had just slapped on a couple pairs of handcuffs, one on the kid's wrists pulled up behind, the other on his ankles—the asshole had already kicked one staff member, catching him in the thigh hard enough to send him flying. Then they'd dragged the footballer into Receiving's padded rubber room, and left him there to bellow and shout himself hoarse, while they all caught their breath and checked themselves for bruises.

That had been a rough time, and Taylor had had six other guys on his side then. That was what backup was all about: sheer numbers, to get the confrontation over with quickly, and minimize the damage all around. Now he was facing the same damn gorilla one on one. The juvenile-hall operations manual had some stern advice in it about avoiding situations like that, of thinking you were so fucking macho you could handle some teenage ape in the peak of physical conditioning all on your own, and winding up getting your head ripped off.

This is what I get. Taylor could almost have laughed, was already laughing mirthlessly inside himself. For being a goddamn do-gooder. He had gone from accomplishing nothing, a flat zero to all his efforts, to this, the imminent prospect of getting his ass kicked.

The footballer spread his feet, planting himself more

solidly, blocking off any way of getting by him and out of the alley. He stood with his hands on his hips, looking at Taylor. "That's my little brother you were throwing around." The sneering smile tightened. "Big man."

Taylor could believe it. They looked like brothers, the younger one even standing the same way, imitating the older one. The same ugly smirk as he waited for action. The other kids in the pack had stepped back a little way, giving the footballer's brother a certain pride of place.

"You like pushing little kids around?" The footballer stepped closer to Taylor, swallowing up the space between them. "Huh, big man?" The smile again, a corner of his lip drawing back. "Guess you don't like kids, maybe. Except for your little friend there."

A couple of the watching kids snickered at that. Taylor knew that the Welsky kid was still standing behind him, against the supermarket wall. He could even have made a break and run off; nobody was paying attention to him now. Not with this much more interesting game going on.

The footballer pushed his way closer in to Taylor. Eye to eye, the same height—he figured the teenager had some fifty to seventy pounds on him, all of it muscle. Plus that dumb-animal attitude of not caring if he got hurt, as long as he got to hurt somebody else worse. Thinking that made a connection in Taylor's head—the footballer had actually said, or rather yelled it out loud, some piece of locker-room advice, the kind of thing a coach would pump into a team during halftime. *Hurt 'em! Hurt 'em worse!* He had been yelling it after they'd had gotten the cuffs on him and dragged him to the rubber room—just seeing and hearing that again, inside his head, brought the rest of it back. The

footballer's name, written down on the booking slip.
It was Dennie something.

There was something else Taylor remembered. What
the charge had been on the booking slip. The same
charge that had been on the other slips, from his previous visits to the juvenile hall. They were all there,
stacked up inside the kid's permanent file. And most
of them, the ones on top, the latest ones, were for the
same thing; he seemed to be making a career of one
thing, getting a specialty in it. And it wasn't stealing
cars, or simple marijuana possession, or any of the
usual bullshit misdemeanors that teenagers got themselves picked up on. It was something else entirely,
something not quite as cool as those other forms of
adolescent high jinks. Taylor remembered this Dennie
kid keeping his lip zipped when the other kids in the
hall had asked him what he'd been picked up for, or
mumbling some lie that would sound better than the
real thing.

But that had been then, back in the juvenile hall.
Now was the alley alongside a supermarket, out of sight
of the parking lot and anyone who might even be so
helpful as to call the cops or store security.

Dennie stepped up closer to him. Close enough for
Taylor to smell the footballer's breath, tinged with sour
beer.

"You like that little punk a lot, don't you?" Dennie
tilted his head toward Steven, still standing by the wall.
Dennie's sneer went lopsided, then level again. "You
and him must be real pals." The sneer curled up in
Dennie's mouth. "But then guys like you like little
boys, don't you? You like 'em a lot."

One of the kids in the surrounding pack giggled.

Taylor gazed coolly back at Dennie. "Just get out
of my way." He kept his voice level, the words just
loud enough for the kids watching to hear. The trick

was to aim for a certain Clint Eastwood soft intonation, as though you had the confidence of such a huge lead pipe up your sleeve that you didn't even have to get excited about the prospect of using it. Plus Taylor was ticked off by the footballer's crummy remark, the big ha-ha homosexual slur. Playing to his audience with fag jokes, the implication that their fun had been interfered with by some big adult fairy.

Dennie's sneer turned into an ugly grin. "Why should I, you fuckin' homo? Huh?"

There, the word was right out in the open, hanging up in the air for everybody to see. Fighting words on the old playground, that little pocket universe of bloodied noses and stupid childish scuffling that the footballer was trying to suck him into, that the big kid had never gotten out of, that Dennie had never wanted to leave because he was king there, rubbing the smaller kids' faces into the dirt, forever and ever, twisting their arms up behind their backs as he knelt on their spines, muddying the ground with their hot, shame-filled tears. The kind of insult made not because it was true, or had even a possibility of being true, but because the other person couldn't back away from it, couldn't leave it hanging in the air unavenged. Right up there with saying something shitty about the other kid's mother— you were supposed to wade right in there, no matter how much bigger than you the bully might be. You'd get your ass handed to you, you'd wind up with your mouth full of blood and the bully's foot jamming down on your neck, and you'd know that was what was going to happen, but you couldn't do anything about it, not under the weight of all those other eyes watching you in the bully world.

It was a pile of shit, the kind that Taylor had thought he'd left behind, a long way back in the dismal prisons of his own childhood's playgrounds. And here he'd wandered right back into it. The sneer on Dennie's face was one he'd seen before, a long time ago, over and over.

And for this fucking punk to use that homo line on him—that was a laugh. Considering what was written on all those little slips of paper in Dennie's juvenile-hall file.

Dennie was still smirking, waiting, blocking off any exit from the alley with his footballer's bulk. The kids in the pack were waiting too, waiting for action.

Cool—Taylor gestured with his thumb toward the surrounding kids. He looked Dennie in the eye, his own lids drawn halfway. Easy, unexcited. "Maybe your little audience here would like to know why the cops brought you into the juvenile hall a couple of weeks ago." Lay it out, just loud enough for everyone to hear. "And all the times before that."

Dennie lost his ugly grin, his mouth dropping slack, as if he'd been caught with a good sneak punch into his gut, instead of just a few simple words. His eyes widened in surprise. Not surprised that Taylor knew what he'd been booked into the hall for—Taylor's knowing what was on those booking slips was one of the reasons Dennie had been relishing this golden opportunity to settle the hash of some juvenile-hall staff—but surprised that somebody would be so cruel and unscrupulous as to use words, the words that would tell everybody, all the kids standing around watching and listening, to hurt him. To gain the upper hand in the fight, instead of just walking into his fists, where he had the advantage. To make it not even a fight at all, but something that was already over before he got to land a single blow. Over because he'd already lost.

It was Taylor's turn to smile. He looked at Dennie, keeping his voice level; it was all he had to do.

"What do you think? Think the gang here would

like to know?'' Taylor glanced around at the watching faces. They were all goggling at Dennie, at the deflation in the footballer who had been so pumped up before. Dennie's kid brother, the one who had been shoving Steven around, was visibly crushed, seeing the reduction in his hero. ''Should I tell them? Come on—you decide. What the cops over in the city keep picking you up for, and how many times they've picked you up. I think they'd like to know. Why don't I just go ahead and tell them?''

Dennie's face filled with rage, too big to squeeze out through the lock of his mouth. He was back in the bully world, too, only now he wasn't the bully, he was the little kid and somebody had just yanked his pants down around his ankles and booted him out in the middle of the playground for everybody to point at and laugh, stumbling out there in his white J. C. Penney's underwear, his hairless nuts shrinking up into his gut from the cutting ice of the other kids' scornful regard.

You stupid shit—Taylor almost felt pity for the footballer. The big cheese to his little brother and these other kids, the neighborhood tough guy. He'd never thought he'd get cut down for something else he did, that he kept secret from his band of admirers. It wasn't a secret, though, if somebody else knew it. The poor schmuck had been counting on Taylor to play by the rules, the ones that would've let the winner be the one with all the muscles and weight. He hadn't known that Taylor wouldn't give a fuck about all that.

Dennie's hands had balled into fists, the knuckles showing white, but they hung uselessly by his side. The pack of kids gazed at him in wonderment. Taylor turned and reached behind, grabbing Steven by the arm. Pulling Steven along, he shoved past Dennie, shouldering the footballer aside. He could feel Dennie and the kids watching him, their eyes burning into his back, as he and Steven headed toward the parking lot.

"Don't look back. Just keep walking."

Taylor kept his own steps slow and unhurried, striding out of the alley—*cool*—and fishing his car keys out of his pocket. The keys felt slick in his hand, from his own sweat. He'd pushed that punk Dennie pretty hard, facing him down like that in front of a bunch of younger kids. There was still a chance that Dennie's none-too-sturdy mind just might snap, and he'd just come charging out of the alley and blindside Taylor, pummeling his tormentor's face into jelly on the parking lot asphalt—so far gone that he wouldn't care what little secrets Taylor might spout off with.

Or if, even at this stage, this close to the car and getting out of this whole bad scene, Taylor's cool facade were to crack and fall apart, and he showed any fear inside by breaking into a sprint for the car's safety . . .

Don't look back, he told himself now. *Just keep walking.*

The kid, this little sad-sack Steven that he'd just risked his ass for, was right next to him. Looking down at the ground, teeth clenched—Taylor could see the lock of the kid's jaw—against the temptation of looking around to see what might be running up toward them, fists raised for a blow to the back of the neck and the kidneys.

The handle of the passenger-side door slid into Taylor's hand. He pulled it open. "Get in." *Take your time . . . move cool—*

Steven hesitated. He stood outside the car's open door, still staring at the ground.

"Come on—" Taylor snapped the order out as he headed around the car to the other side. "I'm not going to hang around here all day."

The kid got in, slowly. Taylor slid in behind the steering wheel and slammed his own door shut. He glanced up at the rearview mirror—he didn't have to reach up and adjust it to see what he wanted. The pack of kids had dispersed, the last of them heading out of the mouth of the alley by the store, and heading off, looking for more fun somewhere else. The big footballer Dennie was nowhere to be seen.

He looked over at Steven. The kid sat there with his hands in his lap, the thin face expressionless, the same mask he'd seen before, back at the juvenile hall.

"Hey—" Taylor put the key in the ignition, but didn't turn it. "—Just try to forget about those assholes. All right? I mean, it's not worth eating your guts out over 'em."

The kid actually turned and looked at him—Taylor was surprised to have gotten that much of a response. Steven shot him a sour look, eyes narrowed, then went back to staring out the windshield.

"What do you know about it?" A low mutter, almost choked off with bitterness. An old voice, not a child's, though the words had come from a child's mouth.

Taylor sighed, feeling the weariness wash up along his spine, draining the life from his muscles.

"Look." Taylor laid his wrists on top of the steering wheel, like dead things that had somehow become attached to his body. "Look, I know what it's like. Okay? I've been there—lots of people have."

"Yeah, sure . . ." Even more sour than before.

This is what I get . . . He'd saved the kid's ass, and this was all the thanks he got. He didn't know if he'd expected anything different, though.

He tried again. To get through. "Hey—come on—I *know* what it's like. I know what a laugh riot it is to be the kind of kid who catches shit wherever you go, and you go home and you catch more shit, there's no place in the world you can go and not catch shit. You don't have to tell me; I've been there."

His voice had risen, in more of an outburst than he had intended. Once he'd opened the lid, the words had come spilling out, unstoppable.

Steven turned and glared at him. "It's different for you."

"Oh? Is that right? Just how is it different for me?"

The kid's sullen voice, from deep inside: "You're bigger." Looking out through the windshield again.

Taylor rolled his own eyes upward, exasperated. This stupid kid . . . "What, you think I started out this size?" As if he were some behemoth, in no danger of getting the stuffing kicked out of him by some seventeen-year-old linebacker. "Everybody starts out small. Believe me. Even those punks." He gestured past Steven's face, toward the side window and the alley beyond. Empty now, the other kids all gone.

Steven's eyes were slitted down as he glared at Taylor again. "You're stupider, too."

That took him aback. "What . . ."

Fury came rolling out, mounting as Steven spat the words at him. "You think you're so smart, huh?" The kid trembled with the rage inside, bigger than a ten-year-old's body could contain. "What are you gonna do—follow me around all day like a bodyguard? Huh?''

''Hey—come on . . .'' Taylor's own voice weak, the words powerless.

Steven's anger kept on, hitting him again. ''If I'd just stood there and took it, they would've stopped after a while. But you had to come along and stick your big nose in it. So the next time they catch me, they're really gonna kick my ass.'' Steven slumped down in the seat, arms folded across his chest, glaring at the empty air beyond the windshield. ''Thanks a lot. Thanks a *whole* lot.''

The outburst had stunned Taylor. He could barely find his own voice. ''Hey . . .''

Steven didn't even bother to look at him. ''You don't really remember how it is.''

For a moment, it seemed as if he weren't in the car at all; Taylor gripped the steering wheel, the smooth curve growing damp in the sweat from his palms, but he didn't see the wheel or the gauges on the dashboard, or the reflection of his stricken face in the angle of the glass. All that had faded away, leaving him somewhere else, time out of memory.

''I remember . . .'' He murmured the words. He could barely hear them, the grown-up voice a faint scratch, unable to reach him, to get through.

Then the other voice, the child's voice that was already old and bitter, that knew just how it was. In this world or any other. ''Why don't you just leave me alone? I can take care of myself.''

Steven's icy tone was like a whip, rousing Taylor. He pushed himself back from the wheel and looked at the kid. ''Fine. Great.'' The words clipped, bitten off. ''Whatever. Just listen to me a minute, okay? Think you can hear me out for that long? I just wanted to tell you that you can get through it. Believe me, one day it'll be over. And then you get to be a grown-up.'' His voice curled in on itself, sarcastic. ''Is that a great deal, or what?''

The kid regarded Taylor for a moment, then pushed open the door on his side and slid out of the car.

Taylor watched him walking away, across the parking lot. ''Forget it.'' Muttering to himself, he turned the key in the ignition. ''What do I know . . .''

10

"Where the fuck's your brain at today? Huh?" The coach gave him a slap to the side of the helmet, hard enough to make his ears ring. "Standing there, fuckin' daydreaming—you missed your fuckin' block by a mile!"

Dennie tasted salt trickling into his mouth, his sweat stinging the corners of his eyes. He felt as though he were broiling inside his football pads, the afternoon sun revved up and squatting like hot bricks onto the practice field. The same summer heat, the tail end of it dragging on into fall, that made the nights so cozy and warm, a dry breeze slipping between the hills from off the desert beyond—good beer-drinking weather, when you could just let it slide down your throat and unbutton your spine as it went, everything going loose inside. He could taste it now, his mouth watering at the thought of it, the cold, sour, sweet wash across his tongue and into the back of his throat, his hands already ripping the next one out of the plastic rings as he swallowed the metal-tasting dregs of the first one, and four more to go after that, and another six-pack to go slower on, once he'd got the buzz going and he could relax and forget everything (*What do you think? Huh? Should I tell them?*—somebody else's voice twisting inside his head), forget that, too, the warm

night air wrapping around him and drying the sweat
leaking through his T-shirt . . .

"Christ all-fucking-*mighty!*" Another slap—
bwanng—to the helmet, rocking his head against the
hump of his shoulder pad. "Are you even fuckin' *listening* to me?"

He wasn't standing around drinking beer with his
buddies, laughing and bullshitting out at the old drive-
in. He was standing out here on the practice field, the
afternoon sun roasting him inside his pads, the grunts
and thumps of the rest of the team sounding in his ears
as they went through some stupid drill or other. And
the coach, who thought he was Vince fucking Lom-
bardi or something, with all that smacking you around
and wind sprints piled on for every goddamn thing
including looking at him cross-eyed—the coach was a
little rooster with a clipboard who'd had to reach up
on tiptoe to smack Dennie's helmet. Face like a
squinting bulldog, and breath that smelled of pint bottles of Maalox. If the little bastard didn't get so worked
up all the time, he wouldn't need that shit—when the
beer had loosened Dennie up good and proper, he
could think about the coach and feel sorry for him.
But not now, with all this shouting right through the
face bars of his helmet.

"Would you care to join us today? Huh?" The bulldog looked as if it had been dipped into a pot of boil-
ing water, gone all red, the vein pumping at the corner
of the coach's forehead. "We're not taking up too
much of your valuable time, are we?"

The other guys had stopped and were looking over
at Dennie and the coach. All that shouting had brought
them around, staring over at him getting his ass chewed
out.

He felt as though his head were going to explode,

from the pressure built up inside it; the helmet was all that kept it from happening. The ringing that had started when the coach had whangged him now went up in pitch, like a dentist's drill biting in, and louder; it surged with his pulse.

Why don't I tell them? Huh? Don't you think they'd like to know? Why the cops—

And it was so fucking hot, the pads and all the other shit had him burning up inside . . .

—hauled you in, what the cops keep hauling you in for, this time and—

. . . it wasn't the sun slamming its weight down on him, it was the heat of his own blood, pumping up so loud and fast that he could hear, could feel it squeezing his eyes shut and clamping his teeth together . . .

—this time and all the other times—

. . . too hot, the blood too loud in his ears, he tore at the chin strap . . .

—Should I tell them? Huh? Should I tell them—

"Goddamn it, listen up!"

—Tell them.

Dennie pulled the helmet off and slammed it down on the ground in front of the coach. The helmet bounced against the coach's shin and rolled wobbling away.

He was able to breathe again. He glared at the coach. "Fuck you." And turned and stalked toward the edge of the field, and the locker room beyond.

The coach sputtered behind him. Shouting: "I'll have your ass on the bench, shithead! For the season!"

Dennie turned long enough to flip the coach the finger, and see all the other guys on the team staring after him. He didn't give a fuck what they thought. He was already stripping off his numbered jersey as he headed for the locker room.

* * *

"You think—" Larry turned to the guys around him, the rest of the team, "—maybe one of us should go after him? Talk to him, or something?"

They looked toward Mick, who'd had his arms folded across his chest as he'd watched the whole scene between Dennie and the coach. Just watching, not saying anything. Now he picked up a football from the grass and began rubbing the dirt that had gotten caked on its pebbled surface, watching his thumb scrape it away.

Mick shook his head finally, the loose chin strap of his helmet dangling against his throat. "Nah—forget it." He lifted the ball and cocked his arm, as if he were about to lob it to a receiver in the end zone. "The big candy-ass'll come back around when he feels like it." He let the ball roll out of his fingers and drop to the ground.

The coach had finally managed to regain enough of his composure to go on with the practice. The defense assistant blew his whistle and started shouting something. Larry stood looking over to where Dennie had gone storming off, as the other guys walked away. Christ knew he didn't give a damn what happened to Dennie—the guy was an asshole who thought his shit didn't stink because he was on the team—but after some of the stuff that had happened the last time he'd blown his top and gone off, it didn't seem right to just let him go like that. If for no other reason than that Dennie was on the first string, a big chunk of their weight on the line.

The guy knew how to get into trouble, though. Big, sticky trouble . . . that was the problem . . .

"Jesus *Christ!* You're not starting up this shit on me too, are you?"

Larry looked over and saw the coach glaring at him, the clipboard jammed against one broad hip, jowly face set in martyred exasperation.

Dennie would just have to look out for himself, for now. In a quick trot, Larry headed over to where the others were waiting.

It was all the fault of that fucking juvenile-hall prick. Dennie stood at the edge of the freeway on-ramp, hands deep in the pockets of his varsity jacket, his face set glowering. Brooding about all the shit that had happened to him, the burning unfairness of it. He took out one hand long enough to raise a thumb as a car turned off the street and onto the ramp; it zipped right past him, accelerating to the swift flow of traffic above. *Fuckers,* thought Dennie; the people in the car were part of the shit, too, leaving him standing here when it was already turning evening and he had stuff to do in the city before the night was over. Stuff that would make him feel better.

He could forget about the bastards in the car, in all the cars that had gone right by him without stopping to give him a ride—or at least let them sink away into the darkness, back where he kept all the things that he never really forgot. He remembered everything, layer upon layer of bad shit, right back to when he'd been a little kid. Thinking about even a little bit of it made his stomach go tight, a fist in his guts. He could taste it, like sour blood on his tongue. If it took forever, he'd pay them back. All of them, even those sonsabitches in the cars.

Another one turned onto the ramp. Dark enough now that it had its headlights on, though there was still enough of the red twilight sun breaking through the freeway pilings for him to see the driver through the windshield. Just one guy in the car, in his thirties or maybe an old fuck, forty or older. It was hard to tell sometimes, until you were right next to them. The man's gaze met Dennie's, and for a moment Dennie

thought that he wouldn't have to go on into the city,
that he'd found what he was looking for right here,
practically on his own doorstep. There was that little
spark, a moment of recognition between two people
who had never seen each other before. Seeing something inside each other.

Then the car was past him, the guy inside not even
looking around at him. Dennie watched the taillights
swoop around the top of the on-ramp's curve and disappear. He put his hand back into his jacket pocket,
squeezing it and the other into fists, tight enough to
pump the muscles in his arms. Maybe the guy in the
car was heading into the city for the same thing. Maybe
he'd see the guy there, on the street. The guy in the
car might be one of those careful ones, who didn't
want to risk anybody he knew seeing him make this
kind of connection. Maybe later, the guy in the car
would be the one for tonight, after all.

That made Dennie feel better, thinking about something like that. The face behind the windshield had
been one of those smooth, round baby faces, like a
little junior exec or something, already moving up the
corporate ladder with the right attachments, wife and
a two-year-old stashed in one of the shiny new devel-
opments, the one with the bullshit phony lake pumped
into the middle of it and the fence all around. The car
had been a Mercedes or a BMW, one of those expensive pieces of shit. So the guy had money, to get whatever he wanted. That little baby face . . . Dennie's
fists tightened, even harder, the nails digging into his
palms, until he could just about feel the blood spurting
out.

"Shit—" He hunched up his shoulders in the jacket.
This was wasting time, standing here with nobody giving him a ride. That bastard with the Mercedes would
get on into the city and hook up with somebody else

for what he wanted, one of the other boys on the street would get him. He was tempted to walk on back to his house and get his own car, the old Fairlane his mom had let him have, and just goddamn *drive* on into the city himself. It'd be faster than hanging out here all fucking night. But he didn't want to—it'd be spoiling the magic of it somehow, to do that. The first time he'd gone into the city to do this stuff—he'd been only fourteen—he'd had to hitch in order to get there. It was part of the thrill, to get into some car you'd never seen before, you didn't know what was going to happen but you were ready for it anyway. Even if all you wanted at the start of the night was a ride, just to get into the city where the real action would be, the cars that slowed down to look you over as you stood under the streetlights waiting, waiting for anything . . . It was still one thing somehow, in his head, from the night's start to its finish; getting into a car just for a ride was like a little taste of what was to come, the real thing, the sliding into a stranger's car with the blue streetlight angling in to show up close some baby face and glittering, expectant eyes . . .

It made him feel good, better and better, thinking about it. "Come on . . ." A whisper to himself, as he saw another set of headlights coming up the street. He'd show them, he'd show 'em all. The fist in his gut twisted and turned, squeezing his guts. That juvenile-hall prick, that smart-ass sonuvabitch. It wasn't some baby face in a Mercedes he wanted, but that juvenile-hall guy—*Should I tell them? Huh?*—but in the meantime some baby face would do, would make him feel better.

He'd recognized the juvenile-hall guy when he'd seen him standing there, in the alley by the supermarket. He remembered the guy; the guy was like in charge or something, whenever the cops had hauled him in.

The guy thought he was so fucking smart, a big man when he had a couple of dozen other guys on his side— the guy didn't have the balls to take him one on one, to try to slap those cuffs on by himself. Dennie would've dismantled the sucker if he'd tried.

So the chance to catch the juvenile-hall guy off his turf, and alone, without anybody to help him out—that had been like a little present, wrapped up and delivered from God. He'd just been strolling across the parking lot, nothing on his mind except the thirst that was already sandpapering his throat, when he'd seen the pack of kids in the alley, his own kid brother among them. And there was that prick from the juvenile hall, acting like he was some fucking hero or something, swooping in to save that mousy little punk. Dennie smiled to himself, tasting how it'd felt to have the juvie guy cornered, to loom over the skinny bastard, *lean* on him, push him around a little bit, the way he'd been pushing around Dennie's brother and the other kids. Say all kinds of shit to him and the guy couldn't say anything back, because he was scared, he knew what was going to happen to him; and then to swing a fist right into the sonuvabitch's face and feel the blood spurt across his knuckles, to double him up with another fist into his gut, rock him back with a knee up into his nuts . . .

Dennie grinned, just thinking about it, remembering the juvenile-hall guy lying at his feet in the alley, all crumpled up, blood weeping out of the sonuvabitch's face, his own muscles all pumped up and tingling, the way it felt to tear through some hole in the line and cream some chickenshit quarterback's ass, everybody shouting and going crazy, the kids in the alley all going round-eyed and saying Wow!, digging it, a ten-yard loss for the other side, pushing 'em back right to their own goalposts . . .

Only he hadn't. He hadn't creamed the juvenile-hall guy. The grin on Dennie's face stretched back across his face as he ground his teeth together. That chickenshit sonuvabitch . . . Why couldn't the bastard have played fair? Instead of lipping off like that, right in front of Dennie's little brother and all those other kids, all of 'em standing around and watching and listening, wondering what was going on. Tears burned at the rims of Dennie's eyes. It just wasn't *fair;* the guy shouldn't have said stuff like that, threatening to tell all those things. Dennie's secrets. It was bad enough that the sonuvabitch *knew.* But to use it against him like that . . .

It had gone on eating away at Dennie's guts, the whole day. Everything going red inside him, hearing the juvenile-hall guy's voice *Should I tell them? Huh? Should I tell them?* over and over, the smug sonuvabitch, the guy thought he was so fucking smart . . . So he'd screwed up in practice, and the coach had yelled at him, and he'd told the coach to fuck off, and who the fuck cared, anyway? Dennie didn't give a fuck—he knew what he needed, what would make him feel better. His fists balled up inside his jacket pockets, and he squeezed them harder, into stones.

The car he'd been watching swung up on the on-ramp, toward him. Not a Mercedes or anything like that, just some beat-up Jap sedan. Some guy heading home from work. Dennie could see right into the guy's eyes through the windshield, and see that this one was straight, and not what he needed. He'd have to go on into the city for that.

He stuck out his thumb, and the car slowed, coming to stop a few yards beyond him. Dennie turned and sprinted toward it as the guy inside pushed open the passenger-side door.

* * *

A lot of the other guys were out on the streets by the time Dennie got there. Working it since before the sun had gone down—in the city, on a street like this one, the action, the little deals, went on twenty-four hours a day. It just got heavier at night.

Dennie walked down the blocks, from one pool of streetlight to the next, nodding to the guys he knew, and the ones he'd never seen before—the glance, the message from their eyes to his, saying everything, recognition of why they were all out here tonight. The blue light, and the glare of the neon above the doors of the bars, drained the human color from their faces, gave them wax masks formed in the features of teen-age boys.

He bummed a cigarette off one, a total street hustler everybody called Scooter, even though he had nearly a full pack in the pocket of his varsity jacket. Just so he could ask, while Scooter held up a lit match in his cupped hands, the flame warming both their faces as they leaned close, how things were going tonight. Scooter shrugged, looking down the slot of traffic lights and crawling traffic. Scooter's face looked as though it were being hollowed from the inside out, the cheeks collapsing to outline whatever teeth he had left, the pink-rimmed eyes being eaten by the dark sockets around them. Pickups were becoming farther between for Scooter; most of the men who cruised the street, coming in from the suburbs or the condos that lined the hills, knew his face already or remembered it from when he'd been prettier. He'd looked like a little angel in faded denim and a Metallica T-shirt when he was fourteen and first started on the street, the same age and time that Dennie had. But—Dennie knew—Scooter didn't love himself enough, not the way Dennie did; Scooter ate whatever came his way and used a needle when there was something to use a needle for, and let the men in the cars do things to him without getting his own back. That was the worst; to let them buy you, and to take the money and actually give them what they wanted, do whatever they wanted, without making them pay for it in something besides money. Dennie made sure they paid. Now he was still big and healthy, and pretty too, the men in the cars slowing down to admire and covet a young hunk footballer, complete to the jacket with the letter on it, and all those hard muscles beneath. And Scooter looked as if he were going to die, which cut his trade down even further, because he looked so sick, and who needed to catch something like that? That *you* could die of? Scooter's dirty blond hair was already growing thin, peeling back from his forehead, the bone of his skull about to break through the skin.

Dennie told Scooter to take it easy, then moved on down the street, even though he knew Scooter wanted him to stick around, to keep him company at his station beneath the streetlight, as though the big footballer's body were a fire that he could stand close to and keep himself warm through the night. But screw that—the other guys on the street, the ones who had gotten out there earlier, had already gotten a jump on the car trade, picking off the first wave of horny suburbanites to hit the street when the sun went down. He didn't want to fuck up his chances by being seen hanging around a germbag like Scooter.

There was already a little transaction going on, a couple blocks up the street. A nice new Volvo station wagon, the kind of car you'd expect to see hauling around a bunch of kids suited up for a Pop Warner league game on Saturday—right now the man behind the wheel was talking to some skinny surfer type, maybe eighteen years old at the most; the kid's long hair fell across his bright-eyed face as he leaned in the

Volvo's side window. Then the kid got in and the Volvo peeled away from the curb—they always drove fast, once the deal had been made, no longer crawling along the street looking over the merchandise, but hurrying off to someplace dark.

Dennie took the surfer kid's station, a nice spot under the streetlight. Far enough from any of the other guys, like slouching sentries posted along the blocks. A solid cement wall to lean against and watch the traffic going by—there was a liquor store a ways up; if you hung around it, some crazy old Chinese guy would come out and chase you with a mop handle, shouting a bunch of stuff so loud that it could bring around the cops. This spot was cool, though. He liked being toward the end of the strip, where the bars thinned out, so that the guys in the cars would already have seen the competition, would have seen that there was no one else on the street as big and pretty as him. Just what they were looking for.

Back against the wall, watching the slow headlights move up the street, the shadows of the other boys turning and shifting—Dennie took a cigarette from his pack and lit it off the one he'd bummed from Scooter. He flicked the butt of the first one away, sparks in the gutter, then settled back. And waited.

11

Steven thought he was dreaming. That was what it felt like: dreaming, when you know you're asleep, and it doesn't matter. When you can just drift with it, the slow waves cradling you in their darkness.

He didn't even know how he'd gotten here, in the back seat of a car rolling through a city's night streets. He'd opened his eyes—slowly, not startled or afraid—and found himself lying here, the side of his face warm against his hands. Looking up, he'd seen the blue of the streetlights sliding by the windows, one after another.

The motion of the car, the deep murmur of its engine, lulled him into a waking drowse. He didn't sit up, but went on lying on the seat, watching and waiting.

He could see the back of the driver's head in the seat up front. Just a black silhouette, outlined brighter, then dimmer, by the headlights of the other cars on the road.

Somehow, he knew who the driver was, though there wasn't a name or a face for him. Steven just knew.

There wasn't anything to worry about. Not now, not here. He drew his legs up, curling around the warm ball of his own heartbeat and breath.

The car moved on, through the dark streets.

* * *

Two hours had passed—or had it been three already? Dennie couldn't tell except from the crick the wall had put in his spine—the sidewalk around his feet was littered with stubbed-out cigarettes. The pack was empty; he crumpled it in his fist and threw it out into the street.

Motherfucking sonuva*bitch*—Dennie glared at the cars going by, his fury churning acid at the base of his throat, hot enough to spit out and boil against some bastard's windshield. The stupid shits—what the fuck did they think they were doing? Driving by, giving him the once-over, their gazes locking with his for a moment, the split second in which everything about each other was read out, except for the exact price—looking at him, then driving on, the sonsabitches, heading right on out into the darkness at the end of the street, or doing a U-turn a couple of blocks on and heading back for another pass at the stuff they'd checked out before.

Not that there was that much stuff left out on the street. This late, getting on toward the hour when the bars would close, the music that seeped around the doors and out onto the sidewalks finally lapsing into silence; the bar types, the ones who knew what they were and didn't try to hide it behind marriage and kids and suburban respectability, would spill out in their leather gear and butt-tucked designer jeans, cowboy boots and thong-tied arm bands, all the costume gear they wore as much for a nostalgic giggle as serious scoring action around the pool tables. Hair graying, and paunches jiggling beneath a shiny black vest looped with chrome bondage rings . . . just a joke now, those rowdy bar days fading into everybody's Polaroid scrapbooks. Maybe, as they climbed onto their expensive Harleys, and into their macho jeeps, they would glance over at the chicken—that was what they called the young street prowlers—and watch for a little while, eyes connecting across the traffic, remembering when they'd done shit like that. And then they'd be gone, the neon switched off, and true dark would cover the street.

Chances would be slim after that, Dennie knew, for the guys who drove into the city to pick up street trade, stopping in the bars to soak up a little blood-alcohol courage and filling their heads with the sweat smell of males all packed together in a small space, that was how they stroked their desires to the point of connecting with some kid under a streetlight. Without that subaudible beat filtering into the cars, and the sense of muscled bodies sliding against each other somewhere, the bastards would go yellow and scurry back down the freeways to home and another long night beside their sleeping wives, in cold waking beds.

Some of the other guys had given up, the ones like Scooter, too street-eroded to have scored, this night or any other night. Dennie could look down the block and see one of them, a kid his own age, who'd just lain down on the sidewalk and curled up, like some old bum or something, tucking his head down against the wall to sleep.

Just fuck 'em all, anyway—Dennie bit his lip, seething inside. The rage that he'd come onto the street with had just kept building up as the cars kept rolling by, the faces glancing at him, then turning away, and he'd lit one cigarette after another. Now he had nothing but his fists in his jacket pockets; he squeezed his eyes shut, seeing inside how nice it'd be to land one right in some little faggot's face, to make him pay, to make them all pay . . .

His blood roared so loud in his head that he almost didn't hear the sound of the car idling at the curb. Right in front of him, pulled over from the flow of traffic and stopped at the sidewalk's edge. Until the low murmur of the engine crept up from the reverberation in his chest and into his skull. He opened his eyes and saw the car, a black shape with the street's neon glinting from the metal.

Nice-looking car, the kind of thing Dennie would've liked for himself, would have someday, he knew, when he got recruited to some big college and some rich football booster forked over the goodies that went with the scholarship. Low, swoopy lines, like a Porsche 924, or a Z car, something like that, the way they made a car look like a knife blade cutting through the air. And plush inside, lots of room to lean back and wallow around in, smiling out through the tinted glass as the stereo massaged you from four different directions. But it wasn't a Porsche or a Z; too dark, he hadn't gotten a look at it as it'd pulled up, to tell just what it was. Maybe some kind of custom job? It looked like money, whatever it was. The engine rumble traveled through the ground and up Dennie's legs, right into some sympathetic nerve in his groin.

The window on the passenger's side rolled down, smooth. The driver was still in shadow inside as he leaned across the seat; Dennie couldn't see the man's face.

A low, easy voice, a gap in the traffic noise letting the words slide across to Dennie's ear: "You're out awfully late."

Dennie could hear the smile in the driver's voice. Even without making connection with the driver's eyes, he knew exactly what was being said. Finally—enough of this shit, hanging around waiting. He knew he'd score; he always did. He smiled, a warm, expectant joy uncurling inside his chest as he pushed himself away from the wall and sauntered across the sidewalk.

The driver leaned back behind the wheel as Dennie

stood beside the car, looking down into the side window.

"Maybe I am." Dennie gave an easy shrug. "So what?"

He could see the driver nod, the shaded face turning back toward the windshield. A big guy, not some little pansy soft as butter wrapped around a stick. Not bulky big, but tall, moving with lean-muscled ease. That was all right—Dennie liked them big. It made it more fun, to show them that all their hours spent pumping away at the Nautilus machines in some men-only gym with all their buddies didn't mean shit. He felt his own muscles grow tighter under his varsity jacket, the first edge of adrenaline seeping out into the flesh.

The driver's silhouette gazed ahead, not looking at Dennie, as one hand reached over and pushed the door open. "Get in. I'll give you a ride home."

Dennie nodded, feeling the smirk grow across his face. He'd heard all these opening lines before. He pulled the door farther open and got into the car, sliding down into the seat.

The driver eased the car away from the curb and back into the street. On Dennie's side, the streetlights swung past, angling in to hit his own face but not the other across the seat from him.

The same low voice spoke again. "Were you waiting for someone out there?" The driver moved his hands over the curve of the wheel, still gazing ahead.

That was all right—Dennie smiled to himself. He didn't mind playing all the little games, the talk that had to be gotten through before they got down to business. "Maybe." He watched the bright part of the street rolling past.

A touch softer: "Maybe you were waiting to make some money." The driver didn't turn to face Dennie, but just drove, sliding through the traffic, thin at this late hour.

Dennie glanced over at the man's silhouette, then shrugged. That was all he had to do, at this stage.

"Somebody might make you an offer . . ." Almost a whisper. "Something you could handle. Something . . . right for you."

Dennie leaned his head back against the cushion. This guy was taking his time, but he was getting there; he knew it.

"Big kid like you . . ." The driver nodded, slowly, as though mulling over some deep consideration. "I hear that some guys—guys who come to the street to meet boys like you—I hear they like a little rough stuff sometimes. Getting slapped around a little bit. Stuff like that."

This was too good to be true; this was absolute fucking heaven. Dennie closed his eyes, his heart feeling like a big warm flower opening inside his chest. The driver, this guy who'd picked him up, was getting right to the point, right to what he really wanted. And when one of these guys talked like that—*rough stuff*—it was easy to tell just what wavelength they were on. *Slapped around a little bit*. What he wanted from Dennie. *Stuff like that*. There wouldn't have to be all the preliminaries, all the usual hustling bullshit that went along with the game. With this guy, there wouldn't be the pulling the car over in an alley and the fumbling around in the dark, the groping to open his fly and closing a fist around the blood heat, head dipping down over the guy's lap to take it in the mouth, the bottom edge of the steering wheel rubbing against the corner of Dennie's brow. Or the other routine, the long-drawn-out one, where they went back to the guy's nice apartment, with all its expensive toys, the big stereo and shit, and beer and maybe a couple stingy lines so thin they looked like they were drawn with a white pencil point on the mirror. And then the bed or on the carpet, it was all the same.

But with this guy, the driver—Dennie knew, could feel it right down in his bones, in the blood pumping into his arms—there wouldn't be any of that bullshit to get through, to get to the part Dennie was there for. The real fun stuff.

He could hear the driver speaking again. "Maybe even something rougher than that . . ." Slow, cool. "Think you're up for that?"

Dennie's fingers curled across the top of his thighs, hands into fists. The blood pumped and sang. He smiled, nodding slowly. "Sure . . ."

The driver's face, still in silhouette, turned toward Dennie. Almost a whisper. "Good . . ."

Good . . .

Steven heard the driver's voice, the single soft word. He raised his head, pushing himself up from the rear seat, listening.

He'd heard everything that had been said, the voices going back and forth, the words that meant more than just the little bit you heard with your ears, words that had deep dark places beneath them, where things moved around in the darkness. He'd still been lying curled up on the seat, keeping quiet, listening and watching, the lights of the city street moving past, little glimpses and fragments all that he could see from the angle below the car's windows. And the back of the driver's head, the dark shape that headlights coming from the other direction outlined, sometimes turning to show the black, featureless profile, the driver's eyes scanning across the street, looking and hunting. The dark and the tearing lights moved by, the car sliding forward in an empty, unending piece of time. Until

Steven had felt the car slowing over to the curb and
stopping. That was when the voices started, the driver's voice, which he recognized before, from his dream
. . . And the other one, who leaned down to the car's
window to speak, to answer the driver's soft, easy
words. He'd known who that one was, too, soon as
he'd heard him speak . . .

Maybe I am. Tough, cocky. *So what.*

It was that Dennie guy, that friend of his sister's.
One of the guys on the football team. The one who
liked shoving him around so much, at their parties out
at the drive-in, and then today over by the supermarket, making trouble for that guy from the juvenile hall.
Lying on the back seat of the black car, where he
couldn't be seen, Steven could imagine the smile on
Dennie's face, the big ugly grin, as if Dennie were
already tasting the fun he was about to have. The kind
of look Dennie got when he was doing stuff out at the
drive-in, like picking Steven right up from the ground,
the big fist bunching up the front of Steven's shirt, and
then tossing him away with a flick of the big, broad-
tipped fingers.

But he doesn't know—the words had whispered inside Steven's head as he'd looked up and listened. *He
doesn't know yet.*

Dennie had gotten in the car, sliding in next to the
driver. The car had moved off into the darkness, into
a place where there were no lights.

Steven held his breath—Dennie still hadn't seen him,
hadn't realized that he was there, crouching on the
back seat, watching and listening. The driver and Dennie talked, the words sliding back and forth in the car's
close, dark space. The whole world was inside the car,
there wasn't anything else outside except the dark.

Think you're up for that? The driver, a black silhouette turning toward Dennie beside him.

A smile in Dennie's voice. *Sure* . . .

He doesn't know. Steven looked up at the back of Dennie's head, tilted against the top of the front seat. Dennie didn't know yet . . .

Good . . . The driver's whisper, the only sound left in the world.

The car had stopped somewhere, far from any other traffic. Dark and silent outside, so still that Steven could hear only his own breath, and Dennie's.

Dennie didn't see it, but the driver's silhouette turned further, past Dennie leaning back into the seat, and around. Until the driver was looking at Steven; he couldn't see the driver's eyes, he never could, but he knew the cold gaze had locked right into his. A wordless message, all that needed to be said. Steven shrank back a little from the dark face, pressing his spine against the seat.

The driver turned again to Dennie. "You ready?" A whisper, softer than all the words before.

Steven knew that Dennie had his hands squeezed into fists, from the way his shoulders bunched up, the muscles swelling inside the teenager's jacket. And that he was smiling.

"Sure." Dennie turned his head. "Come on—"

Dennie's words were cut off as the driver's arm shot out, swinging in a flat arc from the steering wheel. The driver's hand flew onto Dennie's throat, gripping tight. The angle of thumb and forefinger rammed under Dennie's jaw, rocking his head back. Dennie's tongue protruded as the fingers sunk into the flesh of his neck. His eyes went round, a strangled gargling noise scraping up in his mouth.

Steven rose up from his crouch on the back seat. Watching. The world inside the car shrank even more, pushing him toward the other faces.

The driver's other hand reached into the pocket of

Dennie's jacket, not fumbling around, but going straight for what the driver must have known would be there. The hand came back out with a knife gripped in it. Dennie's big clasp knife; Steven had seen him with it before, had seen him unfold the shining blade from the chrome-ended handle. Dennie had always used both hands to open the knife, but now the driver, in one smooth, fluid motion, flicked it open with one hand, the blade sweeping out from the handle and snapping into place. A thin light seemed to radiate from the sharp-edged metal, held up to Dennie's face. Dennie's eyes went even wider, as though they were going to pop from their sockets, when he saw the knife; his fingertips scrabbled futilely at the hand locked around his throat.

The driver turned his dark face around to Steven. Now the driver's whisper was to him, for him alone to hear.

"Steven . . ." The driver held the knife up, a spark threading along its edge.

Steven's gaze moved from the face he couldn't see to the point of the knife in the driver's hand.

The whisper curled at his ear. "Steven . . . give me your hand . . ."

He couldn't stop himself from leaning forward, toward the knife. The light gleaming from the blade fell inside him, to the center of his heart; it held him there, and pulled him toward its hard, sharp purity.

There were only the two of them now, the driver and himself. There was another thing inside the car with them, a frightened thing with round staring eyes that darted from the face in shadow to the child's face. The scared thing gagged for breath, a sob of fear retching out onto its tongue. Tears spilled across the reddening face. The scared thing was afraid of the knife.

It didn't know. Not yet.

"Go on . . ." The knife turned in the driver's hand. "Take it . . ."

The knife drew his hand. His fingers slid around the handle, then curled. Then the knife was in his hand.

The driver wrapped his hand around Steven's, tightening his grip upon the knife.

"Like that . . ."

He had leaned so far forward, from where he knelt upon the back seat, that he had to balance himself with his other hand upon the seat where Dennie was. The collar of Dennie's jacket brushed against his knuckles.

"Go on . . ."

Steven looked at the blade as the driver pulled his hand away. His own hand stayed tight on the knife's handle, squeezing it in his fist. He could see his face in the shining metal, one eye pulled into a thread at the knife's edge.

Then the metal grew brighter, dazzling in a light that started from a cold blue and mounted to a silver white, flooding the inside of the car, washing away his face reflected in the blade, and the driver's silhouette beyond it, and Dennie's scared, pleading blubber. Steven turned his head toward the car's side window, and looked up.

The sky was filled with light—it took a moment for Steven to see through the glare. He squinted and saw the metal poles towering up on either side of the car, lifting banks of lights against the night sky. He knew what they were, he had seen them before—they were the lights they used out at the high school, at the football field for night games. The lights blotted out the stars and the darkness around them. An eye-aching artificial day washed over the field and the silent, empty bleachers; in the distance, the goalposts stabbed into shadows stretching out to the surrounding night.

The inside of the car was lit up, making Steven's hand a white thing that held a shard of fire, and Dennie's face a bleached clown's mask, bright tears trickling down to his open mouth and the hand that squeezed into his throat. Light, but still he couldn't see the driver's face; the dark had condensed behind the steering wheel, but didn't go away.

From that dark, the driver's voice came again, the whisper falling lower and more intense. "Go on . . . go on, Steven . . ."

Steven turned away from the dark face and looked down at Dennie. The footballer's eyes met his; at the edge of the darkness in their center, Steven saw the reflection of the knife, a sharp-pointed sliver, burning with its own radiance.

Dennie slumped down lower in the angle of the seat and the door, scrabbling to get away from the knife, his hands still struggling futilely with the grip that had locked onto his throat. Under the lights' glare, his face had darkened with blood, his tongue welling upward in his mouth, gasping for breath. Something—a word, a name—slid through the gagging sound; Steven could almost hear it, hear what Dennie was trying to say, to beg for . . .

Then the knife fell. The point of light plunged downward and the word bubbling in Dennie's throat became a scream, throttled into silence, only a hiss of pain and shock escaping. Dennie's face contorted, the eyes squeezing shut, the lips drawing back from the teeth. The driver's hand clamped harder upon Dennie's throat, the scream dying inside the fingers sinking into the flesh.

Something hot washed across Steven's hand. He looked down and saw the handle of the knife—the blade had disappeared into Dennie's chest, the metal cutting through the jacket and the shirt beneath it.

Steven's hand was still holding the knife, his grip hard upon the handle. Something wet and dark surged up from below his hand, pulsing across his fingers and thumb. It spread across the front of Dennie's shirt, soaking into the jacket.

The bright flow pulsed again, streaming up from the hole the knife had sunk into, bursting up to Steven's wrist. The driver had let go of Dennie's throat, but Dennie didn't move, didn't try to get away. His head lolled back against the door, the striped print of the driver's grip fading on his neck.

And he couldn't let go. The thing that had been Dennie fell, sliding down to the car's front seat, but Steven couldn't let go. His hand stayed locked upon the knife as it slid out of Dennie's chest and the bright flow surged higher, leaping up at him . . .

His own scream woke him. From the glaring light, into the dark of his own bedroom—the scream snapped dead in his throat as he gasped for breath.

Steven felt his heart pounding in his chest. Beating at the same speed as the pulse of blood in his dream, which had come surging around the knife and up over his hand. Black in shadow, and then bright red as it had flowed across Dennie's chest and over the wrist of the hand holding the knife. His hand, squeezing the knife tight, fingers locked onto it, unable to let go . . .

He sat up in his bed, raising himself up from the sweat-damp pillow, onto his elbows. His right hand was squeezed into a fist, the bed sheet twisted into a knot against his palm. He let go, his fingers slowly spreading apart, stiff, the blood inside seeping back into the flesh that had been pressed white. The marks of his fingernails were red crescents in a line across the skin.

Silence in the bedroom; Steven turned his head, listening. Far off, toward the living room, he could hear his mother snoring, the deep liquid rasp in her throat, and the murmur of the television. No one had woken, had heard his quick, gasping cry. Underneath the room's silence, he thought he could still hear the scream's echo, fading into the corners, dim in the moonlight sliding beneath the curtain.

He turned his hands over, looking at them. A dream, Dennie and the black car, and the driver inside it. Always a dream . . . The driver's whisper, the voice right at his ear . . . *Go on* . . . *like that* . . . *go on*, *go on* . . . He could still hear that, too. Not as an echo in the room, but in his head. Still there, still whispering.

Go on . . .

The voice, the driver's whisper—that was inside his head. But the other sound he heard . . .

He turned toward the window by the bed. The sound was out there, in the distance.

The low murmur of a car engine, coming nearer.

Steven pushed the blanket away, and stood up, the floor cold against his feet. He stepped to the window and drew the curtain back, just enough so that he could see out.

The street was lit blue, the moonlight filling it, like an unmoving sea between the houses. No other light, the windows all dark as far as he could see, in a silent hour, when everyone would be asleep.

No other light, until the sound of the car's engine grew louder, the murmur tracing against Steven's ear. And two points of light swung into view, a black shape turning the corner. Headlights—Steven felt them brush across his face. He drew back from the window, but couldn't stop watching their approach.

The headlights came closer. Now he could see the black car, and the dark figure behind the wheel. Looking back at him, though he couldn't see the driver's eyes. But he knew.

There was something else inside the car. Slumped against the passenger's side door, across from the driver. It didn't move.

The black car rolled toward Steven's house. Now he could see the other thing inside it. Something white, a face drained bloodless, flopped against the glass of the side window. Dennie's mouth gaped open, the tongue lolling to one side. His eyes were unseeing slits, only white showing. Steven couldn't tell if Dennie were still alive—as the car approached, the white face slid down the window glass, leaving a smear of red leaking from the open mouth.

Steven shrank away from the window. The car kept coming, down the street and toward the house.

He dropped the curtain. He crouched down below the window, hugging his knees to his chest, as the sound of the black car's engine grew louder, not a murmur but a roar. Until he knew it was right outside the house, and he could hear the voice inside the sound . . .

Steven . . . go on . . .

Then it faded. Outside, the black car rolled on past, and down the empty street. Back into the darkness.

Even when the night was silent again, the only sound the heartbeat thudding up from his chest, Steven remained where he was, curled into a ball, his face pressed against his knees.

12

Zero period smelled like wet grass. The kid with the clipboard dug the smell, and the other, which wasn't a smell at all, but just the crisp, cold sensation of the early-morning air, everybody's breath coming out in puffs of steam. The weather had turned, zap like that, the desert winds shut off and real fall weather socking in. The kid carried the clipboard in the crook of his arm, digging his hands deep into his jacket pockets to keep them warm, and listened to the drum major blowing his whistle, a sound that cut right through the air.

The high school called it zero period because regular classes didn't start until first period, including phys. ed.—so if the school's marching band wanted the football field to practice on, they had to get out there early. The kid with the clipboard didn't mind; hardly anybody in the band did, even though it meant getting up an hour earlier than anybody else in the school, getting dressed and eating breakfast while it was still fuckin' *dark,* for Christ's sake—the kid with the clipboard was developing a serious black-coffee habit—and working out all sorts of car-pool arrangements to get everybody there, because the buses didn't run that early. But nobody minded anymore—they had all gotten to the point where they would have done it just for fun, even if they hadn't been getting class credit for it. The only problem was that it was the high point of the day, and you had to drag your ass through all the rest of your classes, just to get to the after-school hanging out and horsing around in the band room.

Most of the girls in the band wore plastic bags over their shoes to keep them from getting stained by the wet grass. The kid with the clipboard stopped to regard the butt of the girl in the flute section he'd been dating, as she bent over to pull up the rubber band around her ankle. Then the kid headed on out to the field as the drum major—the only thing that marked him as that was the big staff with the chrome ball on the end—blasted away on the whistle, getting everybody into their ranks and files. A couple of the tubas nearly collided, the wide bells sliding by within inches of each other. The guys wrapped inside the big horns got a laugh out of that—the bass sections in marching bands were always such fuckin' clowns, and the kid with the clipboard had never been able to figure out just why.

"Come on, come on—" The drum major had given up on the whistle and had started shouting. "You're wasting *time*, man . . ."

The kid with the clipboard heard the drum section finally rap out their starting cadence as he walked along the service road that led to the field. He dug the music director's ring of keys from his pocket—he got trusted with the keys even when the director wasn't back in the band room, writing out parts—and opened the padlock on the field's gate. He pulled the rattling chain out and swung the gates open, folding them back onto the surrounding chain-link fence.

That was the kind of stuff the kid took care of, plus writing out the narration for the band's half-time shows and reading it from the announcer's booth at the top of the bleachers, Friday and Saturday nights during the

football season. He didn't march with the band anymore—he hadn't since back in his sophomore year,
when he'd taken over writing the half-time shows—
mainly because he was useless at playing anything except the bassoon, which was all right for the school
orchestra, but which was a fucking *joke* in a marching
band—who could hear a bassoon over three rows of
trumpets blowing their brains out in a Sousa frenzy?
It was like being a mime with a hunk of lumber hanging from a strap around your neck. He still got to wear
the cool band uniform, including the high furry hat—
a busby, like you saw in pictures of the guards around
Buckingham Palace—plus do all the other cool band
shit. In this school, at least, being in the band carried
a certain amount of prestige.

In a way, the kid with the clipboard figured, it was
too bad they had to have the excuse of a football game
in order to do the half-time shows. Back when he'd
been a freshman, the marching band had been some
kind of pathetic appendage to the football team, grinding out the school fight song every time the team
scored and droning the alma mater when the game was
over. The half-time shows were so wretched that everybody in the bleachers, even the parents of the kids
in the band, all got up and went to the refreshment
stand for hot dogs and Cokes. The kid with the clipboard remembered being torn between embarrassment
and relief that nobody was watching and listening to
the orchestra. Plus the football team had been this big deal
then, going to the district and state playoffs and everything, mainly on the shoulders of the star quarterback,
a real natural who'd already signed a piece of paper
saying he was going to go to one of the big colleges,
the kind you saw on television, and play for them.
Then two things happened: the star quarterback had
gone ahead and graduated and gone off to that big

school—and hadn't been heard from since—and the high school had gotten a new music director. Who kicked butt. At the same time the football team was going straight into the toilet, and staying there, the band was becoming this wild crack outfit. Not just marching in straight lines for a change, but playing their fucking asses off, arrangements that the director whipped up of the flashier classical bits—Christ, this year their signature piece, what they played when they took the field before the start of the game, was the goddamn "Soldiers' Chorus" from *Faust*. With big thundering drums, and a brass riff that spun through the autumn air like rockets going off, the Fourth of July come early. Too fucking wild to believe—but from his viewpoint up in the announcer's booth, the kid with the clipboard had seen the change: now people went to the refreshment stand during the game—why hang around just to see the home team getting its tail whupped?—then packed the bleachers to see the half-time show. Wild, just wild.

The kid leafed through the sheets of paper on the clipboard, checking out the formations and drills they were going to rehearse. The band was already coming up the service road, left-right-left, swinging along to the drum cadence, heading for the gate.

In way, he felt sorry for the poor dumb bastards on the football team. High school wasn't turning out for them the way they'd expected it to, the way everybody had probably told them it was going to be. They had smacked their thick skulls right into one of the cold facts of human behavior: nobody gave a fuck about losers. There were probably better athletes to be found in the school than some of the sides of beef they had playing on the varsity squad—but who wanted to sign on with an outfit that was a major embarrassment to everybody? Christ, the kid with the clipboard was

buddies with a couple guys who'd dropped off the team
to join the band. Which pissed off the coaches no end—
the kid had seen them staring daggers at the music
director from the sidelines.

Fuck 'em, anyway—he really didn't give a shit about
the broken hearts of a bunch of beer-swilling Neanderthals. Not even *good* Neanderthals, at that. Right
now, the band was marching on through the gate, the
drum section was pounding away like mad, the little
flute player had given him a smile as she'd gone by
with the others—good thing she hadn't caught him admiring her can right out in the open like that, she had
a bit of a temper—the cold morning air sang in his
head, and if he could've made this little bit of his se-
nior year last forever, zero period on and on, that
would have been absolute fucking heaven. When the
tubas, the last row of the band, marched on through
the gate, the kid followed them onto the field.

"Hey—what's that junk over there?" The drum major took one hand from his staff and pointed toward
the center of the field.

"What?" The kid with the clipboard had to cup a
hand around his ear to hear the shout over the drum
section.

"Over there—" The drum major pointed again. He'd
gotten the band into formation in the end zone and
was now marching them down one side of the field,
crossing the ten-yard lines one by one. He was stepping backward, facing the front row of the band, as
he called over to the kid with the clipboard. "That
crap right over there."

The kid turned and looked across the field. A hurdle, one of the set that was usually kept locked up in
the track equipment shed behind the bleachers—somebody had dragged it out and left on the fifty-yard line.
And something else, draped over the hurdle's cross

bar, that looked like one of the black canvas sacks full of footballs that the team hauled out during practice. The canvas was soaked wet with dew.

"Beats me," he shouted back to the drum major.

"Well, for Christ's sake, get it outta here." The drum major had the staff raised in both hands, ready for a downbeat to a roll-off. "It's right in our goddamn way."

It wasn't yet, but when the band turned around at the other end zone and came back across the field, it would be. He laid the clipboard down on the bottom row of the bleachers. "Hey, Ed—give me a hand, will ya?" His buddy in the French horn section dropped out of rank and laid his instrument on top of the clipboard. They walked over together toward the hurdle; behind them, the opening bars of "El Capitan" blared out.

"What is this shit, anyway?" As they'd gotten closer, the kid had seen that the canvas sack was empty, but draped like a blanket over something beneath it. He could smell it—really like shit—and wondered if some of the jocks had put something disgusting out here for one of their dim-witted pranks. He wouldn't put it past them.

Ed reached out and pulled a corner of the canvas sack away. "What the hell—"

The kid recognized the beefy face hanging upside down, the body doubled over the hurdle's cross bar. It was one of the footballers, one of the bigger and stupider ones that nobody in the school had any use for; a real asshole named . . . His thoughts ticked slowly around, as though time had come to a stop with the revelation of the face with its mouth dangling open. Dennie; that was the guy's name.

The big jerk must be sleeping it off. That was why he was out here, so fucked up that he didn't even know his own friends had left him draped over a track hurdle like a bag of cement or something. The whole team seemed to spend most of their time getting wasted, not even doing dope or anything they might have to pay for, but just gallons of beer that some fan kept laying on them—the whole school knew about it. Fucked up all the time . . . sleeping it off . . .

Then the canvas slid the rest of the way, falling onto the ground.

"Jesus fucking Christ!" The two of them stared at what had been revealed.

The hurdle toppled over, in slow motion. The football player's body hit the ground, the side of its face sliding across the grass, a thick red clot smearing out of the open mouth. They could see it then, everything, Dennie's jeans pulled down to the ankles, the flower of blood splashed across the white buttocks, the red opening that ran from there on up through his gut, and higher, the blood soaking into the ripped shirt and jacket.

Dennie lay sprawled on the grass, one idiot eye gazing at them, seeing nothing.

The music stopped. The kid heard it, dying away in squawks and random drum strokes. A few yards away, the others had seen it now, the thing lying on the field. The kid turned around, the words frozen like a rock in his own throat. Then there wasn't time to say anything, because somebody, one of the girls, had started to scream, and it filled the air solid.

Steven watched them taking the body away. There were a couple of police cars pulled up on the track around the field, and something that looked like an ambulance, one of those big vans painted white and with lights on top. He hooked his fingers into the links of the fence, pressing his face into the wire, trying to see what was going on.

The police had circled the football field with that yellow-tape stuff, the kind they always had on the news on TV, where it said over and over Do Not Cross— Police Investigation—Do Not Cross . . . They'd strung it right around the chain-link fence that surrounded the field, keeping back a crowd of teenagers that had gathered near the gate. Steven could hear their murmuring hubbub, the rapid whispers, words practically tripping on each other, of the girls with their books held against their breasts and their foreheads practically touching as they stood in little knots and pairs. A lot of the guys stood on tiptoe, stretching their necks to see over everybody's heads.

The crowd of students was over in the distance; where Steven stood, there was nobody around him. Right at the edge of the high school, where another fence ran alongside the service road, dividing the school from a long strip of empty, weedy ground and the house beyond. Whenever Steven went to school— he didn't go as often as other kids did, and nobody seemed to mind—he took this shortcut. But that hadn't been where he was heading this morning; he'd known already what he was going to see when he got over to the high school.

A whole bunch of people out on the field now—ones that he knew were cops because of their uniforms, and the others, who were like cops, really were cops—he knew because of the TV shows he watched—but who did other stuff. Like the ones who'd been taking pictures of Dennie, taking pictures all around, the cameras flashing little bursts of light. And the other ones, with tape measures they reeled out, or with plastic bags that they scooped stuff into and labeled, from where they knelt down on the wet grass. There was all kinds of things happening out on the field.

It seemed to be winding down, though. Finally—

some of the police had left, taking their stuff with them. The thing that had been Dennie, that was now just a shape under a plastic sheet, was being lifted onto some kind of a cart thing. They were starting to wheel it over to the open back doors of the ambulance when the noise from the crowd of kids suddenly went louder.

Steven looked over there. A bunch of footballers, all of them in their varsity jackets, had shoved their way through to the front of the crowd. One of them—Steven recognized him from the parties out at the drive-in, but didn't know his name—was out of control, shouting something, maybe Dennie's name, but with his face all twisted and wet from the tears running down his cheeks.

The guy was probably drunk, even this early in the morning. Steven felt a little sick watching him. The footballer was trying to break through the yellow tape and run out onto the field, out to where Dennie was; the cop who had been stationed at the gate and a couple of the guy's teammates were having a hard time holding him back. He was acting like he was in a movie or something, the way he probably figured he was supposed to act. To get all upset like that, make a big show out of his grief and all. It was stupid—carrying on like somebody had killed his blood brother. Steven listened to the guy yelling, big sobbing cries carrying across the distance. What was stupid was to try to make something up like that, to try to put something where there was just a hole, a blank space with darkness at its center. That was what it was really like.

That was the way it had been in his dream. Just dark . . .

They didn't know . . . not yet . . .

The dream—Steven looked up, above the field and

the people moving around on it. To the side, where the bleachers were. Above, towering overhead on the metal poles—the banks of lights were shut off now, rows of them like blank circle faces, faces with no eyes. When he'd seen them before, they had lit up the sky, tearing away the night, flooding the field and the inside of the car, the whole world, with a light that had made Dennie's face into a flat clown's mask, the tears of fright and pain dribbling down it, the light washing away all the shadows except for those around the driver, that kept his face dark and unseeable.

Where it had happened . . . This was where, he knew now. In the dream. The lights had been blazing down like fire, on the field and the black car, and the world inside it . . .

"Hey—hey, kid—"

Steven had been gazing up at the lights so hard that he hadn't heard anyone coming close to him. The voice, an adult's, startled him. He jerked his head around and saw a policeman towering above, reaching out for him with a heavy, broad-fingered hand. The cop laid his hand on Steven's shoulder.

But he was already running, away from the cop and the fence and everything he'd seen on the other side of it. Running down the little strip of empty land beside the school and out to the streets beyond.

He heard the cop calling after him: "Hey—hold on—"

He kept on running.

Taylor was late heading home. When the graveyard shift at the hall had ended, and the day staff had signed on, he'd been crossing the parking lot to his car when he remembered he was out of milk, back at his apartment. He'd left the carton Anne had brought over sitting out on the kitchen counter, and it'd gone off, smelling suspicious when he'd held it up to his nose. There was a Seven-Eleven over by the freeway; he'd gotten in his car and headed for that.

Then the clerk at the convenience store turned out to be a juvenile-hall vet, a kid Taylor had seen off and on, going in and out the probation department's revolving door, for a couple of years. Now the kid was eighteen, almost nineteen, and was doing well enough, as far as keeping out of trouble went, to be pulling down a regular job. The prospect of getting tried as an adult for all the little bullshit crimes he'd been doing before had done wonders for his attitude—you didn't have to be a genius to know that doing time in a real jail wouldn't be the piece of cake that the kiddie lockup had been.

So he'd had to get into a big conversation, the kid asking about other juvie staff he remembered, just as if he were some prep-school graduate reminiscing about his old instructors. The juvenile hall, Taylor had figured when he'd finally managed to disentangle himself and head back out to his car, was about as much of a real school as this guy was ever going to get. Given the family background of most of the kids who went through the system, the hall had probably been the store clerk's happiest hours.

The trip to the Seven-Eleven had taken Taylor around by the high school. He spotted the commotion going on from a couple blocks away—anything that involved teenagers and police together triggered his professional interest. He pulled over to the curb, across the street from the school's athletic field, and rolled down his window to get a better look.

Black-and-whites, and a sheet-draped body being loaded into a meat wagon—he knew what the equipment looked like, from the one death in custody he'd had on his shift. Something had happened out there

on the football field that had left a pile of cold flesh
staring up at the sky.

The crowd of teenagers piled up behind the yellow
police tape was watching the proceedings with interest. Maybe one of theirs? Hard to say—could've been
some old Sterno-drinking bum who'd come wandering
out from his nest under the freeway and whose heart
had decided to give out in a nice public place. These
kids with their morbid tastes would've found that just
about as fascinating.

Some teachers had come out from the school buildings and were breaking up the crowd, herding them
away from the chain-link fence around the field. A bell
rang to hurry them along.

Taylor glanced up at his rearview mirror before pulling away from the curb. A figure darted out across the
street behind him. A kid, running; younger than the
ones who had been clustered around the fence, watching the dead body being taken away.

He thought he recognized the kid, but he wasn't
sure. The kid was already gone, dashing up a side
street lined with houses, before Taylor could turn his
head.

Across the street, the doors slammed shut, the cargo
inside the van hidden away. Taylor dropped his car into
gear and headed home, feeling tired.

13

Not much of a party. Felton had hauled out plenty of
cases of beer, and everybody was helping themselves
to them, but nobody was laughing and carrying on
they way they usually did. They just talked in low
voices to each other, sitting on the fenders of the cars
around the old snack bar, and kept knocking the beer
back, sinking under its slow weight.

Felton had popped a couple of new tapes into the
players inside the office, ones he'd gotten from some
guy back in New Jersey, some sleaze-o who'd done
prison time for some of the shit he used to send out,
but who'd now scaled his operations back to what the
U.S. Postal Service would abide. Still—Felton had
gone through a whole wink-and-nudge routine, elbow-
ing some of the guys on the team in the ribs and leering at them with his red, sweating gaze, still you didn't
know what kind of hard-core stuff might be locked
inside the videotape cassettes. Felton made it sound
as if seeing some old whores with stretch marks and
dead eyes jerking each other off was something worth
getting excited about. But nobody wanted to see the
old fuck's crummy tapes, not now, not with a death
sitting like a rock inside everybody's guts. It pissed
Felton off—sitting around watching dirty films with a
bunch of teenage guys was the party for him—and he

retreated into the office, sullenly working through one of the cases and watching the tapes by himself.

The girlfriends all stood over in a bunch by themselves, too. As though they were allowed to be there, but not to be a part of it. This was something just for the males, something shared out among them, swallowed down and allowed to seep through their veins like a common blood, like the beer in their fists and throats. Not grief, but brooding and muttering anger.

One of them was weeping, though. He'd been at it for so long, his face had swollen, like a little kid, getting all snot-nosed and dribbly. To the point where everybody else was embarrassed by it, a sour off-key note playing under the sharper one of their anger. Larry wished the guy would just shut up; he leaned against the chrome grille of somebody else's car and watched the blubbering jerk. The can of beer in his hands had gone warm, only half of it killed. He hadn't wanted to drink anything at all, but he'd known he had to, in order to be there with everybody else. The team.

The weeping guy—the same one who been carrying on that morning at the school when the police had been doing stuff and taking away Dennie's body— wiped the sleeve of his jacket across his nose, getting a shiny smear like a giant snail track on it. It'd taken three of his teammates to haul him away from the fence around the field, the way he'd been shouting and bawling.

"I told him . . ." The guy's voice was all boozy and sloppy. "I *told* him not to do that shit no more . . . I told him . . ."

Larry sipped at the warm beer. Everybody was sick of this bastard. Even the girls, standing a couple yards away in their little whispering pack, glanced over at the weeper, then shook their heads.

Another guy, a second-string tackle, rolled an empty

can between his palms. His muttering cut through the silence: "Now everybody in the whole damn school will know . . ."

Mick, the team captain, shot this one a look of disgust. "Shut up." He looked like he was about to push himself off the fender of his car and go over and paste the guy one. The guy who'd spoken looked suitably shut-down, staring into the pull-tab opening of his own beer.

Stupid thing to say, anyway—Larry wondered if anybody in the school hadn't known. About Dennie, and what he liked to do. The kind of trouble he went looking for. And found.

Maybe he'd finally found just what he'd been looking for—the thought drifted up from some dark corner of Larry's mind. He didn't have any head for beer— just the taste made his tongue curl back in his throat— so half a can was enough to let these little things loose, out in the open, that otherwise you'd never say, even inside to yourself. But inside, everybody had known that Dennie was that way. Not just being a homo— Christ knows, nobody gave a shit about that sort of thing anymore, not really—but being fucked up in a different way. Really being sick, and liking sick things.

Sick things . . . Larry rubbed the beer can against his forehead, but it had no power anymore to cool the blood underneath the skin. That was what everybody was thinking . . .

With a sharp crackle of metal, Mick crushed an empty can in his fist. He threw it into the darkness. "Fuckin' queers . . ."

The dizziness from the beer drained away from Larry. For a moment, he didn't feel as if he were there with the rest of them at all. As though a little world had wrapped around him, with all the others, the team, in another. That he could see, that he could look into, but the thoughts rolling around behind the faces were something different, not like his. Mick looked like he was ready to kill somebody. *Fuckin' queers.* The others had nodded, scowling and murmuring agreement, when Mick's angry words had spilled out into the night air.

But it was Dennie . . . Larry wanted to shout it at them, to break into that little world that he was no longer part of. It was what Dennie had gone looking for, and had found.

He clamped his mouth shut, sealing the words inside. It wouldn't do any good, to try to tell them what they already knew.

No good at all. He folded his arms against his chest, pushing away the cold. Even if he was alone, he was still surrounded by the others. They wouldn't want to hear anything different from him, different from what they'd already decided and set down in their hearts.

He closed his eyes. He felt more sick than afraid. It was better to just shut up, and let it all slide away.

Steven sat in the dark, watching the football players. And their girlfriends, Kris among them. All standing around, talking and drinking. They didn't know. Not yet.

He leaned back against the speaker pole, hugging his knees to his chest. Just like all the times before, his mom had made him go along with his sister, out to the party—the whole stupid chaperon business. It had flashed on him tonight, when he'd been in the back seat of Mick's car, that his mom really wasn't sending him along to keep his sister out of trouble, to keep her from doing the kind of shit she'd do if her little brother wasn't there, seeing everything. Even his mom couldn't be that fucked up, that fogged with her drinking. Christ, his mom had already gone into Kris' room and found Mick there in bed with her, the two of them sleeping away, still all sweaty from what they'd been doing. Their mom knew what Kris was doing all the time. And—this was part of the big realization he'd had—she didn't care. And if she wanted him to go along with Kris, wherever she was hanging out with Mick, it was just because she wanted him out of the house. That was all. So she could be alone with the TV, and the big silent space all around her, the house filled with the shouting television, and the whispering bottle. So she could just slip down into her dreaming, without anyone else around, fuzzing up the reception.

He'd just realized all that, for the first time, and he felt stupid for not having known it sooner. But all sorts of things were becoming clear to him now. Everything was different, as though he were seeing it all for the first time.

Like the footballers, Mick and the rest of them. They weren't the same, not anymore. He almost felt sad for them. Because they didn't know.

They all went on talking and drinking, the big blubbering one in their midst still carrying on. Just a big show, that was all that was. Steven was glad he'd slipped away from them, soon as Mick had pulled his car up to the party. Away from them, and into the darkness, where their voices were tiny and faint, coming from a million miles away. Nobody had paid any attention to him; they were all wrapped up in what had happened to Dennie. The way he'd been found, with his pants pulled down around his ankles, and his ass ripped open like that. Steven knew that was what was inside their heads, a picture all red on pale white flesh, Dennie's flesh—even though they hadn't seen it with their own eyes, the picture would be there, where they couldn't get it out. So they hadn't been watching him, they weren't in the mood for the kind of games they usually liked to play. It was like he was invisible, they didn't see him at all.

There were other things they didn't see. Real things. Steven turned his head, away from the teenagers silhouetted in the light spilling from the snack-bar door. Out toward the darkness that surrounded the drive-in. They didn't see what was out there. But he did.

Way out there, beyond the fence; on the road that circled around—a pair of headlights. Just sitting out there, not moving. Waiting.

Steven looked back around at the footballers. They hadn't noticed.

He got to his feet, slowly and quietly, drawing his legs under himself and pushing up from the asphalt with his hands. He kept his eyes on them, watching to make sure. The footballers and their girlfriends—none of them saw him. He was hidden by the dark. He turned and walked, making no noise, farther away from them. Until he couldn't hear them talking at all.

The shadow of the fence extended in diamonds toward him, the headlights shining through. He could see the shape of the car now, the black thing against the night's blackness. He could even see inside, past the windshield, to where the driver sat. Watching, and waiting. Waiting for him.

A glance back toward the center of the drive-in, and the little pool of light there, tiny now, another world. The figures of the teenagers could just be seen, shadows arranged around the circle of cars. Steven turned back toward the fence. Slowly, he walked the last few yards, until he could reach out and touch it.

The links of wire were cold in the crooks of his fingers. He brought his face close to the fence, looking beyond to the black car. One of its doors opened—no light blinked on inside it; everything stayed dark—and

the figure behind the wheel slid out. The driver walked
toward Steven.

He squatted down on his haunches as the driver approached. He hung on to the fence, anchoring himself
there, the cold wire cutting into his fingers, to keep
from running away. The driver's silhouette crossed in
front of the car's headlights, blanking out each one in
turn. Steven squinted against the glare of the lights,
the figure's shadow brushing quick across his face.

Then there was only the fence between them. He
looked up at the driver, the black shape, the face with
eyes that couldn't be seen, making a hole against the
stars. The driver's gaze pinned him to the spot.

The last time, when he'd been inside the black car,
when he'd seen everything that had happened, the knife
and Dennie's face, and his own hand on the knife . . .
that had been a dream. That was what he'd decided
after he'd woken up in the darkness of his own room.
A dream of real things, true things. But he hadn't been
there, not really. People saw things in dreams, things
that really happened, but they weren't there—everybody knew that. But now, looking up at the driver, he
didn't know, not anymore. The way it had felt inside
the dream, the narrow space wrapping around him, the
little world of shadows, which moved and gazed at
him . . . it closed around him again, the same as it
had in his dream. But he knew he wasn't dreaming,
not now. He was out in the night's cold air, at the edge
of the drive-in's empty field, far from anyone else.
Except the driver. The only other person in this world.

Slowly, the driver turned his head to one side, then
the other. Steven saw the sharp-edged profile, like a
blade. He knew the driver was looking to see if anyone
were around, or if they were alone out here. Drawing
in the night air, tasting it for the warm trace of other

people—he could sense the driver's gaze scanning across the dark.

The driver turned his shadowed face back toward him. One hand touched the fence—Steven felt it in his own hands, not a tremor, but a soft pressure bowing the wire. The driver crouched down, bringing his face close to Steven's. The car's headlights framed him on either side, their glow outlining the dark figure with a pure blue-white radiance.

The driver's back arched like an animal's, the face only inches away. The gaze locked on Steven's, piercing to the center of his skull. Inside, as though that world had gone in there.

"Steven . . ." The driver whispered, the words just for the two of them, and no one else. And there was a smile, soft and inviting, in the driver's voice. Inviting him farther into their little conspiracy, the world wrapped around them.

He felt strange, as though the other world, the big one, had tilted and ran out from beneath his feet, like beach sand drawn away by the falling waves.

The driver spoke again, his face an inch away.

"Steven . . . Are you happy now?"

Taylor had been waiting all night. Until it was time to go out in the dark again.

He waited until after midnight, when all the paperwork with which the graveyard shift started—making out the new room rosters, counting out the med's from the nurse's station—had been taken care of. Then he'd dug the flashlight out of the desk drawer, and left Repken in charge, thumbing through a magazine as usual.

As he was crossing the juvenile hall's athletic field, he thought perhaps the football team had decided to skip their regular partying. Because of what had happened out at the high school, with one of their number found dead like that, slit open with the blood crusted down his bare legs. The stupid kid had been into rough trade—that was what was in his probation-department file, a history in booking slips, of cruising and making connections with the men who liked and paid for that sort of thing. Not that they could ever pay enough to somebody whose tastes didn't also run that way.

Still, that little discovery out on the high-school field might have been enough to put off the kid's teammates from their usual good beer-soaked time. In the silence of the dark, empty spaces surrounding the hall, he couldn't hear any laughter and shouting drifting across the night air.

But he had other reasons for going out there, besides checking up on what the crowd of footballers might or might not be up to. There were other things in the night.

Taylor reached the gate, and stopped. He thumbed on the flashlight and played the beam through the fence. The light swept along the length of the service road, lengthening into a slanting oval as he directed it out toward the entrance. He could just make out the chain dangling between the low steel posts on either side, blocking any access to the road. He swung the beam back over the road's gravel surface. If there were fresh tracks, of a car or anything else, he couldn't see them.

He switched off the flashlight. Pulling the keys on their lanyard from his pocket, he unlocked the gate and stepped on through to the service road. The loose gravel crunched underfoot as he turned and snapped the padlock back through the links of the chain. His shadow, thrown by the perimeter lights up above the fence, stretched ahead of him as he crossed the road and mounted the first low slope of the hills. Within a couple of yards, his shadow was lost in the surrounding darkness.

Pushing through the dry weeds, he reached the top of the hill. His eyes had adjusted to the dark; he kept the flashlight off as he looked down into the distance.

The football players were out there, after all—he saw them, tiny figures lit by the glow from an open doorway. The usual party hadn't been called off, but was proceeding in a subdued fashion. A wake, Taylor supposed. Like savages mourning their dead, they had their little rituals. If they could've gotten the body from the police morgue, then they could've shared it up among themselves, eating the flesh to preserve the sorry bastard's memory.

There was nothing worth calling the police about, making a complaint. As long as they were all like this—chastened, maybe, the evidence of their own mortality carved into the skin of their friend—then he didn't give a fuck. And in a way, it was somewhat satisfying to think of them down there, with their heads all messed up. Grief, and fear, and other things they were too stupid to figure out. It made up for the cat that had been pinned to his door.

He was about to turn around and head back down the hill when he spotted the other figures. They were so much nearer, at the base of the slope before him, that he had come close to overlooking them. A section of the fence around the drive-in was lit up by a pair of headlights shining through. A car was parked some distance away from two people—a child and a man—crouched down on either side of the fence. They hadn't spotted him, standing above them in the dark. He recognized the child—it was that Welsky kid . . . Steven, that was the kid's name. The man, on the near side of the fence, had his back to him. Even in the beam of the headlights, the man appeared black and featureless, as though the kid were speaking to a man-shaped shadow that had squatted down in front of him. The two figures, the child and the man, had their faces so close together that they were almost touching through the links of the fence.

They were talking. Taylor knew that; he could see the kid's mouth moving, his head shaking in denial. But they were too far away for him to hear what was being said.

He didn't move. He drew his own breath in slowly, soundlessly, not wanting them to look up and see him. In the dark, he went on watching the scene below.

"Steven . . . you're happy now—aren't you?"

He listened to the driver's voice whispering to him. Even if he closed his eyes, he could still feel the driver's gaze pressing against him. Seeking him out, waiting for his reply.

The driver's words went on, like a kiss at his ear.

"You don't have to worry about anything now, Steven. You don't have to worry anymore." The voice tightened, twisting with fervor. "I'll take care of everything." The promise burned like a heated wire. "That's why I came. I'll take care of them all." Then softer: "You know I will. Steven . . . you know that . . . don't you?"

He had to hold on to the fence to keep from falling. The wire pressed against his cheek as he leaned against it. He kept his eyes closed—he didn't want to see the dark face gazing into his own.

"Steven . . ."

He forced his eyes open, and glanced back over his shoulder, at the distant light. They were all back there, in that other world. He turned his head, drawing away from the fence, so he could meet the driver's gaze.

"But . . ." The words came out slowly; he had to

work each one out, from some place deep inside. "But
. . . you killed him . . ."

Silence. The figure of the driver, crouching down
on the other side of the fence, hunched its shoulders.
The hand at the fence curled, the fingers drawing toward the palm. The driver's face leaned closer.

"Isn't that what you wanted?"

The voice sounded almost childlike in its earnest-
ness. And puzzled, as though there were something
that couldn't be understood, a mystery even to the
driver.

Something inside him wanted to scream, to shout
out a single word, one that would burst open the little
world that had squeezed down around them and cut
through the darkness, flying like a knife blade . . .

"Isn't it?"

Yes. Steven's hands tightened on the fence, the wire
digging into the crooks of his fingers. The word filled
his mouth, so big it was choking him—*Yes!*—so big he
had to get it out or it would kill him . . .

He bit his lip until he tasted blood, his eyes clamped
shut, holding the dark inside. A tear squeezed out from
one corner and trickled hot down his cheek.

He shook his head, opening his eyes again, to look right
into the other's face. "No . . . you have to stop . . ."

The driver regarded him, the eyes still in shadow,
unseen. "I can't stop, Steven . . . not now . . ."

The other word, the one that had filled his mouth,
still lay in his throat, something that he couldn't swallow. All he had to do was to say it, to let it out . . .
It'd be easy.

He saw his own hand, a fist straining at the wire. In
the dream, the dream of true things, his fist had tightened around the knife's handle, the blade turning into
fire and his reflection, the light blazing up and filling
the car. The other face, Dennie's face, shiny with the

tears his fright had poured down it—that had been there, too. In the dream, in that world inside his head that he couldn't get out.

The driver was waiting for him. Here . . .

Steven swallowed, the spit sour with the leak of blood from his lip. His whisper edged out. "Go away . . ."

The driver shook his head. "Steven . . . you don't want me to stop. Do you?"

He couldn't speak at all then. There weren't any words.

The driver whispered, softer. "I'll take care of them . . . I'll take care of all of them. You wait and see . . ."

His hands let go of the fence. He scrambled to his feet, then turned, away from the other's face, the shadow and whisper, and ran. He saw his own shadow stretching ahead, the black car's headlights pushing into the dark. Then another shadow, the driver standing up from his crouch on the other side of the fence. He kept running, until the dark was all around him.

Behind him, he heard the car's engine start up. The drive-in's asphalt lit up for a moment as the headlights swung around. Then they were gone, and the engine's noise faded, and all Steven heard was the pumping of his own blood as he ran and kept on running.

Taylor watched until the kid was gone from sight. Swallowed up by the darkness over the drive-in's empty space.

The car was already gone. He had gazed after it, the red taillights slitting two lines through the night as it had gone down the narrow road. It'd turned out onto the street beyond, and he'd lost it then.

For a moment longer, he tapped the flashlight in his palm, the weight of it cold against the flesh. The night had fallen back into silence; he could even see, in the distance, the footballers' party breaking up, the kids getting into their cars and pulling away from the snack bar. The night was coming back, like a tide slowly obliterating a barren spot that had emerged for a few hours, only to disappear beneath again.

He watched, letting the slow movement of his thoughts go on, wordless. Then he turned and walked back the way he had come.

14

His friends dumped him off because they couldn't stand all his moaning and sobbing any longer. The fucker had been bad enough before he'd started drinking, going right back to this morning when the news about the body being found had hit everybody. Like he and Dennie had been big pals or something—it was embarrassing. And then when the big slob started drinking—and he'd always been one of the real beer hogs out at the drive-in parties—then he'd just gotten worse.

"Fuck you—come on, just get out. You make me sick." The other footballer in the back seat shoved at the drunk one's shoulders. He was being literal about the sonuvabitch making him sick; the drunk had puked up his guts, leaning his red, sweating face out of the side window and leaving a trail of beer vomit down the car's fender, and a trickle of it running inside the door. The smell of it filled the car. "Come on—" The other footballer reached past the drunk, pushed open the door—Christ, it was all over the handle—and brought up his foot to help shove against the small of the guy's back. "Just get lost, man."

They'd pulled over to some downtown street. They didn't know where, they'd just been cruising around. The store windows were dark, the signs overhead switched off. From a couple of blocks away came the sound of a street sweeper, its big swirling brushes scouring out the gutters.

Their teammate, the big sloppy drunk, stumbled out of the car, barely managing to keep from falling, his legs giving way beneath him. He caught hold of a parking meter and held on to it, swaying as his hands plastered onto the little window with the dial inside. He goggled at his buddies back inside the car, his mouth hanging open. The front of his shirt was glued to his chest with his vomit.

The drunk managed to lift one hand from the parking meter. "Hey . . ." His tongue was a thick weight. "Wha—"

"You asshole—just go fuck yourself," the one who'd kicked him out shouted through the car window. He and the other two guys sitting up front were still pissed about the stink; they looked at the drunk in disgust. The car jerked away from the curb, one of the guys giving their drunk buddy the finger.

Holding on to the meter, he looked around. Everything inside his head had mired into place, bogged down and immovable. Maybe he was going to be sick again—he knew he had been once already, though he couldn't remember it, because he could taste it in his mouth. His fingers started to slide against the metal of the parking meter, and he gripped it tighter, desperately. If he fell, he didn't know that he'd be able to get back up.

And he couldn't figure it out. He'd been in the car, with his buddies, safe there, his head wobbling back and forth while all the roads spun around and twisted underneath. And now he was out here, in the cold, and his buddies were gone. They were all gone . . . That started him weeping again. A sob broke in his throat, and he had to gasp for breath around it. Dennie was gone, everybody was gone now, and he was all alone.

He pushed himself away from the parking meter, the hot tears spilling down his face. All alone . . . He dug into his jacket pocket and found a can of beer, nearly half-full. The rest had slopped out, wetting the jacket and the side of his jeans. A sheet of glass buckled and swayed toward him; there were things on the other side of it that looked like shoes. He leaned his shoulder blades against the store window and managed to get the beer can up to his mouth. It was sour and warm, and made the sick taste bob around at the back of his tongue. He couldn't swallow—most of the beer ran down his chin and trickled onto his collarbone.

The empty can clattered out in the street when he threw it away. He tried to move, but his legs gave way. His back slid along the glass, the jacket and the shirt underneath hiking up. Then his knees buckled, and he toppled over.

Something salty leaked into the corner of his mouth when he raised his face from the sidewalk. But there wasn't any pain, just the dulled pulse of his blood.

"I told 'im . . ." The cold seeped into his hip and shoulder where he lay. He drew his knees up, wrapping his arms around himself. "I told 'im, I *told* 'im . . ."

He didn't see the flashlight beam when it played over his face. His eyes were closed tight, the tears squeezing under his lashes.

One of the two cops reached down and grabbed hold of the football player's hair. Out in the street, the black-and-white sat with its engine idling, the police radio squawking and murmuring, the dispatcher's crackling voice loud in the empty dark. The cop lifted the kid's head up and shone the light full into his face. The kid mumbled something, squinting and pawing at his face.

"Christ almighty—" The cop's partner shook his head, disgusted. The vomit stink had reached his nose.

The first one had managed to get the kid—a big one, like a ton of bricks—sitting up, with his head lolling forward, a string of clouded spittle looping down to his shirt. The cop turned the flashlight onto the kid's jacket. A big letter M showed, with a little football set inside.

"Hey—" The cop turned where he squatted down by the kid, and looked up at his partner. "This clown's on the team over at Midford."

That was another town over; the police force there was a real bunch of doughnut lovers and coop artists. If the kid had been from one of the other towns in the county, they could have radioed a call over and gotten somebody to come and pick up this wandering lad, take him home to his mommy. But Midford P.D., there was no telling how long they'd wind up waiting around for one of their cars to come by and collect. Screw it.

"I think I recognize him." The cop with the flashlight brought it up into the kid's face again. "He's on their starting lineup." His own son played, so he'd been going to the games.

The other cop glanced at his partner, then back down to the drunk kid. "Yeah? Well, he's headed for the showers now."

The first one switched off the flashlight, then reached under the kid's arm to pull him onto his feet. "Come on, Rambo—let's go for a ride."

"Lemme alone . . ." The kid stayed sprawled against the wall under the store window. He took a looping roundhouse swing at the cop, not even coming close to connecting.

"Shit." The cop sighed, then took the footballer's hair in his fist again. With one sharp movement, he banged the back of the kid's head against the wall. The kid's eyes opened wide, unfocused. "There's a touch-down for you, turkey."

The kid didn't say anything more. He let the two cops pull him to his feet and drag him to the car.

They dumped him onto the bench in the shower room like a sack of potatoes. The footballer wobbled to either side, mouth open and eyes rolled up in his head, his hands cuffed behind his back. One of the cops pulled the kid forward far enough to unlock the cuffs. The metal left red marks, as though some small animal had nibbled all the way around the kid's wrists.

The two cops came out of the shower room, one of them fastening the handcuffs back onto his belt. His partner tossed a plastic bag up onto the counter around the desk. Taylor glanced over from the intake unit's log book—the bag held the usual stuff: a wallet and belt, keys and some coins. A pack of cigarettes, crumpled up and spilling flakes of tobacco. On the other side of the counter, sitting at the desk, Repken kept his nose in the copy of *People* he'd read once already this shift, as though he were looking for something he might have missed. Repken got nervous around cops, like most people did, and froze up until they were gone.

"Big one—" The cop pointed with his thumb toward the shower room. "But he's pretty out of it. Shouldn't give you too much trouble."

Taylor nodded, checking out the booking slip. These guys were okay, professionally cool. Not every police department in the county was stuffed with assholes. This pair had even run the kid past the nurse's station to get him checked out, make sure he wasn't ODing on something that would leave a blue-faced corpse on their hands. Also, they hadn't revved the kid up, jerked his chain around to get him into a fighting mood, ready to deck the first adult that came into range after the cuffs were off, or at least make the attempt. Some cops thought that was funny, to fire off some gorilla they'd poked into a maniacal fury, while they split to some goddamn Winchell's and laughed about it. But these cops had been cool.

The two of them headed down the long corridor leading out of the intake unit. Taylor walked over to the door of the shower room and looked inside.

It looked like the party was over, long over, for this kid at least. One of the jerks who were always hanging out over at the drive-in—Taylor didn't recognize him. Not one of the regulars, like that Dennie kid had been. This kid sat slumped over on the bench, his head hanging low between his shoulders. His varsity jacket was dirty and stained, a long tear in one of the sleeves.

Taylor nodded. It figured—he would've bet money on some of that bunch showing up tonight. Something else pulled the look of disgust on his face even sharper.

He walked back out to the counter and picked up the kid's paperwork. "Your turn." Repken lowered the magazine and looked up at him. A nod toward the shower room—"Get him under a shower. He stinks."

Repken swung his feet off the desk and laid the magazine down. He pushed the chair back, then headed off toward the shower room.

Taylor could hear him in there, Repken's voice bouncing off the tiled walls.

"All right—" Repken started the usual litany. "Shoes, jacket—let's have 'em."

Taylor spread the logbook on the counter and started writing in it, taking the information off the kid's booking slip. Drunk in public. Big surprise, there. He wrote it down. If he just went on automatic, one thing after another, he wouldn't have to think about anything else. About what he'd seen out there tonight, out by the drive-in. It unreeled at the back of his thoughts, behind everything else, a little movie: the car on the narrow strip of road, the headlights shining through the fence, the boy running away, running into the dark while the figure that was just blackness watched him . . . and another figure, on the hillside above, watching that . . .

The drunk's footballer's voice sounded from the shower room. "Oh, man . . ." He didn't sound as if felt too well.

Then the kid lost it. Taylor heard the noise, and knew the little bastard was puking his head off.

"Aww, Christ—" That was Repken. A martyr to his job.

The sounds went on, the kid gagging and moaning. Taylor looked around at the shower-room door, then went on with what he was doing.

The girl at the front desk called down to the receiving unit. "There's a man up who'd like to talk to you." She sounded rattled. "He's kind of upset."

Taylor glanced at the wall clock. At three in the morning, they were always upset when they came to the juvenile hall. They'd usually just found out that their darling angel had been brought in and was sleeping it off in one of the little rooms with the doors that locked from the outside. All of which was a travesty of justice, of Geraldo Rivera proportions, and never the fault of their doped-up children.

"I'll be right there." He set the phone back down on the desk. "Hold the fort." Repken, on his third go through *People*, nodded.

He saw the crowd around the front desk as he walked down the hallway. The guy, whoever he was, had backup, some four or five good-sized teenagers standing around him. They were all wearing those goddamn

varsity jackets, with—surprise, surprise—the letter M
on them. It looked as if some committee from the
nightly beer party had come to pay a visit.

On the other side of the counter, the girl gave Taylor
a look of immense relief as he walked up. She didn't
look scared from all the shouting that had been going
on, but just weary of dealing with jerks. He leaned a
casual elbow on the counter. "I'm the duty officer
here. Something I can help you with?"

The man, red-faced, forties bumping on into fifty,
glared at him. He had on an overcoat over a pajamas
shirt—at least he'd managed to pull on regular trousers. Shoes still untied, though. He shouted, jowls
trembling: "You got one of my fullbacks here—"

So this was the head coach over at the high school.
Come to the rescue. Presumably, the team members
around him had pulled him out of bed, told him what
had happened to their buddy, the big drunk.

Taylor rubbed his own chin thoughtfully. "No—"
He made a show out of his deliberations. "We got
some load-o's and some DIP's brought in tonight . . .
usual sort of thing . . . but I don't recall anyone busted
for being a fullback."

The coach and the pack of footballers glared at him.
"Cut the shit." The coach jabbed a finger at Taylor's
chest. "The kid's name is Hoffman, and I want him
released right now. This instant. The school's got a
big game tomorrow, we got practice in the morning—
I don't need him hanging out with the kind of assholes
you got in here."

Taylor had to bite the inside of his lip to keep a smile
from showing. He shook his head, slow and regretful.
" 'Fraid I can't do it. Your kid's been charged and
booked. The only person who could cut him loose now
is a full-fledged probation officer. And we unfortu-

nately don't have one on the premises at this hour of the night."

"Come on—" The coach stuck his chin forward. "You can hand him over to me. I'll take full responsibility for him."

Another shake of the head. "Sorry. That's the rules."

The coach looked as if he were about to cock his fist back and take a swing. His jaw clamped as he pulled himself under control. "All right—if that's the way you want to play it. What time's a probation officer get in here, then?"

It was all rolling along nicely. Taylor drew a breath in through his teeth. "Well, you got a bit of bad timing—when a kid gets busted on a Friday night, it's not till next Monday morning that he actually gets to see a probation officer. They don't come in during the weekends. I'm afraid your fullback's gonna be here for that whole time."

The coach's fingertip hit Taylor's chest. "Okay, buddy, you want your ass in a sling? Fine. Judge Rendell of the Juvenile Court is head of our booster committee—all I gotta do is give him a call, and my player's out on the street and you're looking for another job, fucker."

This was too good. Taylor gazed coolly at the head coach, then glanced up at the wall clock behind the counter. Almost three-thirty. In the morning. He reached down to the desk, picked up the telephone, and set it on the counter.

"There you go." Now he smiled. "If you think the judge would enjoy hearing from you at this hour, then be my guest." He pushed the telephone toward the coach.

Silence fell over the reception area. The coach's eyes

narrowed down into slits. One of the footballers behind him bristled, balling his hands up into fists.

"Don't forget—" Taylor kept his voice level as he
went on leaning against the counter. He swung his
gaze on all of them. "You're standing in a county facility. We've got about a five-minute response time for
getting the sheriff's department over here. By the time
all the assault charges get sorted out"—he looked back
to the coach—"this little squad of yours could wind
up spending the weekend keeping their buddy company."

The coach's face grew redder, swelling up as if the
blood were going to burst through the skin. Then he
turned and stomped off; the footballers looked at each
other for a moment, then followed after him. The girl
behind the counter buzzed the reception-area door
open—the last of the bunch tried to slam it after himself, but the pneumatic arm wheezed the door to a
crawl.

Taylor pushed himself away from the counter. With
a smile for the girl at the desk—that had been a good
night's work. For a moment, he didn't care what might
be going on in the night outside. These assholes
shouldn't try to screw around with him on his own
turf. He'd remembered a couple of the faces—he'd seen
them sitting in the car outside his apartment building,
that morning with the cat. He'd enjoyed sticking it to
them.

He turned and headed back down the dark corridor
to the intake unit, feeling good.

Larry saw them coming out of the juvenile hall's
front door. The coach and a bunch of the guys—they
didn't look too happy.

He pushed himself away from the car's fender as
they came walking across the parking lot. He'd been

one of the last to hear about Hoffman getting picked up by the cops—the guys who'd dumped him out on the street had turned back around after a little while, to go get him, only to pull up in time to see him being loaded into the black-and-white. They'd started phoning people up then—Larry had probably been at the bottom of their list. So he hadn't gotten over here in time to go in with the coach and the rest of them.

There had been another late arrival. Mick had pulled into the lot a couple minutes after him. The two of them hadn't said anything to each other, but had just waited, arms folded across their chests, slouched against their own cars.

"Well?" Mick sounded belligerent, and a little drunk. "They letting him go?"

The coach jerked open the door of his car. He glared at Mick, and around at all the rest of them. "You know, if you shitheads would think about the game once in a while, instead of jerking off with this kind of shit all the time, we wouldn't have these problems." He got into the car and slammed the door shut.

Larry stood with the rest of the bunch, watching the coach's car head out of the parking lot. Mick was a little ways off, his face heavy with brooding.

"That fuckin' prick," muttered one of the guys who'd gone inside the hall with the coach.

Mick swung around and looked at him. "Who ya talking about?"

The guy tilted his head toward the hall. "You know—that sonuvabitch who's always calling the cops on us."

Mick nodded slowly, looking over at the hall's door and the light spilling out from the lobby area.

"Come on—let's get outta here." Larry didn't like that last bit of talk, the way Mick was glaring at the juvenile-hall building, and everything that might be inside it. He'd already heard about the shit that Mick and his buddies had pulled on the guy, the one they'd taken a special disliking to. Right now, he could practically see the wheels turning inside Mick's head, the dark thoughts working their way up. He looked around at the other guys. "We might as well split. There's nothing we can do about it."

He turned and walked back to his car. Some of the other guys did the same, but most of them—he knew, without turning around to look—stayed over by Mick. He heard Mick's voice as he pulled open the car door.

"That little prick . . ." A low mutter, deep inside. "That fucking little prick . . ."

Larry turned the key in the ignition. He didn't want to be out here any longer.

The drunk footballer was sprawled out on the bed. Here in the intake unit, the beds were concrete shelves that jutted out from the walls of the little rooms, with the mattresses laid on top. It prevented new kids who hadn't yet gotten their heads into the juvie mode of doing things from getting ideas about wrenching a piece of iron off the old-fashioned kind of bed frame, and doing something stupid with it, like attacking one of the staff. Same with the one-piece toilet-and-sink combo every room had—all those smooth edges helped to keep the kids mellowed out while they were locked up. Though this one, Taylor figured as he looked in the little window set in the door, didn't need much assistance along those lines. Once they'd gotten him cleaned up and changed into the standard hall gear of jeans and T-shirt, he'd nodded off like a baby. A big ugly two-hundred-pound-plus baby, with breath that still stank of beer. But any more trouble he was going to cause would wait until the day staff got there.

Taylor stepped back from the door. As he walked

along the corridor, toward the dayroom's light, he let himself smile a bit. The memory of shutting down that red-faced, shouting coach, and his little entourage of thugs, still tasted sweet.

Repken looked as if he'd finally hit the snooze point with his gossip magazine. He'd laid the magazine flat on the desk; his head hung low over it, as if any moment his face would slide off the heels of his palms and hit the glossy pages. Taylor didn't go over to wake him. He liked being alone in the quiet.

He stood by the dayroom windows, looking out. There were still a couple more hours to get through before the first light started edging over the hills. The dark still filled the world.

There was something out there. He knew what it was, even before he saw it. Beyond the perimeter, out on the service road. Waiting, and watching. He looked past the hall's athletic fields, the black expanse of grass, his gaze scanning along the fence, already knowing what he'd see.

It was there. A pair of headlights, the beams slanting across the darkness. He could just make out the shape of the car, a silhouette against the hillside. Taylor knew there was someone inside, watching and waiting. Looking back at him, through the windshield of the car. His gaze met with the driver's, somewhere out in the night.

He didn't turn away from the window. He didn't go over to the desk, pick up the phone, and call the sheriff's department to send a black-and-white over to investigate. He didn't do anything but go on watching, the headlights' unblinking glare reaching toward him.

The wood of the apartment door splintered with the first kick. Right around the lock—another kick snapped the deadbolt free, and the door swung open.

Mick and the rest of the guys stepped into the apartment. He stopped and looked around. The glow from the dial of a stereo receiver cast a faint green light through the room. It was pretty much what Mick had expected to find: bookshelves, crammed to overflowing. Records, probably all that classical kind of shit; that was what was oozing softly out of the speakers up on top of the shelves. A desk over to the side of the living room, with a typewriter, and papers all over the top of it. A file cabinet, and more crap like that—just the kind of faggotty highbrow shit he'd figured that prick from the juvenile hall would live with.

Somebody in one of the other apartments might have been woken by the noise of them breaking in the door—they'd have to work fast. But there was always time to do a good job.

Mick looked over his shoulder at the other guys, and smiled. "Game time," he whispered.

He stepped over to the side of the bookshelves and pulled them away from the wall. They toppled over, the books sliding out and tumbling across the floor. The stereo sparked when it hit, the light going out and the music dying even before the speakers crashed down.

The other guys started in, laughing as they swarmed into the room.

15

He came home and found the door open. For a moment, he thought Anne might be there, that she had let herself in with her key and was waiting for him inside. That would've been all right—he could've used her company. His shift at the juvenile hall had left him wearier than usual, as though the night had lasted years, grinding through the dark and into the morning light.

The door stood ajar a couple of inches—Taylor half-expected Anne to show herself, to lean out from her hiding place and smile at him. Then he saw the wood splintered around the shiny metal bits. The bolt of the lock still stuck out, but at an angle, the dull end pointing toward him; the socket in the doorframe had been ripped loose, dangling by one brass screw. Around the door knob were two muddy footprints, the wood crushed around the heel marks.

There was nobody inside the apartment—he knew that already. The silence oozed out through the narrow opening. Whoever had kicked the door in had already left. He supposed he shouldn't go in, he should just go over to the building manager's apartment and call the police. After a moment, he pushed the door open— one of the hinges grated, pulled out of line—and stepped on inside.

It didn't surprise him. What he saw on the other

side—he stood in the middle of the living room, beside the overturned bookshelves, and looked around. There must have been several of them, and they'd worked fast. So they could get in and out before somebody might have called the cops. The nature of apartment life—people only got concerned if noise went on too long, disturbed their sleep; a few minutes was nothing to get worked up about.

Taylor stepped over the books strewn across the floor. Some of the records had been pulled out of their jackets, or the thin cardboard ripped open, then thrown around or snapped in two. He bent down and picked up the two stiff black wings that had been a collection of Mozart piano concerti, then let them drop back onto the rest of the rubble.

He took a mental inventory, checking things off one by one, as his gaze went around the room. The couch had been slashed, the stuffing protruding from the long slits in the cushions and across the back. The top of the desk had been swept clear, the typewriter lying upside-down on the floor like an overturned tortoise. All the papers had been scattered, leaves in a whirl-wind; he scuffed one over with the toe of his shoe, looked down, and saw that it was a page from the first draft of his book. He realized he hadn't seen it in years, it had just been sleeping away in a manila folder buried in the desk's clutter. The sentences on the page were dead strings of words, as though it were a letter from someone whose name he'd forgotten. He closed his eyes for a moment, letting the words on all the scattered pages fade away.

The morning sun slanted in through the window, and across his face. He turned away, looking back across the room. The stereo was a write-off—even if it hadn't been damaged when the bookshelves had been toppled over, one of the intruders had then stomped

the metal case, flattening it enough to spill out the
sparkling bits of transistors and circuit boards. The
speakers as well, the grille cloths kicked in, split open
to show the ruptured cones and multicolored wire guts.
Something caught his eye, and he looked up.

He read the words that had been written on the wall.
They didn't surprise him, either. He stood looking at
them for a while longer, then he bent down beside the
desk, searching until he found the telephone, pulling
it by its cord from the books and other rubble. The
tone sounded in his ear, and he began to dial. He knew
this number by heart.

The cops showed up in about a half-hour. For Midford P.D., that was pretty good. Taylor hadn't touched
anything in the apartment, had just left the mess the
way he'd found it. He turned away from the window
he'd been gazing from, still wearing his jacket, when
he heard the knock.

He'd left the door open. "Mr. Taylor?" The door
opened wider, pushed by the cop's hand. The two of
them stepped inside.

He almost had to laugh when he saw which ones
they were. Naturally—of all the cops on the Midford
force, these would be the ones he'd get. The two
clowns who always came out to the old drive-in whenever he called in a complaint from the hall, and who
always wound up doing fucking nothing about it.
Maybe the city's budget cuts had left these guys the
only car working from midnight to morning; they'd
probably been winding up their own shift when they'd
gotten the call from their dispatcher to swing around
here and make out a report.

The two cops walked farther inside the apartment,
looking around. The short Hispanic-looking one already had a pad and pen out. Behind him, the beefy

one, the real asshole, nodded as if he were admiring the work.

"Looks like they did a pretty good job on you." The beefy cop pushed a couple of books along the floor with the toe of his shoe.

Taylor glanced at the cop, then looked back out the window. It wasn't worth saying anything to the big jerk.

The other one cleared his throat. "You have any idea who did it?"

He didn't turn around, but went on gazing out the window. "It was the football team." His voice sounded emotionless even to his own ears. "From the high school."

A disgusted groan came from the beefy cop. "Do we gotta go through all this again? All the time, you're bothering us with complaints about those kids—why don't you just lay off?"

Taylor saw the short cop, reflected in the window, give his partner a warning glance. The beefy cop ignored it.

"What's it this time?" The cop's tone got more belligerent. "What makes you think the football team did it? Huh?"

He turned around and looked the cop in the eye for a few seconds, then indicated with a tilt of his head the kitchen wall behind the pair.

The two cops turned and looked. The words they hadn't seen when they'd come into the apartment, the sloppy letters a couple of feet high, smeared in shit— a crumpled piece of newspaper, stained brown, lay at the foot of the wall.

DON'T FUCK WITH THE TEAM.

The beefy cop stood with his hands on hips, looking at the scrawled message. He shook his head. "Well, I tell ya, that doesn't mean much. That doesn't mean anything at all.'' His voice rose. ''Everybody knows you've got it in for those kids—Christ, you might've written that up there yourself. Just to get 'em in trouble.''

This guy was as much a jerk here as he'd been out at the old drive-in. Taylor looked at the folds of the cop's neck, squeezed over his collar. ''Give me a break.''

The cop looked around the kitchen, then picked up a dish towel lying on the counter. Balling it up in his hand, the cop stepped close to the wall and started wiping the words off. The shit smeared under the towel.

''What the—'' The other cop freaked out. It took a second for him to recover from the shock of what he was seeing. Then he grabbed his partner's arm and stopped him. He looked over his shoulder at Taylor. ''Excuse us a moment.''

The short cop, face darkening with fury, tugged the other one toward the door. A moment later, Taylor heard them outside.

''What the fuck do you think you're doing?''

Pineda didn't care that Harrelson outweighed and outranked him—he was so pissed off that he'd slammed the big tub of lard right up against the wall of the building, a couple of yards away from the door of the apartment they'd been in.

''You trying to get our asses hauled in front of the review board?'' Pineda shouted into Harrelson's face. ''You know what you were doing? Huh? You were destroying *evidence*, man—right in front of the guy!''

Harrelson looked stunned by the sudden outburst, coming out of nowhere and blindsiding him. It took him a moment to find his voice, and then the words could barely crawl out. ''Hey . . . don't sweat it . . .''

Pineda went over the top then, like a rocket going off. "Don't sweat it? You're out of your fucking mind! You got such a hard-on for those stupid little football jerks—I can't believe this." He let go of the front of Harrelson's uniform and stepped back, shaking his head in disgust. He looked up at Harrelson again. "Well, you're not gonna have to wait for that guy in there to report this—I'm writing this one up myself. It's *your* ass that's going to be in a sling, not mine."

That stung Harrelson; he managed to pull himself up. "Go ahead—" Blustering. "Go ahead, turkey— and you're gonna find that everybody in the department is on my side about this."

"Bull-fucking-shit." If the guy wasn't such a disaster, threatening to get them both bounced off the force, Pineda could almost have felt sorry for him. "If you weren't walking around in such a fucking fog, man, thinking about all this goddamn sports shit all the time, you'd know they got a stack of complaints on you a mile high. Everybody knows about it. You've been giving those little fucks a free ride, and everybody's been cutting you slack about it, and letting you go on, thinking that maybe you'd wise up . . . And now we're all sick of you, and all that 'support the school team' horseshit you've been bending everybody's ear with." Pineda shook his head again. "It's over, man. You might as well go back to the station and clean out your fuckin' locker." He turned on his heel and walked away from his partner.

Back inside the apartment, the juvenile-hall guy was still staring out the window. Pineda cleared his throat before saying anything; the guy still didn't turn around.

"There'll be an investigation crew coming out from the station. I'll call in from the car right now and try to get them to hustle on out here." He couldn't tell if the guy was even listening to him. "The photographer

will want to take some pictures—so if you could wait
until they're finished before you start cleaning up, we'd
appreciate it. Maybe you could start making a list of
anything damaged or that might have been stolen . . ."

The guy just went on gazing out the window. That
spooked Pineda; he wondered what the guy was thinking about. With some of these quiet types, you never
knew.

"That's about all we can do right now." Pineda
stepped back toward the door. "We'll get back to you
as soon as we've got something."

No response. Pineda hesitated a moment, then
turned and headed out, back to the car and all the
details that had to be taken care of.

Their mom had to go over to the county social-
services department that day, and meet with her caseworker—some bullshit about job training, seeing if she
wanted to study to become a beautician or something.
Which was a laugh; Kris couldn't figure how anybody
would want somebody working on them who was as
much of a wreck as their mother was. But she had to
go in anyway, or they'd screw with the AFDC check.

The best part was that she'd be gone all day. She
had a friend who lived in one of the crummy apartments over by the county buildings, with whom she'd
been a nurse's aide a long time ago, back when she'd
first gotten out of high school. She always combined
seeing her caseworker with a visit to her old buddy,
sitting around gassing and getting stewed while a
bunch of little dogs—flea allergies had stripped all the
hair from their tails—yapped around their ankles. Kris
had gone there once, to pick her up when she'd gotten
too fucked up to navigate; the apartment had smelled
like dogshit and her mother had been weeping, her
face all puffy and red, and a little trickle of blood at

the corner of her mouth, like somebody had slapped
her or something. She'd told her mom to get her own
ass home after that.

But it meant Kris had the house all to herself, for
the whole day. Except for her creepy little brother,
which didn't really matter, because he was at least
smart enough to stay in his room and not come around
hassling her. The first thing she'd done had been to
call up Mick and tell him the good news, that it was
private party time for the two of them. He came zooming right over, all revved up over something he and
his buddies had been up to during the night—she could
smell the sweat of excitement on his skin, then salty
on her tongue when she'd gotten his shirt off. Something that made him hornier than shit, slipping his hand
into her pants even before she could lead him back to
her bedroom. They tumbled onto the bed, with her
giggling and not caring if her stupid little brother could
hear them. Mick had a six-pack with him, and he
popped one open and drank, a little of it leaking out
the corner of his fierce clenched-teeth smile; then he
set the cold bottom of the can down right on her tit
and she slapped the side of his head, hard, to make
him mad. Mad enough for him to give it to her the
way she liked.

All that had just been in the morning, right after
Kris' mom had taken off. After the first time, as soon
as Mick had finished, he'd fallen asleep—he'd already
been drinking, out there horsing around with the rest
of the team. She had lain in her bed next to him, snug-
gling up close to him, their skin damp between them.
Dennie getting killed had set all the guys off, made
them crazy. She didn't care, not really. It had nothing
to do with her, and Dennie had been kind of an ob-
noxious asshole, anyway, and everybody had known
about him doing all that fruit stuff—she was glad he

was gone, and she figured all the rest of the team's girlfriends felt the same way. There was something creepy about faggots, anyway, like they were horning in on territory where they didn't belong—she had never liked the idea of Dennie taking showers with all the rest of them, checking out Mick's and everybody else's butt. She squeezed in under his sweaty arm; with his face against the pillow, he grunted and mumbled something. As long as she had him, she didn't give a fuck about the rest.

He'd gone on sleeping, heavy enough that she'd finally slid out of the bed without waking him, and gone to take a shower. That must've been noon, because she saw stuff out on the kitchen counter that showed Steven had been creeping around and fixed himself lunch. The little slob had left a scraped-empty mayonnaise jar sitting there. He was probably back in his own bedroom, moping around—she could tell he was in the house, even though he'd gotten the trick of staying so absolutely quiet down pat. Their mom had drilled that into him. What Kris couldn't understand was why he just didn't disappear, just split and leave the house nice and perfectly empty for her. Maybe he'd gotten to the point where he liked having his butt kicked all the time.

When she got back from her shower, Mick was awake again. He reached out and grabbed her, pulling her back into the bed, his big hands knocking the towel off her wet hair. He was all hot again, and that was nice, even though she was still sore from the first time. And he'd been prowling around, too, while she'd been in the bathroom; he'd scored a bottle of her mom's cheap supermarket vodka—Kris hated the stuff, it always tasted like gasoline to her. But it was like gasoline being poured on a fire for Mick—he was all over her, slamming her back down into the mattress like he was going to break her in half.

That went on for a long time. They were both worn out by the time he was done. The next time she woke up, it was already dark outside.

She hated that, too, waking up in a dark room. Night came on so early this time of year; if you weren't careful, you got caught, the whole day fucked away.

Mick was out of the bed, pawing through the beer cans scattered around. That was what had woken her up, the sound of the clattering metal, and the drained vodka bottle hitting the carpet with a thud. He hadn't even put his clothes on, but was crouched down, the bumps of his spine all in a row as he lifted up each can and tossed it aside. Finally, he found one with something left in it; he tilted his head back, thirstily downing the warm beer dregs. Then he tossed the can away with the rest.

Kris pushed herself up on one elbow and watched groggily as Mick pulled on his jeans, then his shirt— the fucking thermostat hadn't kicked the heater on, and the evening's chill had settled into the house. Mick's skin was all gooseflesh from the cold. She felt ruined; she'd gotten into the bottle of her mom's vodka, too, pushing it straight down her throat to get past the taste of it. She wondered dully if she was going to be sick.

''Where ya goin' . . .'' She mumbled it, the heel of her hand shoved against the side of her face. Her hair dangled into her eyes.

Mick didn't answer. He shoved his feet into his shoes, without lacing them up. His shoulder hit the doorframe as he stumbled out of the room.

Fuck him. She rolled over on her back, pressing the cold back of her hand against her hot forehead. The vodka's taste crawled around in her throat. If she concentrated, with the little bit of strength she could find, maybe she could hold it there. In the distance, she heard Mick clomping down the hallway. She closed her eyes and breathed through her mouth.

There had to be more booze around. There always was, in this house. Kris' mom was such a fucking drunk—that was where most of the money, the checks from her dad, went. Mick came to the end of the hallway and put his hand against the wall to keep his balance. His eyes felt like they'd been boiled or something; the living room was blurred and tilted.

He lurched toward the sofa. He almost fell across it as he pawed through the cushions. Nothing . . . "Shit." His eyes stung, as though they were about to start leaking tears. "Mother*fuck*—" He grabbed the back of the sofa and pulled it away from the wall.

The glint of clear glass rewarded him. He dropped to his knees and grabbed it, tilting it to his mouth. Nothing came out; he saw now that it was empty, nothing but a brown stain, Scotch or something, at the bottom. His hands felt the fur of dust on the glass; the bottle must've been sitting for weeks back there. He dropped it in disgust, and pulled himself back upright.

He'd have to go get more. Somewhere—it was dark outside already; if somebody hadn't left the lamp in the corner of the living room on, he wouldn't have been able to see his way at all. Maybe Felton was already out at the drive-in; he could score off that old bastard. Because he had to have it—there was too much stuff going around inside his head, pictures of Dennie, the way he'd been found out there on the field, pictures that were all red on cold white flesh. Even when he'd been banging Kris, he could still see them, no matter how hard he squeezed his eyes closed. When he and the rest of the guys had been trashing that juvenile-hall guy's apartment, it'd felt good, as though he were getting his hands on the pictures inside his head, as though they had been as big as the walls and the bookshelves and all the rest of that crap, and he'd been able to rip and tear them up. But then they'd come back.

The alcohol made the pictures go away. It made everything go away. That was what it was for. He'd already learned that much.

He rubbed the side of his leg, feeling through the denim to make sure his keys were in his pocket. That was okay, then; all he had to do was make it out the door, and to the car. Then everything would be fine.

Somebody was watching him. He could feel it. He looked across the room—it swam and tilted again with the turning of his head—and saw Kris' little brother standing at the end of the hallway. Looking at him.

"Stupid . . . little twerp . . ." He mumbled the words, feeling the anger heat his face. It pissed him off, the way the kid was looking at him, just standing there and watching him. Mick squatted down and found the empty bottle, then stood up and flung it at the kid. Steven didn't even flinch as the bottle crashed against the wall a couple feet from his head.

Who gave a fuck . . . Mick turned, pushing himself away from the sofa and stumbling toward the front door. Something grabbed him by the arm, stopping him.

"What the . . ." He looked around, squinting and shaking his head. Steven had come striding across the front room, quick, and had latched on to him, the kid's hand gripping his forearm tight, just below the elbow.

"Don't go."

Mick couldn't believe it. The kid had snapped out the words, an order, the voice firm, like an adult's. His face looked like an adult's, too, the eyes glaring up at Mick.

"Huh?" Weaving unsteadily, Mick looked in amazement at Steven. "What the fuck . . ."

Steven went on speaking, like an adult to a child. "Go back to my sister's room, and lie down." Slowly, firmly. "But don't leave here."

The little punk was telling him what to do. Mick aimed a swipe at Steven with his free hand, nearly losing his balance as his fist swung around. The blow bounced off Steven's shoulder as if he didn't even feel it.

"You don't want to go out there." Steven's level gaze stayed locked onto Mick. "It'll be better for you if you just stay here."

Mick tried pulling his arm away, but the kid's grip was stronger. "Get the fuck away from me . . ." Mick's voice went shrill. "Ya little shit . . . ya fuckin' little homo . . . What the fuck do you want?"

Steven's face clouded with anger. He suddenly threw Mick's arm away from himself.

"Okay—" Steven held the anger tight inside, a little bit of it leaking out in his words. "Go ahead."

Mick goggled at the kid for a moment longer, then turned. He managed to fumble open the front door and stagger outside. Behind him, Steven watched as he pawed at the door of his car.

". . . showed 'em . . . showed 'em all . . ." he muttered groggily as he dragged himself behind the steering wheel. There was something here, something he needed, that he'd just remembered. He leaned across the seat and hit the glove-compartment button. The little door dropped open and he scrabbled inside, coming up with a crumpled scrap of aluminum foil. He tore the foil open; two red capsules fell into his lap. He scooped them up and slapped them into his mouth, swallowing them dry. He could almost feel them unlocking inside himself, the slow, dulling warmth flooding up through his spine.

Eyes heavy-lidded, Mick slumped behind the wheel and stared out the windshield. ". . . fuckin' bastards . . ." All of them; every single one—they all thought they were so fucking smart. But he'd show them. He dug his keys out of his jeans and managed to get them into the ignition. The engine roared to life.

Steven stood in the door, the cold night air flowing around him. He watched as Mick's car squealed away from the curb in front of the house. Its headlights came on a couple of blocks down the street; for a while, he could follow the taillights dwindling away, then Mick swung the car too fast around a corner, barely missing the one parked there, and it was gone from sight.

He went on looking out at the dark. He'd tried to tell Mick, to warn him. But it hadn't done any good. Still, he'd tried; now, whatever happened, it wasn't his fault. Not really.

Something was moving out in the dark, far away, where he couldn't see it. But he knew it was there.

He leaned his head against the edge of the door, watching. And waiting.

Part Three

Party's Over

16

He was still standing at the window, gazing out at the dark. Anne sat in the middle of the floor, glancing over at him from time to time, then going back to sorting through the scattered LPs and putting them in their sleeves.

Most of the damage to the apartment had been cleaned up. The sharp tang of Pinesol hung in the air, from his having finished scrubbing the message off the kitchen wall. The rag and the stiff brush he'd used had already been taken out and thrown away in the building's dumpster. The bookshelves had been pushed back upright, but the books hadn't been returned to the shelves; when she'd gotten there that evening, they'd been stacked up in untidy mounds, as if he'd started putting them back into alphabetical order and had then lost interest in them.

She'd known what to expect, because she'd called him from her office to say she was coming over, and he'd told her what had happened. She looked at the black disc in her hands, the name on the label. *Happened* made it sound like an accident, like the branch of a tree blown in through the window during a storm. What had been done—that was more like it. She slid the record into the stiff cardboard and set it on the pile beside her.

He sipped at the cup of coffee he'd carried with him

over to the window, even though, she knew as she
looked at him, it must've gotten stone-cold by now.
She'd expected him to be still angry about these punks
tearing up his place, but he'd already gotten past that
point by the time she'd gotten there. His long, brooding silence was worse. She'd come to the apartment to
tell him something—that was why she'd called in the
first place. Now, with all this . . . it would take a little
more effort on her part. But she would still have to tell
him.

Not yet, though. His silence still lay too heavy on
both of them, on the entire room. Anne picked up
another record from the floor. "That boy . . ." She
gazed at the back of his shoulders. "The one they
found out on the field, at the school . . . he was one
of the ones you've had trouble with, wasn't he?"

She knew the answer already. Her voice had fallen
into the silence like a stone down a well.

For a moment, Taylor made no response. Then he
nodded slowly, still gazing out the window. His voice
was soft: "Got just what he deserved . . ."

That took her by surprise. The coldness of the
words—she stared at him. "What?"

He turned and looked at her. He shook his head, as
if he'd just realized what he'd said.

"No . . . no, I don't mean because of this." With
one hand, he gestured at the mess remaining in the
apartment. "Just because it was that kid's friends who
did all this . . . I don't care about that. I just meant
. . . No, forget it."

He turned back to the window. Anne watched him
for a few seconds longer, then turned back to her task,
searching about for the sleeve to the record she held
in her lap.

"You know . . ." His low, meditative voice came
to her ear. "I can understand why they did it . . . I

know why. They did it because they're scared . . . and nobody's ever shown them how to handle being scared. They've never had an education in that . . . in being scared.'' He nodded as he looked out at the night. ''But now they're scared, because of what happened to one of them, and when they're scared, they get erratic—they just hit out at anything. They do stuff like this, to prove they're not scared, they're not afraid of anything at all.'' His voice went lower, almost to a whisper. ''But they're still scared. They've been scared since that first one was killed. They know something's—'' The words broke off, the silence reclaiming the room for a moment. ''And they know they deserve it. In their hearts—they're still children. The people around them have kept them from growing up. But they know they've been bad children. That's why they're scared.''

The skin on her arms tightened. The sound of his voice, the things he said—they scared her. She bit her lip, looking down at her empty hands in her lap. When he spoke again, she knew he was smiling, that thin, humorless smile he sometimes got.

''When I was a kid . . . when stuff happened to me . . . that I didn't like . . . you know what I used to dream of?''

Anne looked up, and saw that he had turned his gaze toward her.

Taylor turned back to the window, as if speaking to his own reflection there. ''I used to dream of a man on a horse.'' He nodded slowly. ''I really did.''

She smiled, gently as possible. Maybe he could be drawn back from the silence, and all the dark things he was thinking about in there. ''You're kidding.''

He shrugged. ''Yeah, well . . . when you're a kid . . .'' He took another sip at the cold coffee. ''I'd lie there in my bed, in the dark, and my shoulder would still be aching from where I'd gotten hit, or my ear would be all red and throbbing, and my face would be all wet because I'd been crying . . . you know, with my face right in the pillow, so nobody would hear, because if they heard you crying, that'd just make it worse . . . and I'd dream about a man on a horse." He shook his head. "I guess I watched too many cowboy movies when I was a kid."

She watched him, keeping her own silence, waiting for the rest of what he was going to say.

"Only this man would be all in black, and his face would be all dark—I never saw what his face looked like at all. And the horse was all black . . . just like they'd been cut right out of the night, like it was a piece of black paper." He smiled and nodded, as if he knew, inside himself, how silly it must sound, to speak of childish things out loud. "And I'd dream about this man all in black, with this black horse . . . I'd dream they'd come . . ." The smile disappeared; his voice dropped lower. "They'd come . . . and help me."

She couldn't look at him any longer. She closed her eyes. These were things, she knew, that she shouldn't have heard. Things that should have been left forgotten, or if not forgotten, then just never spoken of.

His voice came back, with a forced edge to it, harsh and loud. "I guess kids today don't watch cowboy movies anymore. They wouldn't know from horses, would they?" He fell silent for a few seconds. "Now a kid would dream about something else . . . something else that would come and . . . help him . . . something else that looked all dark, like it was cut right out of the night . . ."

She couldn't help him. She never could; she knew that now. When she opened her eyes, she saw him standing at the window, still there, still gazing out at the night.

There were only a few records left scattered on the floor. The black discs shimmered, their edges blurring, as she looked around at them. She hid her face from him, even though she knew he wouldn't see it, he wouldn't see anything—she rubbed her eyes with her fingertip.

She stood up. She could've reached out and laid her hand on his shoulder. "I've got to leave now."

He nodded, but didn't turn around to her.

"I'm . . . sorry this happened." She looked at the mess, the dead stereo receiver that had been pushed up against the wall. "Maybe you should try and forget about it. Just clean it up and . . . not think about things so much."

He shrugged, absorbed in his own dark, silent thoughts.

There was never going to be a good time. To tell him. "I won't be coming back here anymore."

He looked over his shoulder at her, his face impassive.

She pushed the words out, one by one. "Richard and I . . . we've decided to give it another shot. You know . . . see if we can work things out. Because of Danny. So Richard told me he wouldn't be seeing . . . her . . . anymore. And . . ." The words stopped, as if there were no more inside her.

He looked at her for a moment longer, then nodded slowly and turned back to the window.

"That's why I came over here . . . to tell you. You understand, don't you?"

The streetlights outside gave his face a cold blue tinge. "Sure." The face in the reflection showed no emotion; whatever it felt was locked inside. "Of course I understand." He looked at her again, then over at the desk. The glass over the photo of his daughter had shattered when it had been knocked to the floor with the rest of the things. The face of the girl could still be seen underneath the shards. "You have to do what's best for Danny." He turned back to the window. His voice sounded as if he were realizing something for the first time, something true. "The kid comes first . . . always . . . You have to do what's best for the kid . . ."

There wasn't any more to say. For either of them. Anne looked at him; his own gaze was far removed, focused somewhere out in the dark. Not here. She turned away, and picked up her coat and purse from the sofa. Taylor went on gazing out the window as she walked across the room. She closed the door after her and hurried to her car, to go home.

Mick tasted salt in his mouth. He seemed to be lying on his back, as though he had woken up in his own bed, or Kris', but somehow he felt the curve of the steering wheel in his fingers.

"Shit . . ." His head ached, the pain swinging back and forth in time to the pulse of his blood; if he closed his eyes, it looked like a red light coming close, then fading away. It made him nauseous to look at it, his gut crawling up in his throat; he forced his eyes open to get away from it.

He was in the car; he saw that now. He even remembered driving . . . he remembered getting in the car, and starting it up . . . after that stupid little brother of Kris' had latched on to him, told him not to go—or had that been part of a dream, something that had drifted through his head while he'd been lying here, all fucked up and out of it? He thought he could smell gasoline, just a trace of it on the cold night air. The kid's voice had been so weird, ordering him to stay.

Or warning him . . . Mick shook his head, though it made the pain leap up to the top of his skull. It must've been a dream.

He gripped the wheel tighter and pulled himself upright. The seat catch had snapped, dropping the back nearly flat. The passenger's seat beside him was where it should be; he balanced himself against it with the palm of his hand. Now he could look around and see where he was, where the car had gotten to.

The headlights had gone out. He must have hit something, smashed the lights into pieces. "Fuck . . ." He didn't care how badly the car was damaged. Sitting upright had made him feel sicker than before; the car's interior tilting around him, getting bigger, then smaller, like everything was painted on the inside of a rubber ball. His tongue curled with the sour taste of his gut fighting up into his mouth.

All he could see through the windshield was crumpled metal—the car's hood? It was the wrong color, gray instead of red—and a brick wall beyond that. He found the door handle, pushed it down and tumbled outside.

He shoved himself up from the asphalt and got to his feet. The smell of gasoline was stronger out here. He placed both his hands against the car to keep from falling, and tried to make out the damage.

The crumpled metal was the side of a trash dumpster. The car had wedged itself at an angle in the mouth of some downtown alley. From the dumpster, its lid tossed back, the ripe odor of garbage mingled with those leaking from the car. Mick could see now that the fender and the front bumper were all fucked up, crumpled and bent, torn away from the frame beneath. A big gouge had been dug out of the alley wall, leading up to where the car's impact had slammed the dumpster against it.

The wheel underneath the torn fender was tilted at a crazy angle. A puddle had formed around it, shimmering with a steady drip from somewhere up in the engine.

"Shit . . ." Mick rubbed his numb, heavy-feeling face. "Fuckin' sonuvabitch . . ." The anger welled up, cutting through the nausea. He slammed the heel of his hand against the fender, nearly toppling himself over.

He flopped around, slumping back against the car, legs splayed out in front. He wasn't so screwed up that he couldn't use more; it would probably make him feel better. If he had it . . . He searched through his jacket pocket and came up with a scrap of aluminum foil. It was empty, the reds long gone into his gut and bloodstream. He threw the foil away and pushed himself up from the side of the car.

The car blocked the nearest exit from the alley; he'd have to climb over it to get out that way. There was no fucking way—his head was still spinning. The other end of the alley was open; blue streetlight spilled toward him, from someplace that looked miles away. He felt like dropping onto his hands and knees, and crawling toward it—that was the only way he'd make it that far.

He stumbled down the alley, toward the distant light. He only got a couple of yards before he tripped, over nothing, and fell heavily onto his side.

It was getting worse—his fingers clawed into the rubble of the alley, digging a hold to keep from falling into the sky swimming above him. The salt taste of his own blood had burst into his mouth when he'd hit the ground; he could feel it dribbling out across his chin. The warm taste made him sicker. He rolled onto his face, the corner of his brow bumping against the alley's brick wall. He didn't want to throw up, lying on his back. You could die that way.

"Showed 'im . . ." The words came up instead into his mouth. He mumbled them into the dirty asphalt. "Showed the little prick . . ."

A shadow fell across him; it blocked the thin edge of the streetlights. Mick felt a hand shaking his shoulder.

"Hey . . . hey, Mick . . ." The voice of the figure bending over him was filled with concern. "Christ, man, are you ever fucked up . . ."

Mick grabbed the figure's arm, holding on to it desperately. Thank God one of his buddies had found him. He felt like weeping in gratitude. "Oh, man . . ." The dark silhouette of his friend, outlined in the streetlights' blue, wavered as the alley tilted in his vision. The tears welled up in his eyes, blurring things even more. "I gotta get to the game . . . we got a game tonight . . ."

"Come on." His buddy pulled Mick onto his feet and held him up under one arm. "Don't worry, man . . . I'll get you to the game."

He let himself be dragged toward the end of the alley. There was a car waiting there, its engine murmuring in the still night air.

"Jesus . . ." Mick's head lolled back against the top of the car's seat. He felt his leg being grabbed and lifted, stuffed inside the car so his buddy could slam the door shut. The door on the driver's side opened, and the guy slid in behind the wheel. Mick rubbed his face as the car dropped into gear and moved away from the alley. "Oh, man . . . I had too much . . . Shit—thank God you guys found me . . ."

He expected them to say something, his friends in the back seat. They always did things together; that was what being a team meant. Like the cat, and then

trashing that asshole's apartment—you did stuff together because you were strong that way, nobody could
stop you. And you took care of each other—wasn't that
why they'd all come looking for him?

But nobody said anything. The car was silent, just
the sound of the engine and the empty streets sliding
by, out of reach beyond the windows. Mick shook his
head, trying to get his thoughts to move, digging at
the stiff flesh of his face, as if trying to wake up. He
dropped his hand, the edge of it dragging across his
open mouth, and looked beside him—

—at the driver, the only person in the car with him,
the only one—

—who turned a black, featureless face toward him,
dark within darkness, even the eyes hidden, though
Mick felt the weight of their gaze, pushing him back
into the seat—

"Hey . . ." His voice sounded weak inside the car,
swallowed up by the dark. Sudden fright cut through
the fog inside his head. He lurched around in the seat,
away from the dark face gazing at him, and scrabbled
at the door handle. He could see the streetlights clip-
ping by outside, the unlit buildings a blur; the car was
picking up speed. But he didn't care, he just had to
get out, he had to get away . . .

A hand caught the collar of his jacket, the hand that
had lifted him up from the alley. The hand pulled him
back from the door, drawing him up from the seat; for
a moment, his face was right up against the driver's,
the glare of the hidden eyes piercing to the inside of
his skull. Then the driver, his left hand still on the
wheel, slammed Mick down into the seat with the other
hand. The back of Mick's head snapped against the
top of the seat. His sight pulled into focus; he now
saw the driver's hand, clenched into a fist, swinging
in a horizontal arc toward him. Before he could raise

his own hands to protect himself, the fist slammed into his face. The blow knocked him into the angle of the door and the seat.

He could taste the blood welling out of his mouth. The spattered drops of red across the window smeared under his fingers as he scrabbled at the glass. He could see the dark street outside slowing, coming to a stop.

"No . . . please . . ." The words were wet bubbles in the flow of blood. Mick cringed against the door as another backhanded fist swung toward him. The blow caught him on the cheek with a crackle of shattering bone. The blood spattered up into his eyes, and his swollen tongue moved across the points of broken things inside his mouth.

He wept, the fright greater than the pain. His legs curled up, his spine bending, as he tried to shrink into a ball, into nothing, something invisible that the dark face could never find, that it couldn't hurt anymore . . .

The driver's hand closed around the front of Mick's jacket, lifting him up again. He opened his eyes, and saw the driver's other hand come up in front of his face. There was something in the driver's hand; with a quick, small motion, something bright leapt out, glittering in the blue light from beyond the car's windows.

The knife . . . Mick had seen it before; he'd had it in his own hands. Dennie's knife—he knew that was it. He saw his own face, wet with blood and tears, stretched out in the shining metal.

Beyond the blade was the face of the driver. The face that he still couldn't see, that was hidden in the darkness inside the car. But he could see the driver's face turn away from him, into profile, looking over the top of the seat and into the back.

The driver spoke, a whisper sliding through the dark space: "Steven . . ."

There was someone else in the car; Mick knew that now. There had always been someone else there, hiding in the back seat. Watching, and waiting. The driver's fist at his throat held him pinned; he couldn't move, but he could roll his eyes and see who it was, the person the driver had spoken to.

Steven . . . The kid was back there, Kris' little brother. Crouched, kneeling on the seat, leaning forward to see everything, one hand placed against the seat in front to balance himself. Steven wasn't looking at Mick; his gaze was fastened on the knife, the light dazzling bright enough from it to burn like flames at the centers of his eyes.

The driver held the knife up higher.

"Steven . . ." The whisper again, an edge as thin as the blade. "Take it . . ."

No . . . Mick tried to cry out, but only a gurgling whimper squeezed past the fist at his throat.

Steven didn't take the knife. He drew back, his eyes still held by the shining blade.

"Come on, Steven . . ." The driver's voice twisted, the urgency rising in it. "Like before . . . This one . . . and the rest of them . . . we can take care of all of them . . ." The knife trembled, Mick's face shimmering in the reflection.

Steven slowly shook his head. "No . . ."

Mick watched as the driver leaned across the top of the seat, toward the darkness in back.

"Steven . . ."

The fist at his throat loosened, enough that Mick could turn his head, and see.

The back seat was empty. Steven wasn't there.

Mick's breath died in his throat as the driver's hand tightened. He grasped the driver's wrist in his own hands, but couldn't halt the strength pushing him down against the door. The dark face rose above him, blocking out the blue light sinking through the windshield.

The knife flashed in the light, a blue spark spinning off the edge of the blade.

Then it was gone. It disappeared, the driver's hand moving too fast to follow. For a dazed moment, the tears rolling into his open mouth, Mick wondered where the knife had gone.

He knew, when he felt the blossom of pain in his gut, the warm singing fire cutting up to his heart. The driver let go of his throat, and he screamed.

Steven stood at the crest of the hill, the night wrapped around him, around the whole world. He could see down to the narrow road that ran outside the juvenile-hall fence.

The black car was parked down there. Even this far away, the car a black shape in the night, he knew what was happening inside it. If he closed his eyes, he could see it again. He could see everything.

The night's silence was broken, torn in two. From down below, from inside the car, a scream reached out. There was no silence then, never again, just the sound of fear and pain battering at his ears.

He stood, and listened. He closed his eyes, and saw. He saw everything.

17

Some of the people were cheering. The diehard fans—
there weren't even that many people in the bleachers,
not after all the shit that had happened lately, but there
was always a bunch that would show up, no matter
what. Aging jocks, still wearing crew cuts and their
faded varsity jackets from when they had graduated
twenty years ago, which they kept mended and patched
even though they could no longer get them zipped up
over their sagging bellies. The way that bunch shouted
and yelled, like they were still high-school kids—it
had always made Larry feel a little weird, but tonight
it made him sick. They must know, all the stuff that
had happened, but they just didn't care. They were up
for the game.

He didn't really have time to think about it. The
shouting from the bleachers had come muffled through
his helmet as the center had snapped the ball to him.
He backpedaled, turning the ball to get the lacing under his fingertips, trying to see where the hell his receiver was, where anybody was—it was like he'd gone
blind, or something worse: he could still see, but it
didn't make any sense, it was just big shapes with
numbers on them, colliding and scrabbling with each
other, the loud whumps of their pads hitting and the
grunts of their breath. Then he was blindsided—the
pocket his blockers gave him might as well have had

a welcome mat for the other side's defense to come in over. He went flying, but managed to hold onto the ball, pulling it against his chest as the side of his helmet hit the muddy dirt.

The coach whistled in somebody else to punt, and Larry stumbled off the field, pulling off his helmet as he got to the bench. He sat down hard, dropping his head low to gasp for air. The helmet dangled between his feet. On either side of him, the rest of the team, the ones who weren't out on the field, were sitting, looking equally exhausted and dispirited—none of them had said anything to him when he'd come off.

The guy next to him spat on the ground. "We're getting our fuckin' asses whipped . . ." His voice was thick with disgust.

Larry stared at the ground, still dazed from the blow he'd taken. He shook his head.

"We shouldn't even be playing this fucking game." He still couldn't believe it. Looking up, he saw the other team returning the punt, making twenty yards without even half-trying. They had brought in most of their seconds, just to keep it from becoming too much of a laugher. What were they all doing here? His thoughts went aloud again. "For Christ's sake, we got a guy dead . . . and we're out here playing some stupid football game?"

The player next to Larry grunted in agreement. From the corner of his eye, he saw some of the other guys nodding. They all looked vaguely ashamed, as if they'd been caught doing some minor but loathsome vice.

It was all horseshit. They should've rescheduled the game for the end of the season, or just fucking forfeited it, or anything . . . Except this coach was so fucking gung ho, like his job was on the line or something, as though they weren't already eight games in the hole, with a lock on finishing last place in the district.

That fucking Mick was an asshole, Larry was firmly convinced, but this time he had to hand it to Mick: the sonuvabitch had the right idea. Just don't show up, even if Mick was the starting quarterback. Which was why the happy assignment of going out there and getting his ass blitzed by the other side's defense had fallen to Larry. Running the plays a couple times in practice made you a regular expert around here. While Mick was out on the streets somewhere, probably getting plastered. Which counted, Larry figured, as a kind of grieving. Better than coming out here and playing football.

Anything would be better . . .

"This is bullshit." He might as well go find Mick, and get messed up with him. That made more sense. Larry pushed himself up from the bench. And started to walk.

The coach grabbed his arm. "Where the hell do you think you're going?"

"Here—" Larry shoved the helmet into the coach's gut, hard enough to rock the sonuvabitch back on his heels. "You call the fuckin' plays."

He headed for the showers, not listening to the coach sputtering and shouting behind him.

The briefcase, the one he always brought with him, sat on the table unopened. Taylor hadn't even touched it, since he'd come to the hall and started his shift. He'd just been waiting, the whole time. He sat at one of the tables in the intake unit's dayroom, listening. To the silence outside, the night slowly working through its paces.

He gazed through the dayroom's windows, to the night's darkness. In the distance, past the hall's athletic fields, he could just see the perimeter fence and the lights spaced along its length. He glanced up at the clock on the wall—already past midnight. That was all right. He could wait.

When he heard the sound of a car's engine, low and powerful, cutting underneath the darkness, as though in the rock beneath the building—he closed his eyes, and listened to it. It was out there. He didn't have to look to know it was.

He looked over his shoulder toward the desk. Repken hadn't heard; he was rocked back in the chair, feet up, working through some fat paperback. This was a slow night.

Taylor got up from the table. He already had the flashlight with him; he'd taken it out of the desk drawer, the first thing after he'd signed into the logbook and the day staff had left. He walked over to the exit door, pulling the keys on the lanyard from his pocket.

He felt the weight of Repken's eyes on his back.

The cold night air came inside as he pushed open the door. He looked back at Repken as he pocketed his keys.

"I'm going outside." Taylor pushed the door open wider. "To do my perimeter check."

Repken nodded, going back to his book. Taylor stepped out and closed the door, the light from the dayroom retreating inside. He left the flashlight switched off as he started across the field.

The car and its driver were gone. By the time Taylor got out to the service road—he had already felt the night's silence, complete and unbroken again, wrapping around him as he'd walked toward the perimeter fence. Nothing out there, only the dark.

He walked up to the fence and switched on the flashlight. He swung the beam through the chain-link mesh,

and up along the road on the other side. Tire tracks—
he saw them, parallel lines in the dust. Whatever car
had been out here, it had turned back toward the gate.

Gone . . . but it had left something behind. The
flashlight beam followed along the tire tracks, until it
came to a stop on something that looked like a pile of
rags.

Taylor leaned closer to the fence. He could see a
puddle of something dark, leaking out of the rags and
soaking into the road's dirt.

He knew what it was, but he had to see it anyway.
He got out his keys and unlocked the padlock on the
gate.

The oval of light moved in front of him as he walked
toward the thing, the bundle of rags. He stopped a
couple of feet away from it—he didn't want to step
into the puddle, which looked black in the moonlight.

Black, then red as the flashlight hit it. The rags were
red, too, the color soaked into the cloth. A pair of legs
stuck out from the bundle, sprawled in a V. The denim
jeans looked like leather, the blood making them shiny.
The front of the jeans had been ripped open with a
knife. What was left of the body's crotch was soft and
red, the blood splashed up onto the varsity jacket
above. A T-shirt had been slashed as well, a gaping
cut from the neck to the bottom, to show the red shapes
inside the chest and gut.

Taylor moved the flashlight beam up to the thing's
face.

The eyes stared up at the night. The mouth was
open, but something was there, as if to silence the
unheard scream. The handle of a knife protruded from
the mouth, straight up. The blade must have cracked
the back of the skull, pinning the head to the soft asphalt beneath.

He recognized the face. He had seen it before, out

beyond the fence of the drive-in. And once, laughing at him from behind the wheel of a car across the street from his apartment; laughing at him as he threw a disemboweled cat into the trash dumpster.

The face wasn't laughing now. It went on screaming around the knife in its mouth.

Taylor turned away from it, and walked back toward the gate in the fence. He had a call to make.

The service road was technically part of the juvenile-hall grounds—the county sheriffs came out for the body.

A red light on top of one of the sheriffs' cars bounced over the hillside like a rapid streak of flame. The road was lit up by the headlights circled around the body. Taylor watched the sheriff's crew going about their jobs, the flash of their cameras breaking the dark open.

He was standing just outside the yellow tape cordoning off the area. A plainclothes officer with a clipboard flicked through the pages of the statement Taylor had already given.

"You didn't see any car out here on the road tonight?" The officer looked up from the clipboard.

Taylor shook his head. "No."

"Have you seen any suspicious vehicles out here? Recently—the last couple of weeks or so."

He had seen them examining the tire tracks, photographing them and tracing them back to the locked gate. He didn't care—he knew they wouldn't find out anything that way.

"Well?"

Taylor brought his gaze back to the officer. "No." It would still be a secret inside him.

The officer folded the pages back over the clipboard.

"There might be more questions later. Depending on how the investigation goes. We'll give you a call."

He nodded. "Sure."

The officer walked away from him, over to where the body was being lifted onto a gurney.

That was the end of this night's business. Taylor turned and headed toward the gate and the waiting building beyond it.

He was lucky. The cops hadn't seen him. He'd been cruising around, looking for Mick, the whole time since he'd walked out on the football game. When he saw the flashing red lights and the cop cars on the service road behind the juvenile hall, he knew somehow, down in his gut, that somebody else had already found Mick.

Larry left his car parked out on the street, a long way from where all the action was going on, and where no one would be able to see him. He scooted up along the hillside, crawling down low in the dry weeds to stay out of sight. From up here, he was able to get one good glimpse of Mick's face, when the old guy the cops brought around, a coroner or something, pulled out the knife from the open mouth. Then they covered the body up with a sheet. Larry had to fight to keep from being sick, clamping his teeth down hard and wrapping his arms around his gut.

The guy from the juvenile hall, the one that Mick and his buddies had been hassling around with, the dead cat and all that shit—he was down there on the service road, getting grilled by the cops. They had all sorts of questions—the guy must've been the one who'd found the body and called the cops. The night air was so still that Larry could hear what the guy and the cops were saying.

Larry wanted to talk to the guy—especially after

hearing some of the stuff the guy told the police. He worked his way down the hillside, well out of range of any of the lights.

The cops finished with the guy, and he came walking toward the gate. Larry was already waiting for him there. He stood up from where he had been crouching down.

"Hey—"

The guy looked up; he had been lost in his own thoughts, walking without watching where he was going. Only a couple of yards away—Larry watched as the juvenile-hall guy looked him over, checking out the varsity jacket. The same as on the body they had just hauled away.

"What do you want?" The guy had a heavy flashlight dangling in his hand.

Larry glanced past the guy—the police hadn't spotted what was going on over here. He looked back to the man in front of him. "Could I talk to you for a minute?"

After a moment, the juvenile-hall guy nodded. "Sure. What's on your mind?" The voice was cool, emotionless.

Larry gestured with a tilt of his head toward the police, finishing up their business behind the yellow ribbon. "I heard you talking to the cops . . . what they asked you . . ."

Impassive, the juvenile-hall guy waited for him to go on.

"You told them you never saw anything suspicious out here. Like a car, or anything."

The guy still didn't say anything. His gaze hardened as he looked at Larry.

His own voice sounded nervous. "I saw a car. You know—suspicious, kinda."

Almost a smile on the other's face, head cocked a little to one side. "Really?"

Larry stepped closer to him. "I've seen it a couple of times. Out by the drive-in—you know, where everybody goes to hang out." You asshole, of course he knows. "It's this black car, and it just comes along on the road outside, and it stops out there—like the guy's watching us or something. And—sometimes—that kid Steven—you know, the kid brother of Mick's girlfriend—I've seen him . . ." He hesitated, then went on, voice lower. "I've seen him go to the fence and talk to the guy in the car."

The juvenile-hall guy gazed coolly at him. "So what?"

Larry shrugged, a twitch in his shoulders. This wasn't going like he'd thought it would. "I don't know . . . I thought maybe—if you had seen a car out here—and it was the same car I've seen watching us . . . maybe we should tell them about it. You know, the police."

The man looked like he was thinking it over. He rubbed the end of the flashlight against his chin. "So, have you told anybody? Like your friends, your buddies on the team? About this car you saw?"

He shook his head. "I didn't think . . . anything was going to happen. I mean, it was just a car out there. Like it was no big deal. And then later, I didn't tell any of the other guys—you know, about Steven going out to the car and talking with the guy—because I thought they might get pissed at the kid. Like he had something to do with what was going on."

A smile rose on the juvenile-hall guy's face. "You're quite a brave lad." Not a real smile. "Aren't you? How do you know it wasn't me in that car you saw? How do you know I didn't find your friend's body out here because I was the one who put it there? Hmm? How do you know?''

That set him back on his heels. It took a moment for Larry to find his voice. ''I . . . I don't know.''

The juvenile-hall guy pushed past him and turned a key in the padlock on the gate. He didn't look around at Larry as he spoke. ''Yeah, well, don't sweat it. It wasn't me.''

Larry grabbed the guy's sleeve. ''You've seen it? The car?''

The guy knocked Larry's hand away. He pushed open the gate.

''Shouldn't you go tell the police about it?''

The guy turned around and glared at Larry. ''Why should I? There's nothing happening that I have any problems with. Why should I care what happens to you punks?'' An arm shot out, shoving Larry in the chest; he stumbled backward as the juvenile-hall guy stepped closer. The man's face had turned angry. ''There's other things you don't know, that I could tell you about. You know what else you don't know? Huh, Mr. Football Hero?'' He gave Larry another shove. ''I'll tell you. You don't know what it's like to be small, and to have people bigger than you pushing you around. Pushing you around and pushing you around, and just never letting up—until you don't want to wake up in the morning, you don't even want to be alive anymore.''

The blows had backed Larry across the narrow service road, right to the edge. He almost fell against the slope of the hill as the juvenile-hall guy strode forward, pushing into his face.

''Huh?'' The outbreak of the man's fury had dazed Larry. ''What're you talking about? I don't . . .''

The man was locked into his own anger, unstoppable. He was shouting so loud that Larry couldn't understand why the cops didn't come running over.

"Because—" The man's eyes had narrowed into slits. "Because something inside you is already dead, it had to die so you wouldn't feel things anymore, so it wouldn't hurt when you got shoved around. You've been lucky, you don't know what that feels like—or else you and your buddies have forgotten. Because you enjoy pushing somebody smaller around, you enjoy killing them bit by bit—it's fun, isn't it?"

Another shove, and Larry fell, sprawling against the hillside's loose gravel. He shouted up at the man: "I don't know what you're talking about—"

The man's voice snarled with bitterness. "Especially when you figure there'll never be any payback for it. That's the best part, isn't it? That you can kill somebody on the inside, and he'll still grow up and be an adult someday, and he'll be walking around with something dead inside him . . . something you and your buddies killed."

He tried to scramble to his feet, but the man's rage pinned him to the ground.

"So what should happen, then? Huh?" The man's voice turned sarcastic. "You tell me. If something happens . . . if something comes along . . . and all of a sudden there is a payback for pushing somebody smaller around, for killing him a little bit at a time . . . what should I do about it? Huh?"

Larry looked up at the man in bewilderment. "What . . . I don't—"

The man didn't even hear him; his voice went lower. "Because maybe it's what you deserve. Maybe you and your buddies better learn how to be scared. Scared right down inside. Because something has come along. And now the payback, the one you thought would never happen . . . now it's started."

He could only watch as the man turned away, striding toward the gate.

Repken looked up from behind the desk when Taylor came back to the intake unit. The door to the outside slammed shut, pushing away the cold and the dark.

"Is that it?" Repken hadn't touched his paperback, still laid open on the desktop, since Taylor had come in hours ago and made his call to the sheriff's department. About what he'd found out on the service road. "Everything all taken care of out there?"

Taylor didn't say anything. He shoved his keys back into his pocket, then stood beside the dayroom table, the one with his briefcase on it. He flipped open the case and stood looking at the sheaf of typed pages inside it.

"That must've been fuckin' spooky—" Repken went rattling on. "Going out there and finding a stiff—"

Taylor picked up the papers from the briefcase. He held them as if weighing them in his hands, then set them down again. For a moment longer, he stood gazing down at them, the cords in his neck tightening.

In a sudden explosion, his fist swept the briefcase off the table, the papers scattering in a white storm and drifting lifeless to the floor.

18

He crept along the road, in the dark. Beyond the fence, the empty space of the drive-in stretched out, dotted with the slender speaker poles in their silent rows.

Steven stopped and raised his head, one hand reaching forward to balance his crouching position. The other people, the cops and the rest of them, had been nearby, just on the other side of the hill; they were gone now, taking Mick's body with them, but Steven was still being cautious. He looked around, but saw no one. But he knew this was the place where it would come.

"Come on . . ." The whisper fell into the dark; he could barely hear it himself. He didn't care then if anyone else heard. His shout broke the night's silence.

"Come on! Where are you?"

Then light grew around him, sending his shadow racing through the fence and across the emptiness beyond. His gaze snapped around, and he saw the headlights yards away, welling up from a dim yellow radiance to the full blaze of their glare.

He shielded his eyes, straining to see past the light. He could just make out the silhouette of the driver inside the car, sitting behind the wheel. It was waiting for him.

Cautiously, Steven circled around the car, keeping

his distance. As he did so, the driver leaned across the seat; the passenger-side window slid down.

The driver's voice reached out to him. Softly: "Steven . . . get in . . ." The driver pushed the door open.

Steven drew back a step, away from the black car. He shook his head. "No . . . go away . . ."

The open door, the darkness inside the car, made his gut tighten. He moved around, slowly, through the beams of the headlights, to the other side. Somehow, his steps brought him closer, as if he were being reeled in on an invisible line. Close enough that the driver could have leaned out from the rolled-down window, and touched him.

Instead, the driver beckoned with a curl of the hand. "Steven . . . it's all right . . . I would never hurt you . . ."

"I don't want you here . . ." He kept moving, back through the headlights, back to the passenger's side. "I don't want you around here anymore . . ."

The dark face, shadowed inside the car, gazed at him. "Come on . . ." The voice slid and twisted, a soft invitation. "Just for a moment . . . I've got something to show to you."

He stood right at the car's side now, the door like a wing around him, drawing him inside. He hesitated. But he knew he had to. He got in.

The driver reached past him and pulled the door shut. Then the dark figure drew back behind the steering wheel. Around Steven, the car's silence closed, wrapping him in the little world he recognized from his dreams.

"Look . . ." The driver pointed toward the windshield. Steven followed the driver's finger, looking to the dark outside.

In the distance, the car's headlights reached across the empty drive-in. The light just touched the snack bar at the center. No one there—no cars parked, none of the football players horsing around and drinking. Empty and silent.

The driver turned his shadowed face toward Steven. "Party's over."

Steven looked back around at the driver. The face was darkness, darkness that he could fall into, fall forever. Darkness that hid the gaze watching him.

The driver had something in his hands that he held out to Steven. A small, crudely wrapped package, the paper stained with some dark liquid. Steven shrank back against the door as the package came closer to him.

"I took these . . ." The driver's soft whisper touched Steven's ear. "To show you . . ."

One hand pulled back an edge of the paper. Then the other edges, like a flower opening. Steven looked down to see what was revealed.

The things were shiny wet. They looked like lumps of meat—now they looked like that—but Steven knew they weren't. Not really. The dark, spattered shapes could still be recognized, pieces that had come from a human body. He knew where they had come from.

He turned his head away, nausea rising up in his throat, choking him. He pushed the package away, the wet stuff smearing sticky on his own hands.

"No . . . no . . ."

The driver's voice tried to soothe him. "I did it . . . for you . . ."

The choking in Steven's throat filled his head, overwhelming any other feeling. The smell of the things made him dizzy, pressing the car's world close around his shoulders. He fumbled beside himself to find the door's handle.

"No . . ." Tears squeezed around his clenched eye-

lids. "I dreamed you . . . I don't want you here anymore . . ."

The whisper curled closer at Steven's ear. "All of
them . . . every one of them . . . for you . . ."

In a sudden spasm of disgust, Steven knocked the
package out of the driver's hands. It landed with a wet
thump on the floor of the car.

The scream burst out of him. "I dreamed you!"

His fingers found the handle and closed around it.
He wrenched it down, the weight of his body pressed
against the door pushing it open. He fell against the
asphalt, his shoulder scraping hard.

As he scrambled to his feet and started to run, he
heard another scream, from behind him. A scream that
choked upon itself, as if from the heart broken at its
center.

"Steven . . ."

The driver's scream washed over him. He pressed
his hands to his ears to blot it out, the tears streaming
across his face as he ran into the dark.

Blind, he ran into something, hard enough to knock
the breath from him. He gasped as he felt hands grab
his shoulders, squeezing tight and trapping him.

The kid's eyes flew open. Larry looked down at the
small face contorted with fear and surprise, gasping
for breath.

After the police had gone, he was still there on the
hillside, where the juvenile-hall guy had tossed him
aside. And had felt the presence not far away, the
things moving in the dark. He'd come looking.

Steven struggled in his grasp, the kid's palms pushing against Larry's chest. He looked down and saw
dark smears of something wet on the front of his varsity jacket.

He held on to the kid tighter, pulling him up to the

level of his own face. Shouting at him: "Who's in the car? Who is it?"

Steven beat his fists against Larry's chest. "I didn't do it . . . I didn't do it!"

The kid stopped fighting when he saw the blood smeared on Larry's jacket. His eyes opened wider in horror, staring at his own hands and the stains on them. The sight brought the strength of desperation to him; with a quick contortion of his body, he twisted free of Larry's grasp and fell to the ground. His frightened glance swept across Larry's face, and then he was up on his feet again, and running. He glanced back over his shoulder as Larry started after him.

The kid was running back toward the car; Larry saw its black shape up ahead on the road. He couldn't see whether there was anyone inside it now.

Steven ran up to the passenger-side door. Larry could see him look inside before he pulled the door open and scrambled inside. The side window started to roll up.

The window had only gotten halfway up when Larry reached the car. As Larry tugged at the door's handle, Steven scooted away from him, back toward the steering wheel.

"Goddamn—" The door wouldn't open; the kid must've locked it. He reached one arm into the car, fumbling around for the lock down by the inside handle. Steven shoved himself farther away, flattening his back against the opposite door.

Larry couldn't find the lock; his hand clawed futilely along the door's thin padding.

There wasn't time—the car's driver had to be somewhere close by. Larry managed to squeeze his head and other arm in through the window opening. He reached for Steven with both hands.

"Steven . . ." The tight squeeze made him gasp. "Come on . . . you gotta get out of here . . ."

Steven shrank back against the other door, one hand shoving against the curve of the steering wheel.

Larry strained forward, rising on his toes, trying to grab hold of the kid. "Come on . . . he'll be back any second . . . I know you didn't do anything—"

He suddenly felt himself jerked backward, the locked door coming open somehow, pulled by somebody outside, behind him.

There was no time to cry out. He saw only the dark silhouette, the figure of the driver, from the corner of his eye as one hand clenched a fist into his hair. The driver's grip tightened into a knot, pulling his head up and back, his shoulders hitting above the top of the door. The hold trapped him, the window's edge cutting across his gut.

The driver pulled the door farther back, then slammed it toward the car. The upper rim of the door opening hit Larry's chest. His breath rushed out of him in a scream, the red pain ramming to the top of his skull and knocking his head back in the driver's grip.

He slumped forward, still trapped in the window opening, as the driver pulled the door open; his feet dragged lifeless across the asphalt. He could feel something warm trickling from the corner of his mouth, down to his chin. He could see the darkness swirling about him, blurred in a red haze.

Behind him, the driver braced to slam the door again, the killing blow this time. Then something smaller scrambled out of the car, past Larry, and into the driver's chest and face.

From a distance, he could hear Steven shouting hysterically—"No! Stop it . . . stop it"—and the sound of blows, Steven's small fists, and the sudden fury of his attack, forcing the driver a few steps back from the door.

Everything was falling away now, happening in some place beyond the curtain that was seeping down from red to black. Larry's head felt as if it were rising, a balloon pumped full of sharp-edged singing that someone had let go of. He could look down and see his own body sliding out of the window opening and collapsing on the road.

Then he was in the body again, struggling to get air past the stone that had been hammered into his chest. He looked up from where he was sprawled and saw the black car's driver peeling Steven away from his neck, Steven's fists still flying but not landing as the driver held him away. The driver tossed the kid aside.

The impact of Steven's fall upon the edge of the road knocked the fury out of him. Larry managed to turn his head, and saw fright well up in Steven's face as the kid pushed himself up onto his hands and knees. Then the kid was gone, running off into the dark.

He couldn't see anything then; the driver's legs blocked his sight. He looked up and saw the silhouette looming over him, the black figure outlined in the dazzling blue-white of the headlights. The light died away as the darkness merged with the night behind it, into a darkness that he felt himself falling into. Falling and disappearing.

He ran.

There was nothing he could do to help the guy, the one the driver was going to kill now. Steven knew he shouldn't have gotten scared and run away from the guy, that the guy wasn't going to hurt him. But it had startled him when he came out of the dark and grabbed him like that, and when he'd seen the varsity jacket, the kind all the footballers wore, and then the blood, the blood of one of the guy's teammates, that his hands smeared on the jacket—he'd been afraid. More afraid of what the guy would do to him, more afraid of that than of the driver.

And he hadn't been just running away. He knew he'd been running back. Back to the driver. Who would protect him. Who loved him.

Then it had all started happening again, too fast for him to think. He'd tried to help the footballer—he'd even remembered the guy's face, the one who'd stopped Dennie from picking on him that time—but there was nothing he could do. The driver was too strong. There was nothing to do but run.

He hit the fence, his fingers clawing into the links of wire, the toes of his shoes scrabbling for a hold. He made it to the top and flopped half over, the up-right ends of the wires poking into his stomach. All the time he'd been climbing, he'd expected a pair of hands to grab his ankles, pull him back down. Up here, he heard the sound of the car's engine starting, a roar in the night's silence. The beams of the head-lights swept across him; he could hear the wheels spitting gravel over the road's surface. Steven swung his legs over the top of the fence and dropped down to the asphalt of the empty drive-in. He picked himself up and ran toward the center of the dark space.

The outline of the snack bar reared up in front of him, a black shape against the night. The moon shone through the dirty banks of windows at the building's front. He ran up to the side wall and squatted down against it, panting for breath and listening.

In the distance, out on the road circling around, the sound of the black car faded away. Heading toward the front of the drive-in, and the entrance to the empty asphalt field.

Steven moved in a crouch along the wall, until he found the door to the office in back. Locked—the cold metal of the knob rattled in his hand.

He could see that one corner of the wire grille nailed over the window had lifted up. He grabbed the wire and pushed, bending it back. Another rusted nail pulled free, enlarging the space. Steven put his hand through, against the smooth glass of the window. It swung inward when he pushed. He ducked his head under the points of the wire, levering himself against the windowsill.

The sharp points of the grille tore across his shoulders, raking through his jacket and shirt to the skin underneath. But he managed to wriggle through, pushing with his hands against the wall underneath the window. The wire caught at the top of his jeans, and he had to reach back to pull it free. Then he was able to drop into the silence inside the office.

Steven crouched under the window and looked out. Nothing yet—he grabbed the wire grille and bent it back into place, as much as he could. The corner of it still stuck out. He left it and scuttled back into the center of the office.

His eyes had adjusted well enough to the dark that he could make out the shapes. A beat-up folding chair, stacks of cardboard boxes, videocassettes scattered around. Against one wall were the tape machines and the TVs ranged on top of them.

They were all dead things, here in the dark. He could hold his breath and become one of them, hidden, so no one could find him. If he made himself small enough, invisible . . .

He squatted down in the corner farthest from the window, in a narrow space between two stacks of boxes. Hugging his knees to his chest, he watched and waited.

Nothing, except the beat of his heart, sounding like it was right up in his throat. He pressed his chin against the top of his forearms, and listened.

He heard the footsteps outside the building. Slow, circling around. The driver must have left the car some distance away and come on foot to the snack bar. Looking for Steven . . . He shrank back into the little space between the boxes, listening to the sound.

It came closer. A silhouette filled the window, black against the night's blackness. The figure of a man, standing there. A hand reached and tugged at the corner of the wire grille. The wire bent upward, past the rusted nail at the side, then stopped. It wouldn't pull loose any farther than that.

The dark figure outside let go of the wire grille, and stepped away from the window. Steven could hear it circling the building, stopping to try the locked door, then continuing around. He held his breath and made himself small, invisible; nothing.

Silence. As though the dark shape he'd seen at the window had gone away, gone back into the darkness he'd come from. Steven raised his head from the cradle of his arms and knees.

The door shook, buckling in its frame from the blow that hit it. The noise battered at Steven's ears.

Another blow, and the door's lock tore free, with the sharp cry of splintering wood; the door swung in and crashed against the wall.

The dark figure stood in the doorway, his hands spread wide to brace himself. The foot he'd kicked the door in with lowered back to the ground.

Smaller—Steven squeezed his eyes shut. He was invisible, he wasn't there at all . . .

The footsteps stopped in the middle of the office.

He can't see me. Steven bit his lip. *It's too dark, he can't see me, he can't . . .*

Steven opened his eyes, a slit just big enough to see the dark silhouette a few yards away from him, looming up in the office, towering toward the ceiling.

He could see the figure's head turn to profile, looking about the room, scanning right past where he was hiding.

The figure turned around, away from Steven. It took a couple of steps toward the door. A hand reached out and felt the wall. Steven heard the sound of the switch being flicked back and forth, twice. No light spilled into the room from the fixture overhead—the socket had been dead for years.

Go away . . . I don't want you here . . . Steven held his breath, watching the figure move in the office's darkness.

The figure stepped toward the door, then halted. It stooped down beside the wall. Steven could hear it fumbling around with something, but couldn't see what it was doing.

A rasping mechanical noise cut through the office; it sounded like a lawn mower being started up. A small engine coughed and sputtered, then died back into silence.

The generator—the little portable one that the fat guy who ran the drive-in left out here, to run his little shows with—that was what had made the noise. Steven could see the dark figure bracing for another pull on the start-up cord. The figure's arm swung back, the handle of the cord in his fist. The generator coughed again, revved into a brief snarl, then settled to a steady murmur. Before standing up, the figure tossed the end of the exhaust hose out the open doorway.

The dark figure moved around the office again. To the other wall, where the tape machines were. It reached down and pushed an ON button.

A jittering gray light slanted across the room. It grew brighter, filling the screen of the TV above the tape player. Steven pushed himself farther back into the pocket of shadow formed by the boxes on either side of him.

A cassette had been left in the machine; a soft whirring noise started as the tape moved across the heads. On the TV screen, the gray light was replaced by moving shapes, the forms of bodies writhing together. Limbs and open mouths, the shining wet of saliva as they tongued each other's skin. The light falling across the room changed color, shading to a pink that coiled and twisted like a slow fire.

The figure's shadow cut across the moving light as he reached out and switched on the rest of the tape machines. The screens above flickered on. Other shapes were there on them, the naked things prying and hammering with sweat-matted groins at the red mouths that welled up toothless and moist. An overlapping prayer of moans and panting squeals fluttered against the walls of the office.

Now the room was brightly lit, the glow from the screens pouring out. Steven could see the dark figure stepping back from the tape machines.

Smaller, invisible, not there at all . . . He squeezed his eyes closed tight, hugging his knees to his chest. The sound of the footsteps tapped at his ears.

With his eyes closed, he felt the shadow falling across him.

Then the voice, soft and even gentle. "Come on—"

He opened his eyes and looked up. A different voice. And enough light to see the dark figure's face.

The guy from the juvenile hall stood above him, looking down at him.

"It's okay, Steven." The man reached his hand down. "Let's get out of here."

19

He could just manage to breathe. It felt like knives stabbing out through the muscles of his chest.

Larry felt that first, the pain of his broken ribs, before anything else. Before his eyes flickered open, and he saw the dashboard and the back of the seat, the bits and pieces of a car's interior floating above him—the pain drew him like a hook up into the narrow space in which he lay.

He didn't know how he'd gotten there. The string of memory had broken, letting him fall into the darkness. There had been something about a car, not this one, but one that had been all dark inside, with the face of a frightened child cowering back away from him, farther and farther away, so that he hadn't been able to reach the child no matter how hard he'd tried . . .

And there had been another face, one that hadn't been a face at all, but just more darkness, another piece of it, a piece with eyes that you couldn't see but you knew they were looking at you.

He remembered that. The little pieces floated around, pieces of ash that floated around inside the car. Everything else had been burned away in a red explosion, flames that had screamed with his voice, that now dwindled to the sharp points buried under his flesh.

Everything . . . The pain had broken him, left him

unable to move. Larry tried to rise, pushing himself up from the car seat with one hand, but it slipped, and the pain danced to the top of his skull, singing, as he fell back down. He couldn't even raise his hand from where it lay, knuckles against the carpeted floor of the car.

Somebody else's car—not the black one, dark as the driver who had come out of that blackness. It came to him, a little thread rising from the hole that had swallowed his remembering. The juvenile-hall guy—he could see the man now, towering up over him. The man had come walking from a car, this car, the one Larry was in now; the car had pulled up a few yards away, the headlights sweeping over Larry's face. The memory brought others with it, the taste of blood and sharp-edged grit in his mouth, the pain across his chest roaring as he'd lain sprawled on the road. The juvenile-hall guy had knelt down—Larry remembered seeing the face, a real face—and then had picked him up, carrying and dragging him to the car, laying him down inside. Where he'd be safe.

That was all he could remember. There was no more. The man had gone away, other business to take care of.

Larry wondered what it was that the man had to take care of; the wondering dwindled away as he fell under the slow dark wave that welled up around him.

As they walked away from the snack bar, the sound of a car engine, a low murmur, came out of the darkness. An edge of light swept across the empty drive-in and touched them.

Taylor looked toward the drive-in's gate. Out past it, on the road circling around, was his own car, where he'd left it. With the boy, the football player that he'd found unconscious on the road, inside—that was all that had remained there, in that place he'd known instinctively to come to, when he'd left the juvenile hall. He'd walked out of the building without saying a word, without turning around to answer the questions Repken called after him. None of that little world mattered anymore.

This was the world now. In the distance, a pair of headlights swung around. A black car moved slowly through the gate.

The car halted, whatever thing was inside it watching them through the dark windshield. Taylor and Steven held still for a moment, waiting to see what the car was going to do.

It moved again, turning from the gate onto one of the lanes that circled around through the field of white speaker poles. The car drove slowly, the sound of its engine a soft rasp. Taylor turned his head, watching the car make its way around.

He and the kid had only gotten a few yards away from the snack bar when the black car had shown up. It came to a stop on the other side of the small building, its headlights angling through a corner of the windows in front. Past the glare of the headlights, Taylor could see the figure sitting behind the wheel. Watching and waiting.

Taylor reached down, his hand touching between Steven's shoulder blades, and gave the kid a push. He kept his voice quiet and level.

"Come on."

They started toward the gate again, walking. He kept his hand on Steven's shoulder, pulling the kid's pace back to match his own slow, deliberate steps.

A voice called from behind them.

"Taylor . . ."

He stopped again. Turning to look over his shoulder, he saw that the side window of the car had gone down and that the driver's shadowed face was looking straight toward him.

Taylor took his hand from Steven's shoulder. "Stay here." The kid looked up at him, but didn't move as he turned and walked toward the black car.

The driver pushed open the door as Taylor approached. Taylor looked down into the car for a moment, then crouched on his heels, bringing his face to the same level as the driver's. Only a few inches separated them, but he could see only darkness, the other's face still hidden.

The driver raised his head, looking past Taylor, out to where Steven waited. Then the driver brought his gaze back.

"Give him to me." The driver's voice a whisper, almost inaudible over the noise of the car's engine idling. "Give me the boy."

Taylor looked at the face, at the unseen eyes that were watching him. He shook his head. "No." The one word, his voice quiet.

Behind the wheel, the driver crouched lower, animallike. "He *betrayed* us . . ." The voice twisted, probing into Taylor's ear. "He let one of them go . . . just when I was going to take care of that one. One of *them*. I was going to take care of him . . . For you."

Taylor gazed at the driver. "No. I won't give the boy to you."

The driver's voice curled, pleading. "Always . . . it was always for you. Not for *him*. I did it for you. All of them . . ." The voice dropped lower. "What's wrong?"

He looked away, out toward the darkness around them. For a moment he was silent, then the words came. "It's not worth it." Taylor looked back at the driver. "It doesn't help. Nothing helps. And when I realized that . . ." Silence, a breath sliding out to the cold air. "Then I wasn't afraid anymore." The darkness wrapped around them, an embrace. "Of anything."

Taylor slowly got up from his crouch beside the open car door. He turned and started to walk away.

The voice, heartbroken, reached after him. "Taylor . . . it was for you!"

He looked back toward the car. His own voice cold now. "Go back where you came from."

The driver raised his head, coming forward from the car's dark interior. Far enough that the faint starlight crossed over the face that had been in shadow before.

Taylor looked into the drawn, distorted mirror image of his own face. Its eyes were holes into another darkness, one that fell away without end.

"I came . . . from here."

The voice's last words, thin and tight as a wire, cutting through the night.

Taylor felt the heart inside his chest slow, as if it were coming to a stop. Between one beat and the next, he and the driver were the only things in the world, everything else seeping away into the night. Then his blood moved again, and he was able to turn and walk away.

Steven looked up at him. He put his hand on the kid's shoulder. "Let's go."

They had gone half the distance, heading for the drive-in's gate, when they heard the black car's engine revving up behind them. Then it dropped into gear, and the tires squealed, the cry slicing through the night.

The headlights swept across them, sending their shadows across the empty asphalt field.

Taylor didn't turn around. "Don't look back." His voice still level. "Just keep walking."

Steven glanced up at him, then kept his eyes straight ahead.

The car leapt forward. On a line toward its target—it struck the corner of the snack bar, punching its way through the banks of windows in front. The glass exploded, a silver, razor-edged storm around the car's hood and windshield.

The thin wall between the snack bar and the manager's office buckled and split. A can of gasoline, the portable generator's fuel, toppled over, its contents spurting across the office's floor as one of the television sets smashed upon it in a blaze of sparks.

Another explosion, a ball of flame, engulfed the small building. Its force, and the impact of the black car, tore the snack bar apart; the walls crumpled outward, vomiting gouts of fire and black smoke. The flames coursed over the car's hood and windshield as it surged through the collapsing debris. It picked up speed as it burst past the glass shards falling in a rain of glistening light.

Taylor felt the heat of the explosion against his back. His shadow, and the boy's, withered and disappeared in the twisting orange glare that flooded over the drive-in's empty space. Still not looking back, he pushed Steven along.

The explosion had scattered the tape machines and TVs across what was left of the office. The flesh on the TV screens writhed, as if it felt the flames leaping up around the images.

From the flanks of the black car, the burning fragments fell away, leaving the gleaming metal unscathed.

It sped forward, tires screaming as it slammed di-

agonally across the ramped hills of the parking rows.
The speaker poles snapped as the car hit them; the
poles flew into the air, the wires ripping out of the
asphalt. The black lines tangled in the car's bumper
and whipped around like frenzied snakes, the speakers
striking out more sparks as they lashed against the
ground and the car's fenders.

The car accelerated, the beams of its headlights
reaching out to gather everything before it.

The gate was just yards away. Taylor suddenly halted
and pushed Steven ahead of himself.

"Go on," he shouted as the kid stumbled a few
steps forward. "Go!"

Steven turned and grabbed hold of Taylor's arm.
"No . . ." He tugged at the arm. "Come on!"

Taylor's face contorted, the calm shattering and falling away. He pulled his arm free with a furious backhand swing, almost knocking Steven to the ground.

"Go on!" The shout a scream now. "Get out of
here!"

Steven staggered backward. For a moment his gaze
stayed on Taylor's face. Then he turned and ran for the
gate.

Taylor turned, looking over his shoulder. The glare
from the headlights blinded him as the car rushed toward him.

The world became nothing but light surging over
him, the roar of the engine tearing everything else
away.

After

Pineda steered the black-and-white through the drive-in's gate. Past the FOR SALE sign that had always been there; sometime in the past couple of days, a SOLD sticker had been pasted over it by the commercial realty agent that had the listing. Felton must've finally gotten smart.

In the distance, at the center of the empty asphalt field, a few thin traces of smoke still drifted up from the wreckage of the refreshment stand. The fire had burned itself out before anyone had made a report on it. Pineda and Harrelson would be the first ones there, in the first gray light of morning.

He glanced over at Harrelson, sitting beside him. The old bastard hadn't said shit through the whole night. Harrelson had had the fear of God, and of losing his pension, put into him; he only had to put in a couple of months to take the early retirement that had been offered to him. That was fine by Pineda—he was already looking forward to getting a partner who wasn't a complete asshole.

There wasn't much left of the refreshment stand. He pulled the black-and-white up a few yards away from the charred circle of asphalt. Maybe Felton himself had torched it, though Pineda couldn't imagine that a low-rent character like that had ever managed to get any insurance for it. Or else those kids, that bunch of football fuckups had done it, while they'd been screwing around out here. No big loss, either way.

Sitting in the ashes were some heat-warped tape players and televisions, the screens blank and shattered. The smell of burnt plastic stung Pineda's nostrils as he got out of the patrol car and looked around.

Farther away, halfway toward the gate, a car sat motionless. Harrelson stayed on his fat ass inside the black-and-white as Pineda walked toward the other vehicle.

As he got closer, he saw how trashed the car was. Black underneath the layers of grime and dust—it hunkered low to the ground, the aged tires split open, letting the wheels sag onto the frayed rubber. The fenders and doors were dented, rotten with rust. The windshield was spiderwebbed with fractures.

Somebody must've towed it in, and abandoned it—Pineda couldn't think of any other way it could've gotten here.

He stepped up to the side and looked in. There was somebody inside, slumped back from the steering wheel, not moving. Pineda pulled open the door; it creaked on its stiff hinges.

Dead—there wasn't much point in checking for breath or a pulse. He knew from the first sight that the man inside the car was cold and lifeless. Spattered with blood, his clothes torn and stained. Around the figure, the interior of the car was as decayed as the outside, the upholstery split open with age, the gauges on the dashboard gutted and empty.

He reached out and touched the body's shoulder. The head lolled on the neck, the face angled toward him. It was the guy from the juvenile hall, the one who ran the place at night.

Pineda ducked into the car, holding on to the door

for balance. He felt under the body's jaw for a heart-beat, just as routine. Nothing. He drew his hand away.

There was something on the body's lap that looked like a small, paper-wrapped package. It was soaked in blood, dried dark now. Pineda used his forefinger to push aside the wrappings. When he saw what was inside the package, he froze, the hair rising on the back of his neck. Slowly, he drew himself out of the car and backed away.

He walked back to the black-and-white. A shake of his head when Harrelson looked up at him. "We gotta phone this one in."

Harrelson reached down to the radio, got the mike, and handed it to him through the window. He took it, leaning back against the patrol car's fender, keeping the car in the distance in his sight.

The kids gathered at the fence to watch. The police had sealed off the drive-in, but somehow the word of what had been found there had leaked out. Things like that always do.

Steven had been there from the beginning, before any of the others had arrived. He didn't say anything to them as they stood around him, pressing close to the fence.

The cops were pulling the body of the juvenile-hall guy from the black car. Behind Steven, a bigger kid, the bully whose brother had been killed, sneered at the sight.

"I always knew that guy was some kind of homo." The kid's voice was bitter. They'd already heard about what had been found in the car with the body. The pieces of the victims. "Big fuckin' pervert."

Steven turned around from the fence. "Shut up." He spoke quietly, his gaze level into the other kid's eyes. "Just shut the fuck up."

The words rocked the bigger kid back. His jaw jutted forward, his fists cocking as if he were about to teach this little shit a lesson.

Then he saw something in Steven's eyes, and it scared him. It scared all of them; the big kid backed away, then the others followed. They huddled together, some yards away, as Steven turned back toward the fence.

He stood at the fence, silent, one hand touching the wire, watching as the body was loaded and taken away.